Skinny Vanilla Crisis

Skinny Vanilla Crisis

COLLEEN ALLES

atmosphere press

for my family

Prologue

"You know you need a hairnet, right?"

It took me a moment to process the words.

I could feel my ears trying to send the words into the hollow space between them—my brain, that is.

My very tired, very hungover brain.

I had always pictured my brain to be like a library: a quiet place with tables and books, filing cabinets off to the side, wherein I had squirreled away many years of memories and facts like pieces of paper that could be pulled out and studied at any time.

My brain, I used to think, was a peaceful space. Organized, even.

But Carmen's words were a cacophony inside my mind.

Nails on a chalkboard.

I wanted to scream.

Recently, a drunk and destructive monster had trampled the grounds of my once-quiet mind, knocking over everything in its path of destruction, completely messing up my mental library.

"I do?" I asked.

Carmen, who had been crouching in front of the bakery case, scrutinizing the layout of the muffins and croissants, turned to look at me.

"Yes," Carmen hissed. "You need a hairnet."

She looked pissed, although in the half a day I had been her employee, I noticed she seemed to wear the expression a bit by default.

The kids had a name for that expression, I thought. What was it? Resting bitch face? Her sleek, black ponytail whipped around as she turned her attention back to the bakery case.

"What about a hat," I said.

It came out more like a statement than a question.

What about a hat.

It wasn't as though I had that much hair—on my head anyway. The stubble on my face, on the other hand, was becoming sizable. And very salt and pepper. Almost all of it was recent, and getting a little out of control.

Carmen stood, brushed her hands on the bottom of her apron, and sighed. Speaking slowly—like I was slow— she said, "Yes, Holden. You can wear a hat."

"I guess it's technically a visor," I offered.

A half-hearted attempt to make her smile.

Carmen glared at me. She was wearing the JavaHut-approved black visor, her bangs bunched up at the top, stuck to her forehead.

It was my first day working at JavaHut, and one thing was clear: Carmen may have interviewed me and hired me, but she definitely also now hated me. She hated everything about me. I could see it in her dark eyes.

"You shouldn't even be out here without something covering your head," she said. "It's against code."

"Right," I said, not wanting to point out that *she* was the one who had told me to follow her from the staff area to the bakery case just moments before this unpleasant exchange between us began.

Not on my way to winning the award for Employee of the Month, was I?

But Carmen continued to stare me down, and I thought it was too bad things had gone so wrong so fast.

Yesterday, when we'd interviewed, she'd hired me on the spot, asking if I could start the next day. I'd taken it as a good sign: we had hit it off, we got along. She'd been a little friendlier the day before. I started to wonder what might have happened to her in less than twenty-four hours.

Of course, I knew maybe more than most that in less than twenty-four hours, your whole life can just implode.

One

Which isn't to say I shouldn't have seen it coming.

Because if I was honest with myself, I probably *should* have seen this coming.

It was a train that had been barreling down the tracks toward my face for months.

We'd been fighting for months—Sophia and me.

Years, if I was totally honest. But it was hard—it feels impossibly hard to decide where, when, or how it all started.

I could say the fighting had been getting worse. In a way, things at home had been getting worse for a long time. Sometimes the fighting was us in a room disagreeing about something, and sometimes the fighting was us more or less ignoring one another for days at a time.

Did it start when she changed jobs last September, took that promotion at the Y? Suddenly, we didn't see each other nearly as much as we used to because our schedules didn't overlap as well as they used to.

We'd talked about that, of course. I remembered sitting at the kitchen table with Sophia as she wrote on a pad of paper, weighing out the pros and cons of taking the position of Lead Supervisor at the YMCA.

Pro: More money.

Pro: More staff (i.e., better work experience).

Pro: More challenges.

Con: Hours not as good.

Con: Seeing me less.

(Perhaps that was actually a pro.)

Con: Seeing Matthew less at home.

That actually *was* a con.

Our son had turned fourteen just a few months ago.

And while new privileges hadn't exactly rained down from the heavens, he had adopted a sudden air of expectation: more allowance, more social events with friends, more staying up late.

On the other hand, Sophia had speculated that maybe this promotion at the Y would be good for Matthew. She had made an entry in the Pro column for that, too.

Pro: Maybe Matthew would spend more time at the Y with his friends, playing basketball, swimming in the giant pool with the twisty plastic slide that was great until a toddler accidentally pooped on it. Which, according to Sophia, happened about once a fortnight.

But Matthew had other interests: namely video games and hanging out at the public library. He'd also joined the chess team at school because it met at the library to practice, in close proximity to a big group of girls who also hung out at the library after school.

Con: Matthew had recently discovered girls.

Although, this had little to do with Sophia making a career change.

I could still remember the three of us celebrating Matthew's fourteenth birthday in January with a pizza and a couple of his friends—no girlfriend yet. Sophia had baked a German chocolate cake from scratch, then iced it, then adorned it with candles. Matthew had pretended to be embarrassed by it, but he had obviously loved the cake. I still had the photos on my phone.

That night had been the nicest one in recent memory,

yet we moved along through the rest of the winter and then through spring like a janky three-wheeled car that hit potholes and veered off the road all the time, even when I felt like I was steering carefully.

We didn't spend much time together, Sophia and me. She was at work, or I was at work, or we were transporting Matthew to or from friends' houses. Or one of us was picking up takeout, or walking our dog, Benny. Often, I graded papers on the weekends. Sophia often had a shift—sometimes two.

How long had we been living through notes on the kitchen table and curt text messages?

Matthew was busy—discovering girls, as I had fully internalized by March.

And then...

And then the implosion of our lives.

Or was it an explosion?

Perhaps Sophia had just been waiting for the school year to end, for me to see my sophomores through exams, for me to get through entering final grades. Then, she felt the time was right to drop the big bomb: she wanted space.

She wanted a separation.

She didn't want to talk about it.

She just wanted it to happen.

"You know this has been coming, Holden," she'd said.

It was the final day of the school year—the middle of June. The students at St. Bridget's had been released at lunch. I'd said my goodbyes and attended the assembly. I would finish the week out with some boring professional development initiatives crammed in on that Friday.

I'd already opted not to teach summer school because

for once, I thought Sophia and I could get away without the extra money, since her promotion had netted us some breathing room in the budget.

So, had I seen this coming?

It happened on a Thursday. Matthew had been at his friend Ricky's house. Sophia had picked up Chinese food on her way home. She'd handed me an uncapped Blue Moon, after taking a big pull of it herself.

Not really like her. Sophia was more of a wine drinker.

"I don't think I saw this coming," I'd said.

The Chinese food was getting cold on the counter, and I hated her so much for making our tradition into something I'd never be able to do again. General Tso's chicken on the last day of the school year was ruined forever.

"We've been fighting like crazy," Sophia had pointed out, sighing, her arms crossed over her chest.

She hadn't changed her clothes from work yet. She was still wearing her standard uniform: her white Y hoodie—not a sweatshirt, but the kind of sleek athleisure apparel popular with so many women now.

And popular with my students. They all seemed to wear leggings all the time—the girls, anyway, like at any moment they might start spontaneously exercising. I hated leggings. They were too revealing. I didn't want to be confronted with fabric showing every single curve on my female students' bodies, particularly the curves around the hips.

And the effect it seemed to have on my sixteen-year-old male students was obvious. I could probably create a graph detailing the decline in grades for my male students directly proportional to the proliferation of soft spandex.

But Sophia—she looked good. She looked great, actually. She had blonde hair that fell almost to her shoulders. It accentuated her skin, which had always been smooth. Big blue eyes. A sharp nose. She was in great shape—an avid runner and yoga enthusiast.

She'd always been interested in fitness, even though she chose a sensible business major in college. Her parents had encouraged her to study something marketable.

After college and after my student teaching assignment was completed, we got married, and I got a job in Grand Rapids, Michigan. She'd landed a well-paying position at an insurance company and had liked it at first. Eventually, though, the work began to bore her, and Sophia hadn't minded leaving that job when Matthew was born. Once Matthew had settled into a steady elementary school routine, though, Sophia had searched for a job that allowed her to incorporate her love of wellness, and the position at the YMCA had been perfect. She'd fit right into the culture there, and I thought she'd never seemed happier.

My wife looked like she could spontaneously exercise at all times, too. Perhaps that was a job requirement for working at the Y.

"I know," I'd said. "But come on. You don't have to move out. This is crazy."

Sophia looked at the kitchen floor for a long time, her arms still crossed. "I won't," she said. "I think you should move out."

"Whoa—what?" I said. "Where the hell is this coming from?"

"Come on, Holden," she said. "I waited until your school year was over."

I was right about that, my brain shouted at me.

"I can see that," I said, not bothering to cover up my anger.

"I think you should find a place. You have time now," she said.

"For how long?" I said, more questions spinning in my head.

"Let's just start with the summer," she said. "It's kind of perfect. You're not teaching summer school. This will allow us to really evaluate our relationship—objectively. Thoughtfully."

Separately, I thought.

I picked up my beer and took a gulp. It was almost gone, so I tossed it back and drank the rest of it in one pull.

This wasn't happening, my brain was telling me.

Six hours ago, I was shooting the breeze with a couple of seniors who had just graduated, who'd stopped by my classroom to tell me how much they'd learned in my English class. They told me that looking back, they were glad I'd been such a stickler for grammar and punctuation, pushing them to choose topic sentences that did the work of the paragraph for them. They told me they felt ready for college because of my class.

Six hours ago, I'd been feeling pretty good about myself. I was a pretty good teacher. I had this gig down.

Six hours ago, I'd been looking forward to Chinese food for dinner.

"Honestly," I said to Sophia, setting the beer down on the counter. "What the actual fuck?"

Sophia sighed, opening the rice in its white carton. I just stared at her in disbelief as she dished out a helping for herself on a clean blue plate, and did the same for me. She grabbed the chicken and vegetables she'd ordered for herself, using some chopsticks to scrape the food onto the rice. Then, she did the same with my entrée.

With my end-of-the-school-year celebration chicken.

The words *what the actual fuck* hung in the air and reverberated in my mind. My students liked to say it. It had never felt so appropriate to me as it did at that moment.

I stared at Sophia as she took her plate to the kitchen table and calmly began eating, taking sips from her water container between bites. She did have extraordinary table manners. She always chewed her food delicately, her mouth closed, elbows never on the table.

I watched her eat her entire meal after I'd grabbed a second beer from the fridge.

After Sophia finished her food, she picked up her empty plate and put it in the sink, rinsing it under the faucet briefly before putting her plate in the dishwasher. I'd taken the liberty of opening a third beer and was drinking it.

Why the hell not? I wasn't teaching tomorrow. I could come in with a champion hangover, and no one would notice as Principal Watson ran us through all the fire drill procedures, then the annual update on the latest in CPR instructions.

"I'm serious," Sophia said softly, not looking at me, looking at the dishwasher door she had just closed. "I want you out of the house by the end of the week."

"The end of the *week*? Do you mean, like, tomorrow?"

Sophia considered, her tongue combing over her teeth, looking for stray pieces of food. She flossed twice a day.

Had she always just been too perfect?

"By the end of the week," she said. "Yeah, Holden. Sunday night will be fine."

Then she turned and went upstairs, telling me over her shoulder she was going to take a shower.

After she left, I stood in the kitchen holding my cold beer. Finally, feeling numb, I turned my attention to my celebratory General Tso's, now cold on the counter. I ate it clumsily with my fingers, standing over the sink, listening to bits of rice falling into the stainless-steel basin like sprinkles of fat, cold rain.

Two

They say that eventually, the things you found adorable about someone when you first met them—well, eventually those are the things that start to drive you bananas.

Like if you meet a girl, and she scrunches her nose up in a particular way every time she laughs—at first you think it's the most adorable thing you've ever seen.

But then after a few years, you're so annoyed. Why does she scrunch her nose up like that every time she laughs? Does she have allergies? Sinus issues? Undiagnosed medical problems?

For Carmen and me, our love story was quite brief.

When she met me yesterday—Sunday afternoon—Carmen had seemed charmed by my smile, my reticence, the English-teacher vibe she said she could catch off me.

"I bet you're the teacher everyone loves," she'd said. "Our regulars will love you."

She already hated everything about me that she once loved: my smile, my reticence, the English-teacher vibe I couldn't help but give off.

Her frustration was palpable by 11:00 a.m. that Monday.

I guess Carmen thought since I was a teacher—since I had a master's degree—I was very smart and would pick up on espresso slinging in a heartbeat.

That didn't seem to be the case.

Maybe I should have mentioned in the interview that I only drank Folgers, black.

The morning had been extremely busy. Monday morning seemed like a terrible time to induct a new person. Perhaps that's why our love story went awry so fast, why my shine had worn off for Carmen so quickly.

This time, it was that I'd forgotten to take the old espresso grounds out of the silver cup thing before pushing the button to begin a brew, so the espresso came out full of grounds and very nasty.

Carmen had to close her eyes and sigh—I assumed to prevent herself from screaming at me. Her annoyance was almost visceral.

"Apologies," I said, grabbing the long silver handle and cranking it counterclockwise, as Carmen had taught me at around 5:15 that morning.

She had to keep a sense of perspective. This was, after all, my first day, and I was, after all, an English teacher.

Not a barista.

She'd seen my application, to which I'd carefully stapled a resume. She'd made the remark that nobody really did that anymore, but then again, nobody forty-five years old had ever applied to work at JavaHut, I was willing to bet.

Without carding Carmen or my new coworkers, I placed the median age of JavaHut employees at around twenty-one.

Which would make me an outlier in a pretty serious way.

"Next time," Carmen said, in a voice that seemed to exhaust itself from having to muster up so much patience, "empty the old grounds into the trash before putting new ground espresso into the tin, and tamping it

15

down, as we went over."

I nodded. "Right."

I put my thumb and forefinger on the rim of my visor and pulled it down in a mock gesture, like a cowboy saying, "yes ma'am."

Carmen did not seem amused, but a woman at the register was ready to order a drink, and I watched Carmen turn her smile on—the peppy one she saved just for customers.

Carmen was probably dragging the median up, I thought. I pegged her as twenty-seven or twenty-eight. Or was it the mean she was dragging up, not the median?

Good thing I taught tenth-grade English, not math.

"Welcome to JavaHut, what can we get started for you?" I heard Carmen say brightly.

I took my white cloth and wiped down the machine, as she'd taught me, making sure it was always ready to brew the next shot of espresso.

I wondered how long Carmen had worked here, and if she thought the JavaHut logo, prominent on her apron, was as stupid as I thought it was.

It featured a cup of coffee, outlined in black, steam rising off the top. It looked like it was trying to be the Starbucks logo—the iconic mermaid holding her tail in a way that was actually metaphysically impossible, but at least carried some degree of visual interest.

The JavaHut logo looked like a toddler had drawn it.

Honestly, a toddler probably would have done a better job.

I also wondered how many Pizza Hut jokes were made at JavaHut's expense.

"Skinny mocha," I heard Carmen repeat. "You still want whip?"

The customer, an older white woman with gray hair and a soft smile, had already pulled a five-dollar bill from her wallet.

Carmen stepped over to me and repeated the order slowly, like I was dumb.

I wasn't dumb.

But I was quite hungover. I'd had a lot of beer on Sunday night, after the interview with Carmen, after realizing I'd accepted a full-time job at JavaHut.

The words bounced around in my mind for longer than they would have, were I not wrestling a hangover.

"A skinny mocha, no whip," Carmen said. "That means nonfat milk, and do not put whip cream on top."

"What about the sprinkles?"

I suspected the answer, but I just couldn't help myself. I was tired and my brain was a foggy mess. I was so ready for my first shift to be over so I could get something to eat—preferably something very greasy.

"No sprinkles," Carmen said through gritted teeth. "The chocolate sprinkles go on top of the whip, so if there's no whip..." She raised her thin eyebrows, which I was pretty sure she penciled in, and let her sentence trail off to nowhere.

"Then no sprinkles," I said, saluting her again with my visor. "Got it, boss!"

Carmen turned on her heels and went back into the staff room, where I was sure she was screaming into a refrigerator filled with gallons of different kinds of milk.

Who knew there were so many kinds of milk: 2%, 1%, skim, almond, coconut, soy. JavaHut had recently even added a vegan milk option—oat milk.

Who the hell drank oat milk?

I glanced over at the nice woman who'd ordered the drink and gave her a smile. It was possible I'd grabbed the wrong container of milk from the mini-fridge under the espresso machine when I did the steaming part. I was having a hard time remembering if we kept the skim milk in the canister with the pink lid, or in the one with the blue lid. JavaHut really should just label its canisters with words, I thought, and not rely on this bizarre color-coding system that could obviously go so wrong if a barista happened to be struggling with a hangover.

Maybe I should suggest that to Carmen.

Oh well, I thought as I handed the skinny mocha, no whip, no sprinkles to the woman who'd ordered it. She took the coffee and told me to have a nice day. She looked too skinny anyway. If I had accidentally switched the milk, she probably could use a few more grams of fat in her diet.

* * *

I'd been anxious for my shift to end at 1:30 p.m. I wanted to go home, get something to eat, and then get some rest.

Then I remembered that home was depressing.

"Home" was one of those hotels that rents by the week—the kind of hotel a person would drive by and think, I will never need to rent a hotel room by the week.

Until you do, and then you're providing your driver's license, a deposit, and a week's rent upfront to a cranky, balding man named Geoffrey who looks at you like it's your fault he works there.

The Scenic View Hotel, South Division. The part that isn't so great. An area of Grand Rapids I wouldn't let Matthew go to with his friends, if he'd ever asked.

Weekly rates.

Monthly rates, too, but I wasn't allowing myself to inquire within about those.

No way Sophia would kick me out for a month.

She had said this would be for the summer, but she couldn't have meant it. Summer lasted a long time. This had to be something temporary she was going through.

She would miss me, wouldn't she?

She'd think that even though our relationship had grown pretty thin in the last nine months, seeing scraps of me around the house was better than nothing.

Right?

I unlocked the door to my new home and stepped inside.

Brown carpet greeted my eyes. Brown paneling. So much brown. The 1970s lived at the Scenic View Hotel.

I should be lucky the carpet wasn't shag.

Queen-size bed. Decent mattress.

Small round table with two folding chairs. Pretty uncomfortable.

Kitchenette: sink (no garbage disposal, no dishwasher); microwave; small refrigerator (no freezer), also brown.

Ironically, no coffee maker, so it was a good thing JavaHut had accepted me so quickly. All the coffee I could drink for free.

Bathroom: shower, no tub. Small vanity.

There was no good place to put my toothbrush, so I had decided it would live in a Styrofoam cup on the back of the john.

I walked over to the small fridge and opened it. Yesterday, a trip to the grocery store had provided me with what I thought I would need, but I'd specifically only allowed myself to buy the essentials: a loaf of bread, a package of smoked turkey, sliced cheddar, mustard—the hot kind, the kind Sophia didn't care for.

To be healthy, I'd grabbed a couple of yogurts—the Greek ones—and a head of lettuce, to be an optimist. I forgot salad dressing, though.

A twenty-four pack of Budweiser—to be a pessimist.

A fifth of whiskey in case things got bad. At home, I kept one above my workbench in the garage, and there were a handful of times that had come in handy.

I felt too tired to make a sandwich, so I opened the loaf of bread and pulled a slice out. No toaster in this room, I realized. I ate it plain, in about three bites.

And then for the hell of it, because what else was I doing, I grabbed a Bud from the small fridge and cracked it, standing in the middle of the shitty kitchenette. 1:53 p.m. on a Monday.

I finished the beer in five gulps, setting the empty can in the middle of the table. I was contemplating opening another one when I felt my cell vibrate in my pocket.

Sophia, I thought instinctively.

Nope.

HOW ARE YOU?

Matthew.

I moved my fingers on the phone's keyboard to reply. DOING OKAY. HOW ARE YOU?

OKAY.

I saw the three little dots that meant his fingers were

typing more, but after a minute of me staring at them, they went away, and staring at the white screen didn't make them come back.

He knew, of course. Sophia thought he was old enough to be told like an adult what was going on with us, but she'd taken the lead on the conversation, and she'd kept it to the high points.

I had little doubt she'd Googled around until she'd found an instructive article on the best way to tell your newly-teenage son that his parents are choosing to spend a little time apart. That's something my perfectionist wife would do.

I could picture her typing into the laptop: *best way to tell a child their parents want a trial separation.*

Well, one of them was choosing a trial separation.

The other had chosen a job that paid a measly twelve bucks an hour and a residency in a depressing hotel. I felt like I could do nothing but watch as what was *supposed* to have been my first summer of decadence in decades turn into JavaHut limbo. I had pictured taking long naps, going on leisurely runs, and playing basketball with Matthew. This was a far cry from that Rockwellian mirage.

I sighed and sat down on the bed, glad I'd brought my own pillows and the spare plaid comforter we kept in the basement for company. The bedspread that had come with Room 204 did not inspire confidence.

It was not something you'd ever want to take a black light to.

I laid all the way back, the beer cooling my nervous system, entering my bloodstream, happily counteracting all the caffeine I'd had on my shift and easing the hangover I'd earned from drinking so much last night.

I started a text to Matthew again, and then erased it, then started another message, and erased that one too, wondering if he was staring at our digital conversation the way I had been a few minutes before.

Probably not.

It was likely he was still texting. It seemed he had a new girlfriend, although Sophia and I weren't completely certain. Katie. One of the library chess girls. She had black hair and seemed nice. Pretty. Easy smile.

I'M SORRY THIS IS HAPPENING, I wrote to Matthew, then erased it.

THIS ISN'T YOUR FAULT, I wrote.

Then erased it.

These were exactly the statements Sophia and I had made to him the other day, in person. What good would it be to repeat them?

Would they be more powerful in writing?

Maybe.

Maybe he needed something he could go back and read and reread.

Maybe seeing it in black and white would cement it in his mind.

I had hated the look on Matthew's face when we'd broken the news—when Sophia had broken the news.

He'd been playing basketball with his friend Daniel that Saturday. He'd needed a shower. I could smell his funk from the chair next to him, but I kept my mouth shut about it and sipped a longneck instead.

He had taken it so well. He had been so calm. I had tried not to read into it too much, tried not to assume he took it so smoothly because it wasn't a big shock.

Rather, I tried to trust that he took the news well because he was a mature kid and because we weren't crying. Our voices had been steady, in control.

And because we hadn't fought in front of him.

At least not that much.

The fighting was usually in our bedroom, and neither of us was prone to yell. The fighting looked a lot like each of us being angry with the other, shooting complaints and insults that didn't do anything to dissolve the tension between us. Fights ended when Sophia, exasperated, would leave to take a bath or a long walk, or I'd disappear to the garage.

But how much fighting was too much?

Was I not being honest with myself about how much Sophia and I fought? How much Matthew overhead? How smart he was?

I could see his face clearly in front of me: his big brown eyes, dark hair, sweaty. His full lips. He'd gotten those from Sophia, not me. His t-shirt, gray, stretched out at the neck. I knew where every freckle and mole were underneath that shirt.

Maybe it went over because the word "temporary" was thrown around a lot—mostly by me, but a few times by Sophia.

Temporary.

Trial.

Live apart for a time.

Just the summer.

To figure things out.

It's really only a matter of weeks—one lousy summer.

I'm sure we'll figure this out before August.

We had stayed away from the S-word—separation.

Certainly, we had steered clear of the D-word.

I sighed again, erasing my last text to Matthew: THIS HAS NOTHING TO DO WITH YOU.

Maybe Matthew had taken the news so well because many of his friends had parents who had split.

But that was conceding that this was permanent, which it wasn't.

This was temporary. JavaHut was only for now. Room 204 with the depressing carpet and paneling was going to be a blip in my long-term memory.

Which is why I settled with just texting my son: MISS YOU BUD. SEE YOU TOMORROW.

Three

"Nice to meet you, Charlie."

I was shaking the hand of a very tall, young Asian man. His smile was large and sincere. I had a good feeling about him right away. I also pegged him at about seventeen, maybe eighteen. Not much older than my son. He was probably still in high school.

"Nice to meet you, man. Your first day was yesterday?"

"Yep," I said.

He raised his black eyebrows conspiratorially. "Did Carmen put you through the wringer?"

I laughed, adjusting my black JavaHut-approved visor over my eyes.

It was 5:05 a.m. We would open our doors in less than half an hour, but for now, it was just Charlie and me, four empty carafes of coffee waiting to be filled, and a mountain of espresso beans to grind.

Carmen would be in soon, as would Kelsey, the young barista I'd also met yesterday.

So far, Charlie hadn't seemed fazed by my age. He also didn't seem to pick up on the fact that I was deep in an internal debate with myself about what to tell him—how much to tell any of my new coworkers—about my predicament.

"No guys," I pictured myself saying. "I have a real job. Not that this isn't a real job. This is an important job. But I do have an actual career. I'm a teacher. This is my summer vacation."

I pictured them nodding, understanding, maybe even thinking it was cool.

But at least for the time being, I had chosen to keep those cards close to my chest.

It would probably come out in conversation anyway, I thought—what my deal was.

That was another phrase my students said all the time— "What's your deal?"

What *was* my deal?

If it came up—the fact that my wife kicked me out and I grabbed the first job I could so we don't go broke this summer while she figured her shit out, since it was too late to commit to teaching summer school—well, if it came up, then I could decide to what degree I wanted to burden these young people.

And considering none of them had ever been married—probably, anyway—it stood to reason none of them would even begin to understand how frayed and messed up things can feel, how complicated your romantic relationship gets after you've been living it every day for more than two decades.

"She's tough on you, at first," Charlie said, donning a clear plastic glove on his right hand. He had opened a box of muffins and began to put them into the bakery case.

I wasn't sure if customers were under the impression that any food sold at JavaHut was in any way fresh, but it most definitely was not. All the baked goods came pre-made, pre-packaged, pre-everything. We just sold them.

He added, "She warms up—I promise."

"How long have you worked here?" I asked Charlie. He laughed, even though I hadn't been trying to crack a joke.

I took his lead and put a glove on as well, grabbing a chocolate muffin from the white box.

"Oh, like four months. I go to CC," he said, referring colloquially to the community college downtown.

"Gotcha," I said. The words *I'm a teacher* were sitting on my tongue. Would saying them make him like me more?

Instead of blurting them out, I took a sip of coffee. Charlie had brewed the first pot and had poured us each a cup. It actually tasted incredibly good.

Unlimited drinks during the shift. One food item per eight-hour shift. Not terrible.

Caffeine was welcome, considering I was exhausted on my feet. I'd slept maybe three hours Monday night, and all of them had been total shit.

I'd taken a nap after texting with Matthew, slept too long, then woke up too late. I ordered a pizza because I'd felt too tired and potentially too buzzed to leave Room 204. Then, because I am a genius, I drank more beer with the pizza. I couldn't fall asleep until after 1:00 a.m., even though I turned off the lights and the television at around 11:00 p.m.

The strange sounds of Room 204 were still too new to me, and I woke up around 2:00 a.m., desperate to sleep more. I had had to remind myself I wasn't at home in my own bed, and that Sophia wasn't next to me.

I couldn't remember the last time I'd spent this much time by myself, without Sophia, without Matthew. Maybe several years ago—the weekend after I had my vasectomy. Sophia had kindly taken a trip to Mackinaw with Matthew—just the two of them—leaving me to rest on the couch with some movies and a few books, the freezer filled with meals Sophia had cooked for me and half a dozen bags of frozen peas. That had been a fun weekend, despite some discomfort.

This depressing hotel wasn't my familiar living room, nor was it like the hotels we stayed in on the vacation we'd taken last year—our epic road trip to the Grand Canyon. We'd debated getting two hotel rooms for that trip. Wasn't Matthew old enough to warrant having his own hotel room?

Where we'd landed, though, was that this would be the last time we would all share a hotel a room, just the three of us, which made the nights that we did feel bittersweet to me. The last family vacation where Matthew would want to share a hotel room with his folks. He wasn't a little kid anymore.

Now...

Who knew?

Would there be any more family road trips to the Grand Canyon? Or anywhere else, for that matter?

"Good, huh," Charlie asked, snapping me out of my memories.

"What?"

"Good coffee," he said with a grin. He looked so well-rested, no drama on his mind. I envied him. There was probably still alcohol swimming around in my bloodstream.

My brain was a dead place.

"It isn't Starbucks," he said.

I chuckled. "It's very good."

"I tried getting hired at Starbucks," Charlie said. "Too competitive. I hear they give you money for college."

"That's great," I said. "I think I heard that, too."

"Yeah," Charlie said. "Don't tell Carmen, but I still apply like every month. I'd love to ditch this place and go work there."

"Don't worry," I said. "Your secret is safe with me." I took another sip of the coffee. It sincerely was good. It didn't need any creamer, sugar, or milk. Better than Folgers.

"Thanks," Charlie said, grinning. "Plus, the girls at Starbucks are *way* hotter than the girls here. No offense to Kelsey, or Lila. Or Carmen."

I chuckled again. "Is that so?"

"*Way*," Charlie said, crouching to nudge an oversized cranberry craze muffin back into alignment.

"Cuter *dudes*, too, if that's your thing," he added, pretty casually, emphasizing *dudes* now.

It took my brain a second to find the right response.

"Oh," I said. "Well, generally, for me, it's ladies."

Nice of Charlie to think I had any game at all for either gender.

I wondered how old he thought I was. For forty-five, I was in decent enough shape. Sometimes women looked at me for a moment or two longer than was necessary.

Or so I sometimes imagined.

A few years ago, there had been a long-term substitute teacher, Ms. Keely. I was worried she had some kind of crush on me. She stopped by my classroom often and lingered.

And she was gorgeous. Maybe thirty. Long black hair.

I had tried not to encourage her, waited for her assignment to end when Hannah—Mrs. Hedges—came back from maternity leave.

I didn't wear a wedding ring, which I had thought on more than one occasion might make me vulnerable to the attention of any woman who wanted to try to bark up that tree.

But then again, I'd *never* worn a wedding ring, and nothing too over the line had ever happened.

When Sophia and I got married, I took my wedding ring off pretty much the moment we returned from our honeymoon in Niagara Falls.

It had made her cry—sob, actually, but I eventually got her to understand it wasn't a commentary on my feelings for her—just a result of the fact that I hated rings, and the gold band had been digging into my skin the entire week we were supposed to be enjoying our new life together. I didn't like the way it felt on my finger. I never got comfortable with it.

Then again, Sophia would say, I never gave it a chance.

"You tried it for a week," she'd say. "Our *honeymoon*." I knew that that was the insult to the injury, that I was literally—in our first week together as husband and wife—giving her a reason to think our marriage didn't suit me.

So, I never really wore my wedding ring. It lived in Sophia's jewelry box next to some brooches she'd inherited from her grandmother. I liked to think about the ring there, safe and secure, keeping her precious jewelry company.

I think deep down, though, even after eighteen years, it still pissed her off that I didn't wear that gold wedding ring.

"Cool, cool," Charlie said. "You wanna get the espresso machine warmed up? You remember how? I can help you if you forgot."

"I think I've got it," I said.

I looked down at my left hand, naked and pale as always. Not even a white space where a ring used to be.

I took another long sip of JavaHut's finest black coffee.

If my wife and I did split up, at least not wearing a ring wasn't something I was going to have to get used to.

* * *

On my break, I took a fresh cup of coffee and let Charlie know I was stepping out for my fifteen minutes. I wasn't very hungry, but I did feel dead on my feet. I decided to walk around to the back of the shop.

JavaHut was situated in a strip mall. Next door, there was a dry-cleaning place. Next to that, a Mexican restaurant, but not an authentic one. It was one of those fake kind of TexMex places that had a habit of springing up around the Midwest. Terrible food. Next to that, there was a place that did dry cleaning.

Depressing. Garish neon signs. Concrete everywhere.

I'd been drawn to its anonymity when I'd applied at JavaHut. It was not in the part of Grand Rapids where I spent most of my time, and it was far enough away from St. Bridget's that I thought I stood a good chance of not running into anyone I knew.

Because the fewer people who knew about this dysfunctional summer, the better.

But there was something else that had drawn me to JavaHut.

When Matthew was a newborn and very fussy, there were a handful of times Sophia had needed a break—like a real break—the kind where she was alone in the house to soak in the tub and then take a long nap.

I'd strap Matthew into his car seat and just drive around—sometimes for hours. He'd fuss for ten or fifteen minutes, and I'd turn on some classic rock. Soon enough, he'd be asleep, and I'd drive around, cruising the parts of town where there were fewer traffic lights so I could keep the Camry at a steady twenty-five miles an hour for Matthew.

I remembered driving by JavaHut in those bleary, sleep-deprived months. I remembered its stupid logo and its lack of a drive-thru because more than once—and since I couldn't get a beer—I thought a cup of coffee might be nice.

But no drive-thru for such a shitty coffee joint on the side of town no one goes to, unless they want, for some reason, to eat at the shitty faux-Mexican restaurant or shop at a dollar store, or perhaps get a paycheck cashed in advance for an exorbitant fee.

Perhaps my brain had been drawn to this place because it had wanted me to remember back to a time in my life when this part of town had offered a kind of reprieve to me, as a new father with a tiny newborn in my backseat. Those were hard times—the early months of Matthew's life when Sophia and I were figuring everything out together—but those times were also the source of many of my sweetest memories.

I couldn't remember feeling this spun-out and exhausted since Matthew was a newborn.

I sat down on the curb behind the dry cleaner's,

thankful for a few minutes off my feet. I was used to being on my feet all day, teaching. But my muscles were getting used to the new things I was asking them to do: crouch, squat, reach above the espresso machine to pour in a fresh bag of whole beans.

I reached into my back pocket for my cell phone.

Without thinking too much about it, I called Sophia. She picked up after the fourth ring, right when I thought it might go to her voicemail, and I honestly had no idea if I should leave her a message or not.

Which was a strange feeling. I'd never thought twice about leaving a voicemail for my wife before.

"Hello?" she said. She sounded a little careful, like she was treading lightly.

"Hi," I said, matching her caution.

"Hi, Holden," she said. It didn't sound like I had woken her. I checked the watch on my left wrist. It was 9:01 a.m.

"How are you?" I asked.

I tried to guess where in the house she might be. Maybe still in bed. Probably not, though.

"I'm fine," she said.

"That's good," I said.

Long pause.

Awkward.

I wasn't used to that either.

It never felt like this—not even during the ugly fights.

"Was there something you needed?" she said.

I stared at a pile of trash gathering at the curb a few inches from my feet. Napkins, wadded up. A black plastic fork with two crushed prongs.

What *did* I need?

"Yeah," I said. "I need to know what's going on."

There was another long pause, and the sound of what I thought might be water running in the kitchen sink. Maybe she was rinsing her breakfast dishes.

"We talked about this, Holden," she said.

"Barely," I answered.

I could feel anger welling up right under the surface. I hadn't realized I was so angry because I was so tired, but there it was, barreling out of my mouth before I could stop it.

Because it was bullshit. She had told me on a Thursday that she wanted me out. We talked to Matthew Saturday afternoon. I took the bare essentials, was out by Saturday. I got a residency in Room 204 on Saturday. I got this job on Sunday morning.

I'd been so busy following her orders, I realized, I hadn't pressed her hard enough to understand where these orders were coming from.

Was *that* part of the test? Was she waiting for me to fight back harder, to press her?

Maybe I was already failing her and didn't even know it.

"What the fuck, Sophia?"

"What else do you need me to say?" she asked.

"I don't know," I said. "But I don't understand what's going on right now. With us."

"We need a break," she said. "We talked about this," she repeated.

"You dumped this on me," I said.

"You seemed to agree," she said slowly.

I closed my eyes and rubbed my face. My cell phone felt hot against my cheek.

"Maybe I agreed to this too quickly," I said. "Maybe I should have put up more of a fight last Thursday."

The more I thought about the idea, the more sense it made.

This was like how she'd drop hints in October about what she wanted for Christmas, and it was my job to pick up on the hints. If I didn't—if I asked her in December what she wanted for Christmas—it demonstrated that I hadn't been listening well enough.

I had finally picked up on that move in year five of our marriage.

Yes, this was it—this was the answer. I hadn't put up enough of a fight. I should fight her now, then I could come home.

"Or maybe you just knew I was right," she said.

"*Right*?" I repeated.

"Right about us needing some time apart," Sophia said. "So we can think."

"Is that what you're doing over there?" I asked.

For the first time, I heard an edge of kindness in her voice. "Right now, I'm making a cup of tea," she said. "Getting ready for work. But yeah. Of course, Holden. I'm thinking."

"Tell me what you're thinking," I said. "I got a job, you know."

"Matthew told me," she said. "That's great. Thanks. That'll help—you know, financially."

In other words, it would fund our separation.

It was too much.

"Sophia, this is crazy," I said.

"It's not crazy, Holden," she said evenly.

"We're married."

"Yes," she said. "And we may still be married when this is over."

"Really?" I asked.

She sighed again, loudly. "Look. Maybe. That's the point, right? I want us to take a summer to think about if this is what we really want for the next...you know, thirty, forty years, or whatever. We've had a good marriage, but these last few years, we fight constantly—"

"Not constantly," I interrupted.

"Close enough to constantly," she said. "Come on, Holden. I want you to be honest with yourself. Be honest with me."

If I was honest with myself, I wished she would stop using my name so much.

I didn't even care for my name. The name Holden was synonymous with phonies. It was unusual enough to stand out, and it seemed oddly prophetic that I would become an English teacher. My parents weren't even fans of Salinger—Holden was an old family name.

And it was why I avoided teaching *Catcher in the Rye*.

Sophia continued. "I'm encouraging you to be honest with yourself, and then you can be more honest with me. We aren't close anymore. We don't have sex. We don't talk, we don't share... our lives... We've become two completely separate people..."

I took a sip of my coffee. I had only about one minute left on my break, but it felt too embarrassing to tell Sophia that.

It would have been easier to teach this summer, like I had been doing every summer. I had my lesson plans already done. The classes tended to be small. And the students who enrolled were missing credits, so they were often highly motivated to get their work done so that they didn't risk not graduating with their friends.

But then again, maybe there was no way I could have taught this summer. Maybe it was good I got this stupid job because maybe for once, I needed to do something where I didn't have to think, or be a role model, or a leader.

Because being a teacher meant caring more about my students than myself, and right now, I didn't want to have to care about anyone other than myself.

"So what are the odds?" I said. "Just tell me that."

"The *odds*?" she asked.

"The odds we'll still be married at the end of the summer. That you're going to want to still be married."

"I don't know, Holden," she said. "I should go."

Please stop using my name, I thought.

"*I* should go," I said.

"Okay," she said.

"When are we going to talk again?" I asked. If I sounded needy, I didn't really care.

"I don't know," she said. "I don't have a schedule. I think the best thing to do would be to take this one day at a time."

"Will you call me tomorrow?"

"I work tomorrow," Sophia said.

Me too, I wanted to scream. I *also* work tomorrow. And I was supposed to get a break this summer. Instead, I went out and got a job at the first place I filled an application out at so we don't have to add financial stress to our pile of problems. At a job that's far beneath me, I wanted to add.

Instead, I simply said to my wife, "Okay."

"Are you still taking Matthew out to dinner tonight?" she asked.

"Yeah," I said.

Pizza, probably, although the thought of more pizza made my stomach turn over. I would need a nap before then—perhaps a beer, too.

What a mess.

"I'll be there to pick him up at six," I said.

"Okay," she said.

"I love you, bye," I said, our standard way to end a phone call.

When I realized she'd ended the call before hearing me tell her I loved her, I crushed the coffee cup in my hand, a few ounces of hot liquid spilling over my fingers, my wrist, and onto the depressing concrete parking lot under me. I stood up, cursing.

I'd overstayed my fifteen-minute break.

Jesus H. Christ.

Four

My head was pounding as I walked back into JavaHut.

Maybe I was just still hungover from last night, but Sophia's words felt impossible to process. They swirled around what was once the perfect library of my mind, which was now a total trash trailer.

I was adjusting my visor back into place, ready to grit out the next four hours of my shift, ready to give an apology to Charlie for being a touch late, when I heard a voice behind me call, "Mr. Averett."

I turned around.

At the cash register, helping a woman holding a baby was a JavaHut employee with dark blonde hair. I could tell my brain was working on putting the pieces together—matching the face with the voice.

I made myself smile. The barista with the dark blonde hair smiled at me. She looked like she wanted to say more. Instead, though, she whipped back around to the customer, swiping a Visa through our credit card machine and returning it. The customer shifted the weight of her baby in her arms to tuck the Visa back into her purse.

I finished tying the strings of my apron behind my back just as my new coworker turned to me and put her hands on my shoulders, squaring up to me.

It was tremendously odd.

She was incredibly beautiful.

"Mr. Averett," she repeated. "Oh. My. God."

"Hi," I said. "You're... Lila?"

Thank you, brain.

That was the right answer.

"Yes," she said. She looked very pleased. "You remember me!"

I didn't, actually.

At least, I didn't think I did.

But I'd found her name, at least, in the messy files of my altered mind.

Between the hangover and Sophia messing with my head, and trying to remember all the ways someone could order a cup of coffee, I wasn't sure what I remembered. Except that my brain had reminded me that this morning, Charlie had mentioned I would meet Lila when her shift started at 9:00 a.m., since she'd taken Monday off.

So I just stood there, grinning at her like the idiot I was.

"This. Is. So. Random," she said, still squared up to me, shaking her head.

I wondered how long she was going to leave her hands on my shoulders.

And if this was even appropriate.

She was nearly as tall as I was, probably 5'9" or 5'10." She seemed to have a way of speaking where all the words in her sentences stood apart, like she was inserting imaginary periods between all her words.

And she was very pretty—would Sophia call her hair color dirty blonde? It didn't look dyed. She had fair skin, very clear and pale. Pink lips—very thick. A lot of mascara, I could garner. Bright hazel eyes.

She had a slim build—not overly skinny. Athletic—like

Sophia. Probably a runner or yoga enthusiast, too. She was a few inches taller than my wife. Her forehead was almost perfectly in line with my chin. She had on a simple gray t-shirt and black pants under her required Java-Hut ensemble: visor and black apron, tied in the back, the hideous JavaHut logo prominently displayed across her chest.

Which I tried not to linger on. Her chest was pretty nice.

"I haven't seen you in like, oh. Man. What. Like. Ten years? Nine?" she said.

Former student, you idiot, my brain yelled.

Oh boy. This was happening.

"Lila," I said, pulling my shoulders back a little, in the hopes that she would now remove her hands from them. "Of course," I said. "It's so great to see you."

"Mr. Averett," she said again. She shook her head slightly.

But thankfully, she did take her hands off my shoulders and run them through the ends of her long ponytail.

"Hold on," she said. She held up her pointer finger and glanced at the door, which had just closed behind a small group. "We've got customers."

Indeed, a handful of coffee enthusiasts had stepped into JavaHut during our odd reunion, and I was relieved. I busied myself at the espresso machine, Charlie popping in and out from the staff room a few times with fresh gallons of milk and clean rags to wipe down the espresso machine.

Wands, as I had learned they were called. The metal arms that steamed milk.

I was thankful for all the mochas and lattes and the

opportunities they offered me to think.

In my head, I made my brain try to place Lila.

Ten years ago...

Ten years ago, I was teaching ninth grade English, not tenth. Western Literature? Was that right?

Or was that the year we tried block scheduling—a pilot that wasn't terribly successful? Our administration had finally conceded its failure and had thankfully abandoned block scheduling a few years later.

Lila. What was her last name?

I had no recollection of her in my class, even though she was probably as pretty back then as she was now.

Not that that was a pervy thing for me to think. I had just noticed over the years that the standouts were the bright kids, the enthusiastic kids, and often the attractive kids—the students who were the easiest for me to remember, if I was honest.

Well, those and the troublemakers, of course.

Lila.

What was her last name?

I couldn't think of it by the time Lila had a break in customers, so I just had to slap on another smile as I stood there in my visor and JavaHut apron.

"So how are you, Mr. Averett?" Lila asked. "And can I ask, what are you doing working here? Are you still at St. Bridget's? I like the stubble, by the way," she said, touching her chin with her fingertips.

Not a look I had gone for on purpose, but I hadn't told her that her formerly clean-shaven teacher was now disheveled and calling the Scenic View Hotel home.

I realized it was highly probable that Lila, whatever her last name was, might have also been doing the math on me.

Was I retired? Did I get fired? Had I had some kind of midlife crisis—career change?

There was another teacher at our school to whom that happened—Mrs. Kenna—err, Ms. Kenna. Shannon. She left teaching after ten years, left her husband, and started a new career as some kind of skincare product salesperson. Something like that. It was dramatic, when it was all unfolding, and I hadn't understood it well at the time.

"Summer gig," I said to Lila with my most polite smile. So far, that was the safest answer for all of us.

"Ah," she said. She seemed relieved. "You don't want to teach summer school? Didn't you used to?"

"Nah," I said. "Not this year. I wanted to take a few months off from teaching, but—you know, the extra income is appreciated. Saving for college for my son."

That last part my brain filled in as a lie, but once it was said, I liked how natural it had sounded. That was a narrative that made total sense, I thought. Thank God. Matthew would be going to college in a few years—that was true enough, too.

"Tell me about it," Lila said, rolling her eyes. "Tuition is *so* crazy expensive. I can't even imagine what it will be in the future." She scoffed a little. "How old are your kids?"

"Just the one, a son," I said. "Matthew. He's fourteen."

"Cool," Lila said. She was playing with a bangle bracelet on her wrist, and I was praying Charlie would come out and join our conversation.

Not that it was awkward, but until I could find Lila in

my memories, I suspected it was going to feel a little weird for me.

What kind of student had she been? What kind of grades had she earned?

How old was she now? Twenty-five? Twenty-six?

Was she going to tell Charlie I was a teacher? That was fine, I thought. If Lila thought this was a normal thing, maybe she could just sell it to Carmen, Charlie, and Kelsey, and I wouldn't even have to worry about my secret life spilling out at the wrong moment.

"Mr. Averett," Lila said slowly, smiling again. "This is like. Honestly. This is the coolest. We get to hang out all summer," she said, with enthusiasm that felt genuine. "It'll be like summer camp. This will be so fun!"

I chuckled.

Dear God, could JavaHut get another customer through that door.

Why was there no drive-thru?

Oh, because JavaHut was located in the most depressing strip mall in Grand Rapids, as though on purpose.

"Should I call you Holden, though?" Lila asked. "Not— not Mr. Averett?"

How did she know my first name? Had Carmen told her? Maybe she'd seen it on the schedule or had heard Kelsey talk about me.

Or maybe it was one of those things where you already knew your teacher's first name because when you're young, teachers are weirdly interesting people. You see them every single day, and they work with you and give you direct and personal feedback, but you never learn too much about them, as far as their personal lives go.

At least, I had perfected the art of not oversharing with my students. It was important to me. No family photos on my desk, no anecdotes about my weekend. I was a friendly teacher and warm, but a bit reticent, and not interested in letting my students know what life was like for me after the end bell.

"Ah, sure," I said. That was the right answer. I wasn't her teacher anymore. I was just another person she knew, a person she worked with.

God, this was weird.

And kind of embarrassing, honestly.

It occurred to me then that my coworkers probably talked about me when I wasn't there, or were going to all summer. What kinds of things would they say?

That Holden. He's nice and all but... He's kind of too old to be working here. He's a bit slow, too, don't you think?

"So, Holden," she said, a big smile on her face. "You like it here at JavaHut so far?"

"Oh, it's great," I said, rocking on my feet a little.

"We're no Starbucks," she joked, rolling her eyes. "We get to hear that from people all the time. Anyway, what's your drink?" she asked.

I almost said, "Budweiser." Then I realized she meant coffee.

"Ah. I like coffee," I said. "Just your basic, black, you know. No added stuff."

"Classic," she said, nodding. "But seriously, the best part of working here is experimenting."

"Hmm," I said.

"Seriously!" she giggled. "You get to mix stuff and come up with your own drinks. I've invented a ton, thank you very much, although Corporate has not been a big fan, so my drinks never make the menu," she said. "Still. My friends and some of the regulars know to ask. I'll have to teach you how to make some of them, but there's also a cheat sheet on the clipboard under the register if you get asked for something special and I'm not here."

"Thanks," I said. I forced myself to take a deep breath.

This isn't going to be that bad, I thought.

Come on. I had bigger problems anyway.

Like putting my life back together and making sure Room 204 wasn't a place I would be sleeping for the rest of my life.

She was just another former student, and actually, since she was from a decade ago, she probably wouldn't even tell any current students I was spending my summer pouring coffee for strangers for a rate that was just a few bucks above minimum wage.

Unless—and hopefully—Sophia and I could get through this crisis, and maybe I could quit JavaHut next week, move back home, and never utter the word "espresso" ever again.

"Since you asked," Lila said playfully, "mine's a Cinnamon Chai Chino."

"A what?" I asked.

"Cinnamon. Chai. Chino," she said slowly. "It's the best. It's chai with espresso and cinnamon. I'll teach you how to make it, the next time we're not busy," she said, nodding at a man with a newspaper tucked under his elbow who just walked in the door.

"Welcome to JavaHut," I heard Lila say cheerfully. "What can I get for you?"

A lobotomy, I thought.
Pronto.

Five

Coffee.

All I could smell was coffee.

The odor had infected my clothes, my hair, my skin. It had found a way to permeate even my fingernails. I smelled coffee every time I took in a deep breath no matter how much Old Spice I slicked into my armpits during my lunch break.

I parked in my usual spot behind the Scenic View Hotel, realizing suddenly how depressed I was that I already had a spot I could consider to be my usual. I was depressed that the black Dodge Ram parked next to me, rusted out by the back wheels, was some kind of a comfort, a sign of home.

For a long minute, I sat in my red Camry, breathing in the coffee smell, picturing the blood in my veins as running no longer blue, but dark brown.

Finally, as I did on some days before I headed to my classroom to teach, I found the energy to get out of the car, shut the door behind me, and walk into Room 204, imagining I was being pushed inside the godforsaken room by some kind of invisible hand behind me.

Since I had set my stay up with Geoffrey at the Scenic View as a weekly deal, there was no evidence of housekeeping having come through to clean.

That was on me.

Bummer, too, because the best part of staying in a hotel is leaving for the day, and coming back to see that someone has carefully made your bed, given you fresh towels, fluffed your pillows.

The feeling that someone was taking care of you.

No one was taking care of me in Room 204.

I was totally on my own.

And not at all hungry, so I took a hot shower in an effort to eliminate some of the coffee smell off my body. No real luck. Standing with a pilled, thin white towel wrapped around my waist in the middle of the room, I raised my forearm to my nose and took a deep whiff. Coffee.

How in two days had it seeped all the way down to my bones?

For lack of any better suggestion to myself for what to do now, I laid down in the unmade bed and shut my eyes.

What surprised me was the face that immediately popped up behind my eyelids.

Lila.

Lila what was her last name?

If I were at home—at my real home—I could consult the bookshelf in the basement where Sophia had neatly lined all my old yearbooks. It had become a habit to purchase a yearbook every year, which Sophia had told me was endearing. A waste of forty-five bucks, maybe, but I always thought I'd appreciate the volumes when I was old, after I'd retired.

Plus, many of the students were really into signing the insides of the front and back covers, and would hover in my classroom like puppies, asking to exchange notes in the pages.

It wasn't a lie that I got a kick out of looking at my

staff picture every year, seeing the subtle alterations each fall add up to big changes over time. Who was that young, skinny kid who taught his first year at St. Bridget's?

A newlywed—that's who.

When things had been so effortless with Sophia.

When we ate out in restaurants all the time and stayed up watching movies or making love. When we didn't have Matthew, or what felt like real responsibilities. When we weren't beholden to anyone else. It was all so much easier back then, and I had the photos to prove what I looked like those first few years.

It was a version of myself that I sometimes remembered—the one with a new wife and a new mortgage on a nice house just outside of Grand Rapids, tucked safely in the quiet suburbs.

After Matthew was born, I can read the lines on my face in the staff photos and see sleep deprivation, stress, the effects of chronic concern over ear infections, stomach flus, and even a case of hand-foot-and-mouth disease that didn't seem to bother Matthew for more than a weekend, but had knocked me off my ass for almost a week.

If I were home, I'd be able to magically travel back in time to Lila's year, look at her picture, try to remember who she was.

Maybe she'd even been one of the students who had written something in the front cover.

I was thinking about Lila, and then I realized I was not thinking about Lila as a student, but as a young woman.

An extremely beautiful young woman. Who had

smiled at me a lot.

I was thinking about her long hair. Her smooth skin. Her eyes. Her legs.

Uh-oh.

Her legs.

I opened my eyes and stared at the ceiling of Room 204—bright white, except for the spots marked by brown water stains.

Not a harbinger of anything good, those water stains. Would I wake up one morning during a heavy rain to water dripping on my forehead?

This was a specific type of hell.

There was no way I could think about Lila like she was a woman.

Obviously, she wasn't the sixteen-year-old she would have been when she was in my class, but once a student, always a student. That was my philosophy.

Not a woman. Not a woman.

Not a pretty woman.

Definitely not a woman I should be thinking about.

Although.

It wouldn't be the first time I had found female students attractive.

Of course I had. I would be lying to myself if I said I didn't, and there's no point in lying to myself. It would be like trying to be something I wasn't. I was a man—a heterosexual man.

As a teacher, if I found that I was starting to sense any kind of attraction to a young female student, I did the right thing, which was to be honest about it, with myself, and keep myself in check, making extra sure I wasn't paying any special attention to her, making sure I wasn't reading her papers with a certain lens and directing my feedback to her in a certain way. Making sure I didn't comment on her clothing or her hair—things I knew better to avoid. I hadn't needed the #MeToo movement to give me the common sense to know if I found a young female student attractive, I needed to do the opposite of ignore the feeling. I needed to acknowledge it, and then make sure I was acting correctly around it.

I needed to set the example and be the role model—especially so in a case where I happened to have a sixteen-year-old girl sit in the front row of my English class who could give even a seasoned supermodel a run for her money.

And there had been a few over the years. Their names were not too far from my tongue, but I couldn't provide them just the same. Not without my yearbooks to jog my memory.

Still. Once a student, always a student.

It didn't matter that Lila had smiled at me, and made me smile today. It didn't matter that she seemed genuinely sad when I untied my apron at the back, threw it in the laundry pile and clocked out—even though clocking out just meant initialing my timecard to assert to Carmen I'd worked my whole shift that day.

Lila had chatted with me most of the early afternoon, and it'd been nice. It'd made the time pass, and if I was honest with myself, it had made me feel less lonely.

It was a welcome feeling, considering my fate was to return to the most depressing hotel room in the Midwest to kill a few hours before I could take my son out to dinner, pretending, for his sake, that everything was fine, that everything was going to be fine, that all married couples go through peaks and valleys and that I'd likely be home before the end of the month.

I sighed and closed my eyes again. But there she was. The soft curve of her lips, the way she scrunched her nose when she laughed. "Godammit," I said out loud.

You are old enough to be her father, my brain told me.

It wasn't impossible, anyway.

A twenty-year age difference.

That was two whole decades of time.

There was no way I should be thinking about a woman I was old enough to parent.

No way.

I got out of the bed and whipped the white towel off and onto the floor, knowing no one but me would be picking it up later, and got into a pair of jeans and a t-shirt. The laundry was already starting to pile up by the makeshift shitty kitchen table, and I realized in a few days, I was either going to have to use the sketchy washing machine at the Scenic View, or ask Sophia if I could come home and do a load or two, like a broke college kid.

A nap was obviously not in my future, and I couldn't just sit in that tiny, shitty room with my thoughts, and with Lila's face swirling in and out of my mind's eye.

I also shouldn't add another beer to the one I had pounded in the shower, so I grabbed my keys from the table, patting down my back pocket to make sure I still had my wallet and cell. I had a few hours before Matthew was expecting me.

Time to get out of Room 204.

* * *

Not that I did anything particularly important.

I started to just drive around, with no destination in mind. I drove for a half-hour with the radio on. Classic rock: Steely Dan, CCR, Springsteen.

I considered going to a movie, but then thought better of it. It was a Tuesday afternoon, during the summer, and there was a high chance I'd run into students at the movies.

Plenty of times, Sophia, Matthew, and I ran into students at the movie theater, but it wasn't weird for a man to be seen at a matinee with his wife and his kid, buying popcorn and Junior Mints—Sophia's favorite combination—at the concession stand.

On the other hand, it would be weird to see your English teacher in a dark movie theater, alone, deep circles under his eyes, looking haggard in a t-shirt and smelling like Arabica beans and Budweiser.

I decided it was too risky.

Instead, I finally settled on driving to a smaller outlet mall on the southwest side of town that had fallen a little out of vogue since Waterfall Pointe opened a decade ago. All the good stores migrated to Waterfall while all the crappier ones stayed in South Hills.

I walked around a Sears for about forty-five minutes, and then managed to do the same at a J.C. Penney that had certainly seen better days. Even the mannequins looked like they wanted to escape the scene.

I settled on getting a soft pretzel at the food court and while eating it, realized I had been holding my phone in my hand since I parked the Camry because I was hoping Sophia would call me. Or text me.

I had initiated our last conversation, and pride would not let me initiate another one until she gave me something in return.

Still. Why was she not calling or texting me?

How long was I going to have to walk around a mall until I could get some scrap of communication from my wife?

Chewing the last bite of the pretzel and throwing the thin wax paper in a garbage can, I also thought about how my body probably hated me for the steady diet of coffee, booze, and carbs I'd been giving it since I left home. Everything I had ingested since Sophia had kicked me out had been brown. That couldn't be good.

No doubt my digestive tract was wondering where the mixed green salads were—the ones Sophia served with hard-boiled eggs. Where was the quinoa, the fresh hummus she made in our food processor and served on flatbread?

She had a knack for making healthy food that tasted good—a knack I had been missing in only a few short days, even if I did sprinkle hot sauce on her kale Caesar salad because come on—it needed something.

Finally, miraculously, it was time to find my car in the parking lot, get back in, and drive to the house to pick up Matthew. I hadn't bought a thing at the mall aside from the pretzel. I felt thankful for the simple blind luck of not having seen anyone I knew.

I texted Matthew when I pulled the Camry up to the curb in front of our house, not certain if I should pull into the driveway. What were the rules? Park on the street? Leave it running?

Thank God for cell phones, I thought. At least I didn't

have to ring the doorbell.

Matthew came bounding out a few minutes later in his gray hoodie, his eyes glued to the phone in his hands. Even though it was summer, the evening had cooled considerably—enough for him to have grabbed his favorite sweatshirt.

The funny thing about teenagers: all of them seem to have developed the ability to walk while staring at their phones, like an evolutionary trick inside one generation. He barely looked up to find the car door before sliding in, reaching for the seatbelt, finally sticking his hand with his phone inside his hoodie pocket.

"Hey, Dad," he said, turning to look at me.

If I had been hoping to gauge his mood by his facial expression and voice, I was out of luck. He was giving me nothing.

"Hey," I said, mustering a smile. "It's good to see you, man."

"You too," he said. I heard a soft vibration coming from inside of his sweatshirt. He pulled his hand out, looked at a text, chuckled, and his thumbs were flying over the letters on the screen to reply.

"Is your mom home?" I asked.

"No," he said. "She's at work right now."

"Huh," I said. I could have gone inside. I could have done a damn load of laundry. Would have been nice for her to communicate that.

"Have you given any thought to where you want to go?" I asked. "It's your pick."

But he didn't seem fazed.

"Old Chicago?" he asked. That surprised me zero. That was the place he always wanted to go, the place with deep-dish pizza and garlic breadsticks.

And a very good selection of beer.

Brown *everything*.

"Sure thing," I said. "Sounds great to me."

We didn't say much after that as I navigated the car to the restaurant, maybe ten minutes away. I couldn't tell who was trying harder to pretend it wasn't weird. I found a parking spot under a lamp in the lot, put the car in park, turned the engine off, pulled out the key.

I sighed and turned to look at Matthew, who was still texting someone. "Hey," I said. "Do you think we can do a moratorium on the phone? It *is* dinner."

We had a house rule that cell phones got put away during meals. Sophia's rule, but a good one. Sometimes, I thought Matthew would burst, hearing his text messages coming from his phone in the next room. He often left his cell on the side table by the sofa—a table made from oak, or cherry, I couldn't recall. But each vibration from his phone reverberated into the dining room. It was almost comical at times, watching him scarf down a plate of spaghetti to get back to his text messages. A few times Sophia and I would laugh out loud and remind him it was healthy actually to chew food.

"Sorry," he said. "I'll put it on silent." He did, and then leaned to the side in the car to put his phone in the back pocket of his jeans.

"A girl?" I asked.

He grinned. "Maybe," he said.

"*Maybe*," I teased.

We walked together into the restaurant, which was busier than I thought it would be, but a nice-looking hostess with a high bun seated us near a window.

Once my beer arrived and Matthew was sipping a Mountain Dew through a clear plastic straw, and once we'd put in our order for pizza and breadsticks, I looked at him. He was staring out the window at other people parking their cars, getting into their cars, leaving in their cars.

"I know this is weird," I said.

Matthew shrugged. "It's okay. I get it."

"Well, that's the thing," I said. "I don't know that there needs to be anything for you to get, Matthew," I said. "Your mother and I... you know," I paused, looking for the words. "We have some stuff to work out. This is..."

"Just a temporary situation," he finished my sentence for me. Rotely. "Dad, it's okay." He took another sip of his Mountain Dew. I took a deep pull from my beer. I wasn't sure which was worse for a man's body.

"I'm still sorry," I said, feeling my voice break a little. It had been a long day. I'd probably gotten one night's sleep stretched over three days at this point. Of course I was tired. Of course I was upset. I was working at a coffee shop, as a grown man, and I was sleeping in a place so deplorable, no one had bothered to list it on Yelp to give it even one lousy star.

Because it had been the cheapest place I could find that would rent me a room one week at a time.

Because I had to take this one week at a time.

One day at a time, actually.

"It's okay," Matthew said, almost sounding impatient.

His eyes darted to the left, and I wondered if his phone wasn't on silent, but rather still on vibrate. Probably, there was a text waiting for him on his phone that he couldn't wait to get to.

I rubbed my forehead with my fingers and prayed the waitress would bring our food soon.

"Dad," Matthew said.

"Yeah?"

"This might be, like, a permanent thing with Mom, you know," he said.

I studied his face. His nose, slightly bulbous—mine. His eyes—definitely mine. His eyebrows—fuzzy like mine, but the shape of Sophia's. He was lucky he didn't seem to have skin issues. Very little by way of pimples and acne. Another attribute from my beautiful wife.

"I'm sure it'll wind down soon," I said.

"I don't know if it will," Matthew said. He got serious. "Dad, I think you should know, even if it's awkward to tell you—"

Right then, the waitress returned to set our pizza on the silver stand at our table, cheerfully pointing out where the grated Parmesan and crushed red chili flakes were, asking us if we were okay. Part of me was thirsty for another beer, but I thought better of it.

Better to see what kind of bomb my teenager was going to drop on me before committing to another strong IPA.

"We're okay for now," I said. "Thank you."

"Okay," she said with a grin. "I'll come back and check on you to see how those first few bites are tasting."

I didn't want to, but I noticed Matthew checking out her ass as she walked away.

"Dad," Matthew said, reaching to grab a piece of pizza. It was still piping hot, but he didn't bother to use the spatula that came with the pie. He licked red sauce off his finger, and I was just about to take the spatula and dish up a piece for myself, when I heard my son say, "I think Mom's dating someone."

Six

"Mr. Averett. I mean. *Holden.* Sorry," Lila giggled. "It's going to take me some time to break that habit, I think."

Oh, God, I thought.

Could I smash my skull with the roll of quarters in the drawer?

I was standing at the register, handing a paper copy of a receipt to a young woman holding a baby when Lila's voice sailed through the air.

There she was, standing at the entrance to the staff room, giving me an award-winning, cover-of-a-dental-brochure smile.

I took a small breath in through my nose and did my best to return the favor.

"Lila," I said. "How are you?"

She practically bounded the few steps toward me, tying her apron strings behind her, nearly bumping into Charlie as he put a cap on the woman's dark roast.

I was taken aback by how beautiful she looked, and I didn't want to be.

She wore a purple tunic, which was a pretty color for her. Underneath, she wore black leggings and thick wool socks that pooled at her ankles under her boots. A small black velvet choker adorned her neck. The whole thing was a little 90s, but that's the way my students had been dressing all year, whether or not they knew it.

"I'm great," she said casually. She'd pulled a tube of lip gloss from the pocket of her apron and smoothed the clear wax on her lips. The smell of cherries hit me even from a few feet away. "How was your night last night?"

We were standing just a couple of feet apart by the register now. Charlie was manning the espresso machine, wiping down the wands. Carmen was probably still somewhere in the back. We felt overstaffed, but Charlie had assured me it was good to have so many people on deck.

Before I could give Lila an answer, Carmen called my name, and from the volume of her voice, I imagined she was sitting at the desk.

"Holden," Carmen said. "Take care of the cold press for the rush. Lila, will you help?"

"Sure thing," Lila said cheerfully.

"Okie dokie," I said, trying to muster a smile.

I wasn't sure I'd ever said "okie dokie" before, let alone in a professional setting.

Although, I was a little relieved to be given something to do. I could take a break from looking at Lila, deciding what to tell her about my night last night.

I shouldn't tell her, for instance, the truth: I'd gotten properly drunk after dropping Matthew off, slept terribly, and spent an hour trying to ferret out who my wife might be dating by looking at her Facebook page, which was nearly impossible to do on my phone with its tiny screen. A tiny screen that had a crack in the corner I was too cheap to fix, and sure as hell wasn't going to shell out a hundred bucks or whatever it was going to cost to fix it right now.

Not when money was tight and everything was in this state of flux.

But I'd wanted to do the nice thing for my wife and

not take our shared laptop with me to Room 204, especially considering how soon I had originally hoped to be out of Room 204. I thought she would appreciate the kind gesture.

Now I just pictured her emailing and texting or whatever it was with some new guy.

My online hunting into Sophia's life told me virtually nothing, except that she was interested in a concert coming up next month at the performance hall downtown. And here I was now, 5:30 a.m., one hangover rolling directly into the next, trying to cover it up with a gallon of coffee and my own will to survive.

I realized I'd never really looked at Sophia's social media stuff in the past. Maybe just every once in a while, when she turned the laptop toward me to show me something—someone had gotten married, or had had a baby. It wasn't something I thought I needed to see.

Maybe I should have paid more attention to what my wife was doing online—who she was talking to, what she was posting, who liked her photos.

Maybe that's how she met this new guy, or whatever, that Matthew thought she might be dating. Maybe I'd been a chump for a long time before this summer started and was just now getting clued into it.

I took a sip of my coffee, carefully labeled with my initials—ironically and comically *HA*—in black sharpie, per Carmen's preference, and turned to face Lila.

Lila who, if I was honest, I would have tried to find online as well late last night, but I still couldn't remember her last name, and I was making it a point not to ask her or Carmen or Charlie, or sniff it out on the schedule.

It was better I didn't know her last name, better that I

hadn't tried to see her face on the small cracked screen of my smartphone.

Because if I was honest, which increasingly I was able to be with myself, Lila was pretty.

Lila was so pretty.

Lila was downright beautiful, and I couldn't lie about it to myself.

And she was smiling at me like I wasn't a broken mess of a man, but instead, was asking me if I wanted her to teach me how to make cold brew, since that seemed to be the new en vogue drink, especially in the hot summer months.

Which was all news to me, I joked to her.

I was a classic man.

Black coffee.

Standard—nothing fancy.

What you'd expect from your old literature teacher.

"It's really easy to make, honestly," she said. "I'll be right back."

She returned a few moments later from the staff room with a pitcher that looked like it was full of brownie batter. I'd remembered Carmen making it yesterday. "This soaked overnight, so now we make it into something you'd actually want to drink."

She smiled at me, and I found myself smiling back and looking at the floor. I could still catch the scent of cherries on her lips.

I watched her slim hands move around in the cabinets, pulling out a black basket and then an oversize filter, and finally an empty pitcher. She talked me through what she was doing, and the irony did not escape me that a former student was giving me instructions.

The way she smiled at me, she probably found it entertaining as well, but she was kind enough to act as though there was nothing patronizing about it at all.

"And people *drink* this stuff?" I asked. "I mean, they order it? They pay money for it?"

She giggled, throwing the used filter into the garbage. "It's good. It really is. Especially if you add milk."

"Huh," I said.

"That's right—I forget, you're a straight black man." She giggled again, closing her eyes and then rolling them once they were open again. "That came out funny. You are not a straight black man. You drink your coffee black," she said. "You are a straight, white, man."

She gave me a look, and immediately, the alarm in my brain went off—that well-trained little bell that had kept me out of trouble and served me well for many years, when it seemed like every few months there was some national headline about a teacher having a relationship with a student that outraged America and made everyone say, "I don't understand how this could happen."

Yeah, I always understood how it could happen—at least with the older students, the seniors.

I was just always careful never to let it happen to me.

The alarm in my brain was cautioning me that Lila, even ten years removed, should not think of me as a man.

I was, but I also wasn't.

In a very real sense, I was not a man.

I shouldn't be, to her.

That should not be something she noticed about me.

I had better be careful. Moments like this could easily turn into flirting.

I needed to treat her once again like she was a student in one of my classes, no matter how the tables were turning and she had the upper hand here.

"Yeah," I answered. "I'm afraid the correct phrase for it is, I'm very boring."

"You're not boring," she exclaimed. "It's just funny that you work here, and you're, like, not interested at all in all the different ways you can make coffee."

"I'm interested in all the different ways I can *drink* free, black coffee," I said.

"You're not gonna try this?" she said, pointing to the two plastic pitchers that held the cold brew.

I hesitated. And traced her arm up to her face with my eyes as I did.

Yup.

She was too attractive now for me to stop actively noticing every few minutes.

Shit. This was bad.

"Maybe later," I told her. "I'm going to stick with my plain old black coffee for now."

"Okay," she said, putting lids on the two pitchers. "You think you can handle the next batch solo?"

"Sure," I said, relieved that she was heading over to the espresso machine to give Charlie a hand with the new rush of latte orders.

Had she picked up on a change in my demeanor, my mood?

Subtle, maybe.

I realized I was far too hungover and far too tired for any of this.

And far too obsessed with the idea that Sophia might be seeing someone else.

When I had pressed Matthew at Old Chicago last night, he'd just told me that he'd overheard her on the phone with someone, and that she'd been laughing and giggling a lot. "Like, way more than normal," he said.

"That doesn't necessarily mean anything," I'd said, feeling a wave of relief in the moment. "Maybe she was on the phone with Aunt Alyssa."

Matthew had given me one of his champion know-it-all looks—the one he'd mastered when he was only ten.

And since when was my son—my awkward teenage son who had not too recently taken the plastic guard off his full-size mattress because Sophia had decided he was finally clear of accidents—more in the know than me?

"That's not how she talks to Aunt Alyssa, Dad."

I'd nodded, taken another big bite of pizza to give myself time to think.

Chewing, I'd added, "So what evidence do you really have?"

Just like with my essay writing unit, my brain flashed. State a thesis. Decide on a topic sentence and make sure it does the real work. Tell your reader what you're going to tell him. Then support your claims with evidence, detail, argument. Support, support, support. You can't just make a bold claim and then expect your reader to follow along on some sort of wild leap.

And this coming from Matthew about my wife of eighteen years qualified as quite a leap.

Disappointingly, he'd only shrugged. "I don't know," he said. "It's not like she'd tell me. She doesn't want to *upset* me," he said, putting air quotes around the word "upset."

Because old habits die hard, I found myself coming to

Sophia's defense. After all, even though we were having marital problems, we still had to present a united front to Matthew.

For Matthew.

"Well, she doesn't want to upset you," I said. "I'm sure she's just—I'm sure it's just a friend."

Which had made Matthew roll his eyes all the way to the ceiling.

"What," I'd said, exasperated.

"If that was just a friend—let me put it this way," he said, and hours later when Room 204 was spinning and I was contemplating a trip to the toilet to try and throw up three and a half slices of pizza and about three pints of the heavy craft beer our lovely waitress had brought me, I was still thinking about this: the way he casually dunked a breadstick into the marinara sauce, and said, "If Katie talked to me the way Mom was talking to this friend, we'd be together, dude. Like, not messing around but like, together for real."

Seven

Great.

Now I had two problems.

Well, more than two.

The first problem: Sophia.

Having an affair?

Or just having fun with someone while we sorted out our mess?

We certainly hadn't talked about this.

Then again, we'd barely talked about anything last week, and my wife was surely choosing to be reticent now.

The act of me agreeing to move out for the summer had hardly been more than Sophia giving me the boot and thanking me for landing a job immediately, albeit one that didn't pay great, so our marital problems didn't affect our day-to-day finances too much.

Which, admittedly she was handling, as always. So I hoped my JavaHut wages were enough, but I guess I had not exactly asked.

Because Sophia handled things.

Sophia handled the bills.

She did the shopping, the groceries.

She did the cleaning, or at least a lot of it.

Every other Tuesday, a woman came in from a cleaning service Sophia had vetted to help with the burden. It was a luxury Sophia told me she very much enjoyed.

Sophia did all the meals, though, the dishes. The everything. She resisted that craze where people pay other people to grocery shop for them, strangers delivering produce and cereal to your doorstep.

Sophia even took care of the lawn for the most part—either personally or by bribing Matthew to do it with a twenty-dollar bill.

But she said she liked mowing the lawn, my brain reminded me.

She said it was good exercise, taking the Craftsman up the incline of our front lawn.

Good for the upper body, she'd say.

How could she even think about being with someone else?

Matthew had to be wrong.

Or maybe I was right, and she was just flirting with someone, rather harmlessly. A man in her life. Maybe someone from the Y.

Lord knows that a harmless flirtation at the right time was a balm that worked wonders.

A harmless flirtation could boost self-confidence, re-mind someone they were still objectively attractive to the opposite sex. Absolutely no harm in that, in my opinion.

Which brought me to my second problem: Lila.

The beautiful young woman who reached over my head with her long slender arms to bring down a new bag of whole coffee beans, who smiled at me when I made my first pumpkin spice whatever.

Who moved around me in the serving area with the grace of a ballerina.

Who told me she'd had a nice night last night curled up in bed reading, her dog cuddled with her under the blanket.

Like that didn't paint a picture I soon wanted to be rid of.

No mention of anyone else with her in bed.

On purpose?

Or was there truly no one in her life, by way of a man?

No indication she wasn't also straight.

Adorably, she also drank three different coffee drinks per shift, it seemed, each seemingly more elaborate than the next.

"I should weigh way more than I do," she'd joked. "I can't help it! I have a huge sweet tooth. Yoga helps."

If I had been assessing her body, I knew right then at that comment that I seriously had to stop. The absolute stupidest thing in the world I could do this month would be to develop some kind of crush on this girl.

Lila.

The other problems...

The other problems felt more temporary at least, and in that way, more manageable. Insomnia. Easy—that was brought on by stress.

I'd always been someone who had trouble sleeping during periods of stress. Finishing my master's thesis under deadline, for instance, had wreaked havoc on my sleep that semester.

When Matthew had a nasty upper respiratory infection that wouldn't go away and required a three-night stay in the children's hospital.

When Sophia had found a lump in her breast and that had led us to a string of a few terrible days waiting for a phone call to confirm it was nothing, as the doctor had assured her that he suspected it was.

When Sophia's father had passed, Matthew had been just six years old. I watched Sophia cry for months. She tried to put on a face brave enough to take Matthew to school. I remembered holding her almost every night, letting her spread tears all over my shirts.

That was real stress, I thought. That was a time in which our family was really in crisis, not just blowing everything out of proportion and making everything feel dramatic.

This was just a temporary hiccup in our lives.

Once life got back on track, once it got back to normal, I would go back to sleeping my usual seven or so hours a night—no sleep aids, no alarm clock, even. No nightmares—just the occasional need to get up and pee in the middle of the night, which was normal for a man my age. It was also a sign of being well-hydrated, which was important.

Or a sign of having imbibed too much.

Which segued to problem number four: beer.

I was certainly drinking too much, but like the sleeplessness, alcohol was my friend in times of stress.

I wasn't an alcoholic, even as I knew that that was the first thing alcoholics often said.

No—wasn't the first thing alcoholics usually said, "I can stop anytime?"

I *could* stop anytime. I had stopped many times.

I'd go a month or two without anything to drink, and I didn't miss it.

Then the pendulum would swing the other way, and I'd have a reckless quarter where I probably drank too many beers—not even to get drunk, just because I love the taste of beer, and the beer I had at dinner tasted so good, it often rolled into one after dinner, and then one while Sophia and I watched a television show or a movie before she slipped off to bed to take a bubble bath or to read a novel.

Or sometimes, with Sophia tucked in bed, I'd wander back down the kitchen table, all clean and quiet now that the dinner dishes had been put away and all the surfaces wiped, take a stack of student essays on Emerson out of my leather bag and grade them, ahead of schedule, because grading was easier after my third beer.

I wasn't an alcoholic, I would think.

I was just a habitual drinker.

Beer was a habit, and one that was only bad if I did it too much. Like if I had made it a habit to eat a piece of cheesecake every day. After a few months, and after probably gaining a few pounds, it was time to say hey, you shouldn't eat a piece of cheesecake every single day.

And a few times, Sophia had told me I should drink less beer—usually quite tactfully, when the small gut in front of me turned from a little charming to a little too big—typically in the months leading up to my annual physical.

Then it was back on the wagon. Jogging after work, maybe one light beer with dinner, but more often lemonade, iced tea.

Sober grading.

Not as much fun, but down went the ten pounds that hung around when I drank a pint or two every day—especially the heavier stuff, the good stuff. The stouts, the porters. The stuff that would get you through the winter, as my dad would say.

Right now, I was drinking way too much, exacerbated

by eating like shit (Taco Bell, McDonald's, pizza), and also compounded by not sleeping, which was exacerbated by working at JavaHut and ingesting a tremendous amount of caffeine every day.

Maybe if I'd thought more about it, I should have worked somewhere that didn't require 4:30 a.m. wake up calls. No wonder they'd hired me so fast. Who in their right mind could keep this kind of schedule?

Young people, I answered myself.

Coffee shops were a young man's game.

Or a young woman's game.

Beautiful young women.

One gorgeous young woman.

Who, I realized as I grabbed my phone, ready to head out the door to at least make an attempt to buy some groceries for the upcoming week, to resolve to eat something a little better—let's say a salad or at least a sandwich with spinach and spicy mustard and lean cuts of smoked turkey—had just texted me.

* * *

HOLDEN, the text message said.

Then a smiley face emoji.

SEE? I'M GETTING BETTER. I HOPE YOU DON'T MIND, BUT I GOT YOUR NUMBER FROM CARMEN. I JUST WANTED TO TELL YOU I LISTENED TO SPRINGSTEEN ON SPOTIFY TONIGHT THE WHOLE TIME I WAS COOKING DINNER, SIPPING RED WINE, AND YOU'RE RIGHT! SO GOOD. SEE YOU TOMORROW!

I read it.

Then I reread it.

I knew about Spotify.

My students had shown it to me, sometimes asking if they could play something from their phones in those last idle minutes of class before the bell rang, to which I typically acquiesced.

I didn't remember talking to Lila about Springsteen, although on Tuesday morning, and into the early hours of that afternoon, I remembered she had been peppering me with questions while my headache and I suffered through a two-hour stint ringing up customers at the register.

Favorite season?

Favorite state?

Favorite president?

Favorite actor? Movie? Musical?

One of those questions had been, Favorite album?

My memory delivered the information to me almost a little regretfully.

What was I supposed to do with these text messages?

How was I supposed to respond?

Also, what was I supposed to do with the image of Lila, that she'd painted of herself so clearly? Didn't she know that English teachers had great imaginations? Now, I could vividly picture her padding around her kitchen, perhaps in some comfy lounge clothes, no shoes, her hair in a big messy bun on the top of her head, a nice glass of red wine in her hand.

Stop it, I told myself, shutting the phone off and throwing it onto the plaid comforter that adorned my shitty queen-size bed.

Stop it.

But a minute later, the cell was back in my hand, and I was wondering if I should say something in return.

Ignore it, my brain yelled at me.

Ignore it.

I sighed. I walked out of Room 204, locked the door behind me, dialed Sophia on my cell phone after I started the car and buckled in.

She picked up on the fourth ring.

"Hello?" she said, as if she didn't know who was calling.

"Hey," I said.

"Holden," she said. She sounded a little breathless, like she was running, or had just finished running.

"Am I catching you at a bad time?"

"No," she said. "Just getting home from work."

"Oh," I said. "Kind of late huh."

"I shifted my schedule around a bit," she said. She offered no further explanation.

"Really?" I said. And I couldn't help myself. "Is that the best thing? Considering I'm not home?"

"Holden," she said, sounding annoyed. "It's fine."

"It's eight o'clock," I said. "On a Wednesday."

"Are you worried about Matthew?" she asked.

"A little," I said. "He's been alone since ... what? Since when?"

She sighed. She did sound frustrated. I felt annoyed she hadn't asked me if this was a good time for me to talk, until I remembered that I was the one who had called.

God, I was tired.

I was just looking for a way to work into the conversation that I was heading to the store to get more groceries for the week.

Although, it was a little late for a healthy person—or

at least a normal person—to eat dinner. I hadn't had dinner, really, just a boatload of Lay's potato chips.

Why did a glass of red wine suddenly sound so damn
good?

Maybe I'd pick up a bottle at the store. I navigated the
car in traffic, heading to the supermarket.

Of course, I'd have to buy a wine opener and a goblet,
unless I wanted to try to uncork a bottle of wine with my
pocket knife and fish pieces of cork out as I drank.

I'd done that before.

Or drink straight from the wine bottle.

I'd done that before, too.

"He's been alone most of the day, Holden," Sophia
said. "It's summer. It's his summer vacation. That's the
point."

"He had his first day of basketball camp today," I corrected her. "He was telling me about it last night."

"Yes, he did," she said. She didn't say anything for a
second. I figured she was annoyed I'd brought it up in the
way that I had, like I deserved a medal of some kind for
remembering something from yesterday. From last night.

"How did it go?" I asked.

She sighed. "It went great, but truthfully, Holden, if
you want to know, you should talk to him. Call him."

"I'd probably get further if I texted him," I chuckled.
No response.

"Is that it?" she asked.

Is that it? What the hell did that mean?

"Can we talk about money? You know. Bills?"

"We can," she said slowly. "If you have any questions.
I'm taking care of everything here. Just like... Well, to be
frank, Holden, just like I always have."

She had a point.

Even after she made the move from working part-time at the Y to working full-time as Lead Supervisor, Sophia was the bill payer, the mail collector, the online accounts manager.

She did take care of everything.

I had grown pretty lazy, I had to admit. I didn't even log in anymore to any of our accounts, except occasionally to see how much we had in our savings.

She tracked our bills and finances on a spreadsheet that she shared with me, but I didn't really bother to look at it, let alone analyze it.

"I don't have any questions, I guess," I said. "I'm putting expenses on the Visa."

"Okay," she said. "That's fine. I'll pay it."

"My paychecks are going to be directly deposited," I added. I felt like a useless loaf. "From JavaHut. Into our checking account. Every place makes you do direct deposit these days, I guess."

"Good," she said. She sounded far away. "Thanks for doing that. That will help."

"And I guess speaking of money," I said, trying to find a way to keep her on the phone. "I'm just on my way to the store, to get some groceries," I blurted out. "I'll put that on the Visa, too."

"Good," she said, a little more gently. "That's just fine. Get what you need. I know you're not going to go crazy over there. I trust you."

That gave me a little jolt, at least. Sophia trusted me. That was a good sign.

I let the phrase reverberate in my brain.

She said, "I was going to walk Benny and then I was

thinking about taking a bath."

"Is Matthew home?" I asked.

"Yes," she said. "But Matthew *is* old enough to be unsupervised all day, Holden. He has a cell phone. He rides his bike to basketball camp. He wears a helmet. He knows to check in with me. I'm not worried about him."

"You still track his phone on that app?" I asked.

This time, she finally did chuckle. I pictured her slipping out of her shoes, finding a clean wine glass in the cupboard, uncorking a nice bottle of red.

Seriously—what was it about red wine tonight? I had a new commitment to find a cheap bottle, and drink the bulk of it tonight.

Then, I pictured Sophia sharing a bottle of wine with some faceless man.

Was that why she had adjusted her work schedule?

A coffee date this morning? God, wouldn't that be ironic?

Mental note to go online and look at the Y's website for clues.

Or go back to her Facebook page to look for more clues.

Maybe she was on Instagram. My students told me Facebook was for old people, and that they spent more time on Instagram, or—what was the other one...Snapchat?

Was my wife on Snapchat?

Was my wife Snapchatting with a man? It sounded dirty to me.

Maybe I could find a subtle way to ask Charlie what social media people use when they want to date other people. No, that would come out weird. There was no way I could find a casual way to ask such a question.

I made my brain list all the men I could remember her talking about from work, but the truth was, she worked with mostly women.

Who were the men?

Come on, brain.

The jealous part of you knows.

The jealous part of your brain always knows, always senses. Right?

There was a Chad... There was an Ethan, right? A Lucas. A Gabe.

No, I was making that up. There was no Gabe. There was a Gage.

That was it. Someone in shape. Someone physically fit. Someone who shared her commitment to the mission of the Y.

Someone unlike me, whose BMI didn't consistently float to the top of the acceptable range—although, in my defense, it really did stay within the acceptable range.

I could picture someone chiseled. Someone with pecs. Someone sensitive, who understood her better.

Who looked at her differently.

Who looked at her like she was interesting.

Like she had something to give, or say, like she could open up a door to something new and fascinating, with ease.

The type of man who wouldn't give up on wearing a gold wedding band after eight days because it cut too much into his skin.

Because he just wasn't used to it.

Because he just refused to make a compromise.

I remembered a guy named Ian from the last holiday

party at the Y. Tall guy. Lanky, even. Drank Scotch on the rocks, and I thought I caught him looking at Sophia a little too long.

Then again, I remembered that I'd had too many beers that night, and Sophia had been so annoyed with me that we'd had to call an Uber home when we hadn't planned to, annoyed she had to take an Uber back the next morning to get her car from the Y when she hadn't planned to.

I thought again about Lila, and cursed myself for mentally rereading her texts as I drove.

My car was closing in on the entrance to the supermarket, and I was flooded with relief: the bright lights of the store, the terrible music, the fact that few people would be there in the evening. Hopefully, anyway.

"Sometimes," Sophia admitted, her voice cracking me back to reality. "Only when he ignores my text for an hour, and then I gotta see where he is. Listen, I'd like to get into that bath, and that can't happen until Benny gets his last call for a potty break."

"Okay," I said, sighing. "Thanks. Talk to you later. I love you, bye."

I ended the call before I could listen to her say goodbye. I wasn't quite sure why.

I guess I thought if I didn't hear her say it, I wouldn't have to rehear her say it later in the evening as I was drinking cheap red wine and trying to forget about the day, trying to forget about everything, and trying not to think any thoughts that would get me into trouble.

Eight

Carmen was gritting her teeth so hard I felt bad for them.

"Try it again." She eked the words out. "Please."

Internally, I chuckled.

With all due respect, Carmen, I thought, *you wouldn't last a week as a teacher.*

They'd eat you alive.

The trick, as I had mastered it, is to make sure your face conveys absolutely no sense of how annoyed you are. This is accomplished by picturing your ire or your frustration as little pieces of confetti, and then putting those little pieces of confetti in a jar, and then you put a lid on that jar, once it's all filled up and you've gotten all your annoyance out, and you go ahead and put that jar high on a shelf, and you ignore it.

You do not let the kid see that he's having any kind of effect on your day whatsoever.

Or, as my mentor Gary told me the year I student-taught under him, Never Let Them See You Sweat.

Not catchy, but neither was WWJD?, and people wore those brightly colored bracelets around for years.

I gave Carmen a winning smile and went back to the drawing board, or in this case, the espresso machine.

I cleaned out the cup component, rinsing it in the sink with hot water. I filled it with freshly ground espresso beans and pressed it down firmly with the tamper, as Carmen had shown me. Then I put the piece back in the machine, making sure to place a small silver cup underneath to catch the espresso as it dripped out.

This was the part I knew how to do, though; this was the part I was good at.

The harder part was remembering the elaborate drinks that customers asked for, specifically the order in which all the ingredients were meant to go into the cup so that said elaborate drink tasted the way our customers expected.

Even though we were not a Starbucks, as Charlie often and quite mournfully reminded me, we had our regular customers, and they were not shy about letting you know if something wasn't up to par.

For some drinks, you started with the pump of the syrup. For others, you started with the espresso and then added the steamed milk. Sometimes, after the milk, another flavor shot was added, and if the drink had whipped cream, dollars to donuts, you also had to sprinkle it with chocolate powder or vanilla powder, or some kind of powder. Or, let's say it was a blended frozen drink; now you had to pour chocolate syrup on it.

And it couldn't just be poured on willy nilly. It had to look a certain way. It had to look presentable to the customer, even though we just put a lid on top anyway, and I highly doubted customers took the lid off to examine my craftsmanship.

Had they, I could also hide behind, *Hey, I'm sorry, I don't really do this. I'm not a forty-five-year-old coffee barista. I'm a teacher. Really. I have real skills. I could explain the difference between a sonnet and a quatrain right here on the spot, or give you five examples of dramatic irony, or tell you a dozen words coined by but not necessarily attributed to William Shakespeare.*

"Pump the syrup into the cup first," Carmen told me, saying each word slowly.

I looked at her to smile again, and observed that the tall woman who had ordered the drink was smiling very patiently at me.

Maybe the customer at the register thought I was an adult with some kind of developmental disability or something. If she took her cues from the way Carmen was treating me, it wouldn't be an outlandish conclusion.

Maybe the tall woman was mentally commending JavaHut for being so progressive.

Whatever.

I finished crafting the drink, put the lid on, put it in a sleeve, and handed it to the customer. She met my gaze and took the drink from me, and said, "Thank you, have a wonderful day," with such deliberation and care, I was beginning to believe my recently-formed theory was spot-on.

When I went back to wipe down the espresso machine, Carmen was already there, cleaning up and rinsing cups.

"I can do that," I told her, but she shook her head.

Then, unexpectedly, Carmen seemed to find a new source of patience, a new ability to deal with me.

"You're doing okay, Holden," she said finally. "The first week is the hardest. You'll get the hang of it."

"Oh. Thanks," I said.

Charlie, who was coming out of the staff room, returning from his break, raised his eyebrows at me upon hearing Carmen's compliment and gave me a double thumbs up.

I smiled and shrugged.

Maybe I'd be better at this job if I wasn't so hungover, though.

Maybe I should give that a try for my next shift.

I went back to the register to take a few more orders.

Hardly anyone paid with cash anymore. I guess that was for the best.

My first job as a kid had been at a hardware store, and those grumpy men who purchased their tools and other supplies loved to give me a hard time if I struggled to dole out the correct change, nervous as I was, a kid around Matthew's age.

Now everything was swipe, or touch, or insert to let the machine read the chip. Everything revolved around those little rectangular pieces of plastic people whipped from their wallets and purses probably five times a day.

The sound of the door opening pulled me from my thoughts. I looked up to see a young man and a young woman walking into JavaHut and the realization hit me slowly, and then all at once.

It was Matthew.

And he was with a girl.

I froze. Was this a flight or fight moment?

He knew I worked here. I hadn't hidden it from him. I had told him the other night when I had taken him to get pizza.

Was he coming in to say hello to me? Or did he forget *this* was the JavaHut I worked at, not the one near Waterfall Pointe, also known as the nice mall.

Before I could move, Matthew looked up and met my eyes. I told myself to follow his lead and above all, be cool.

NLTSYS.

Easier said than done.

WWJD? would be easier.

Jesus would just give away free coffee, or turn ice water into lattes. He would perform veritable miracles.

Bet he couldn't master cold brew, though.

"Hey there," Matthew said, giving me a big smile. "Two medium caramel lattes, please."

I repeated the order more loudly, over my shoulder for Charlie's benefit.

I nodded and smiled at Matthew, and began to punch their order into the cash register.

The girl next to him was pretty. She had fair skin and long red hair.

Not Katie, my brain said. *Katie has black hair. Don't call this girl "Katie."*

The girl he was with looked up at me for a second and smiled, but then went right back to staring at her cell phone, using both thumbs to type something into the phone's glowing keyboard. I couldn't help but notice how close she was standing to my son, and I couldn't help but notice how weird it was for me to see a girl stand so close to my son.

If I tried, I could recall his whole childhood in one flash in front of me—everything. Diapers to baby teeth to fourth-grade musicals to needing to be told to take a shower every day.

At the register, I punched in the wrong drink, and then punched in the wrong quantity. I realized I had messed up the sequence so badly, Carmen was going to have key in with her supervisor code and fix it.

This was so embarrassing.

I put my hands on the counter in front of me and

looked at Matthew, trying to salvage my face with a smile.

"Oh, you know what? These are on the house," I said with a wink.

This made the girl look up at me, and then Matthew, flashing us both a big grin.

"Thanks!" she said. "That's so nice of you."

She pulled a crumpled dollar bill from her pocket and stuck it into the tip jar, still smiling at me.

This was humiliating.

"No problem," I said. "Thank you," I said, to her, about the dollar.

I made a mental note to enter Matthew's drinks into the register later and pay for them with the cash in my wallet—nearly half of the money I was making that hour.

Matthew smiled at me, and the two of them moved aside to make way for a man talking on his phone, interrupting his own conversation with whomever he was talking to in order to bark an order at me: quad white mocha, extra whip.

Matthew and the girl left a minute or two later, coffees in hand. I'd text him later, I thought. He'd wanted to play it cool.

Maybe he wanted me to scope this girl out, and then give him my opinion about her.

Or maybe...

Another very real thought came to mind.

Maybe he'd just wanted to play it cool for *my* benefit, so that when I resumed teaching in the fall, a limited number of people knew what I did with my summer vacation.

So far, all I had managed to do was go on a bender

and entertain a dalliance with depression.

All I had done so far with my first week of summer was have a midlife crisis.

A venti-sized, skinny vanilla midlife crisis, with an extra shot of espresso.

* * *

Lila came into JavaHut right as I was dumping a fresh bag of espresso beans in the top of the large canister.

I noticed her printed floral leggings and the long black tunic she wore over it. She had her long hair neatly braided in what my students had schooled me to be a French braid, and it was cascading down the side of her shoulder. Her full lips were stained like berries. Large gold hoops hung in her ears.

She looked effortlessly beautiful, even as I tried to tamp that part of my brain down, again. Not successful.

I said hello, and smiled.

"Hey, Holden," she said, smiling back. I remembered right then, too, that I had never texted her back from last night—Wednesday night—from when she told me she had listened to The Boss with her red wine while making dinner for herself and had agreed with my choice of music.

Texting her back had seemed like the wrong impulse.

What would I even have said?

Wouldn't texting Lila back just encourage her to start a full conversation with me via text, and why would we need to do that?

Also, as my memory served, at that time, I had been on the horn with Sophia talking about grocery money and battling the feeling that it seemed oddly easy for my wife of eighteen years to kick me out and keep going on with business as usual, with her work and her baths and her letting Benny out for the night.

Why was it weirdly easy for my wife to transition her life to a place where I wasn't there, and it didn't seem to matter?

Maybe she was still in denial about it. Or shock. Certainly, I was still in shock.

Maybe not, though, my brain countered. Who knows how long Sophia had been planning to kick me out on the last day of the school year.

After all, we had been sleeping apart for... a long time.

Months, truthfully. Since the previous fall.

At first, it was my back, which had started to act up. The mattress on the full-size bed in the spare room treated my back better. That was true—it really did.

Then, it was Sophia's new hours at work, and how it was easier for everyone's schedule if she could get up earlier than me, not wake me up.

Then...

Then the weeks bled into months, and I never came back to the bed. Benny took my place, sleeping on my pillow every night. Eventually, Sophia stopped asking when I was planning on coming back to our bed. Eventually, I stopped bringing it up altogether, too.

Lila slipped on her apron, pulling her braid through the shoulder straps, and jumped right into shocking the hell out of me.

"I wanted to ask," she said. "What are you doing after work?"

"Oh. Umm. Today?" I asked.

What did my plans consist of? It was a Thursday.

I was thinking about taking my car through the car wash. The Toyota Camry was sinking to an embarrassing level of dirty. I should clean out all the McChicken wrappers. Sweep it out, maybe even splurge to have it detailed.

I used to tell Sophia it was a waste of money, that I was perfectly capable of vacuuming and wiping down the interior of my own car—even though I seldom actually did. But she'd gradually won me over to how nice it was to leave your car somewhere and come back a few hours later, and for just thirty bucks, get to feel like you'd suddenly upgraded to a brand-new vehicle.

Then again, my brain chimed in, that amount of money that was close to what I made in two hours of slinging espresso. That thought depressed me in a pretty profound way.

I looked up at Lila and saw that she was still looking at me quizzically.

I felt glad no one else was really within earshot, not even an anonymous customer.

She giggled. "You know, it wasn't meant to be a hard question, Holden," she said playfully. She reached out and balled her right hand into a fist, gently punching my arm.

I lurched. I couldn't recall another time in my life where lurch was the right word to describe my body's reaction.

I chuckled. "Sorry. I don't know what my plans are," I said.

I thought about making up a lie. A credible one could

be about Matthew—maybe taking him to a movie, or shopping, or something. Maybe the mall—the nice mall.

But I held my tongue.

"I was thinking about going to the beach," she said. "I had plans to go today, but my friend just bailed on me. I was wondering if you would want to go. With me."

She stood there, playing with the end of her braid, turning the light hairs over in her fingers, looking at me, expectantly.

"Do I want to go?" I repeated, still dumbfounded.

"Yeah," she said. She laughed lightly. "We both get out at 1:30 p.m. Come on—it'll be fun. We can just walk around for a bit. It *is* summer, you know."

"Oh," I said. A vision of Lila in a bikini flashed through my brain. Quickly, I shooed it away.

"Well. I—I probably should pass. But thank you. Thank you so much." I was being way too polite; it was coming out as desperately awkward. I could feel myself cringing inside.

Lila shrugged a little, flipping her braid back behind her. I thought I saw her bottom lip start to protrude in the tiniest pout. "Okay, some other time."

I stood there praying for a customer—or if not a customer, some other easy way to escape the situation.

That was the right answer, wasn't it? *No?* Just like refusing to text her back had been the right thing to do.

Not going to the beach with Lila was the right thing to do.

WWJFD.

After a few silent seconds, I was, in fact, saved by a small wave of customers, one after the other, who suddenly all wanted blended frozen beverages, which were a pain to make and required a lot of blender rinsing between orders.

A half-hour quickly passed this way, and then Lila asked for a break for lunch, then Carmen called me in to ask some scheduling questions, and then the whole conversation seemed to edge out of my memory.

If I had hurt Lila's feelings, she wasn't showing it—not really; I was, likewise, trying to keep my face from giving away anything at all.

* * *

On my break, I called Matthew, but I got his voicemail. I left him a message telling him it was great to see him, and that of course, I was curious who his companion was.

He texted me less a minute later, which made me chuckle.

Typical teenager. He was just like all my students. Deign to answer an actual telephone if it rang, but he could text back immediately, like the house was on fire.

THAT'S PORTIA, Matthew texted. I LIKE HER NOW.

It took me a minute to type out that she seemed nice, and then to ask if he had any plans with her. NOT YET, he'd said, but he was hoping to ask her to a movie on Friday. Immediately, I offered to drive the two of them, if he wanted.

Then I wrote, I THOUGHT YOU LIKED KATIE.

KATIE HAS A BOYFRIEND. I HAD SPANISH WITH PORTIA.

OH, OKAY, I texted back. WELL. LET ME KNOW ABOUT DRIVING. I'D BE HAPPY TO BE YOUR WINGMAN.

MAYBE, he wrote. He followed that up with the smiley

face emoji with sunglasses. LET ME GET BACK TO YOU.

I'D BE COOL, I texted. He laughed at that.

I wondered what I would do when my son got old enough to get his driver's license, when he wouldn't need me to drive him anywhere at all. I wondered if I'd still be his wingman then.

I guess if I were single, it would feel even weirder to be a wingman to my teenage son.

YOU MEAN YOU WOULDN'T SIT A FEW ROWS BEHIND AND SPY ON US? he texted.

NOPE, I wrote. I'M COOL.

He sent me the yellow smiley emoji that had hearts for eyes.

Next, I called Sophia. I wasn't sure why I called her when I knew I only had four minutes left on my break and with Carmen around, there would be no skulking in tardy.

Maybe that was part of the appeal. This was a time-bound event, and there was only so much damage that could be done in such a short amount of time.

Her voicemail picked up, too, but I didn't leave her a message.

Her text flashed on my phone a minute later. SORRY, WORKING, she wrote.

I typed NP as Matthew had taught me. *No problem.* Then, on second thought, I added, I HOPE YOU'RE HAVING A GREAT DAY.

I looked through my other text messages. The top threads were Matthew and Sophia. Typically, the next thread was my sister, Judy, but I realized that there was another conversation with an unknown contact staring me right in the face.

An unknown number, although not an unknown area code.

616.

Grand Rapids.

Lila's message.

I read it, and then I read it again.

I should delete this whole chain, I thought.

I should delete this strange conversation she started with me before I did something crazy, like write her back, which would be a particularly stupid thing for me to do after I'd had a few beers, which was likely to happen that night.

But for some reason, I couldn't bring myself to delete it.

I didn't like this idea that her number would just disappear if I did, and I'd have no way to get it back other than asking her for it (which would be insane), or asking someone else at JavaHut for it (which would also be insane).

With my right thumb, I clicked on the little "i" icon next to the text, and a field popped up, asking me if I wanted to create a new contact or add the number to an existing contact.

I held the phone for a long minute, letting the time left on my break just expire so I didn't have to decide, so I would have an excuse not to have decided.

I tucked the phone in my back pocket as I stood up from the curb.

Back to the grind.

Nine

Knowing that Lila and I were both done at 1:30 p.m., I was admittedly a little careful when the time approached, giving Lila the benefit of a head start, so it wouldn't be awkward.

I took extra time putting my apron in the laundry pile in the staff room, made some additional small talk with Charlie, and then went to the bathroom just to be safe, even though all I did in there was wash my hands and give myself a cold stare in the mirror.

These people at JavaHut didn't know me well enough, or they were too polite to tell me, but I looked sincerely like shit.

Lila must know.

She must have a memory of me ten years ago, when I was her teacher, and I was well-rested and optimistic, and I didn't consistently look like I'd crawled out from beneath a trash pile.

I got to my car and fiddled in my pocket for my keys.

Maybe I would go take it for that detail—the place over on Salisbury Avenue. You didn't need an appointment over there, and they did a really good job. They were cheaper, too.

As I opened my car door, though, I looked at the car next to me, to the right.

It was a Jeep—a hunter green one. Lila was sitting in the driver's side, poring over her phone.

And she looked like she was crying.

She didn't notice me—at least not at first, but when it was clear that I was staring, that at least fifteen or twenty seconds had passed with me just fixated on her face, she looked up at me and wiped away her tears with the back of her right hand.

I walked over to her driver's side and crouched down a little so I wasn't quite as tall. My ass was flush against the side of my car. *Great*, I thought. *Now my pants can be filthy, too.*

She tried to roll down her window, but it wouldn't budge. I saw her laughing and shrugging, then heard her engine start.

I missed the old-style window cranks, the kind that didn't require the car to be on. I remembered those from being a kid, but I knew Lila wouldn't.

"Are you okay, Lila?" I asked cautiously.

She sighed and shook her head. "This is embarrassing."

"It's okay," I said. "I just—sorry, I just saw you there, and I didn't want to drive away without checking on you. I saw you crying."

"It's been quite a day," she said with a bit of dramatic flair.

At that moment, something kicked alive in my memory.

The way she said it.

"You were in the Spring play," I said suddenly, proud of my memory. "*Romeo and Juliet.*"

She looked at me like I had two heads. "You mean, my senior year?"

"Yeah," I said. "I remember now. You were—wait, were you Juliet?"

"No," she said, shaking her head. "I wanted to be. I auditioned to be. Mr. Briggs gave it to Rosemary Sanders. Whatever. I'm not bitter about it. I was cast as Nurse."

"That's right," I said, perking up, nodding my head hard. Lila looked at me again, but it seemed like I had managed to make her smile.

"Why?" she said.

"Oh—the way you said that, it reminded me that you loved to act."

She stared at me, studying my face. "Yeah. I was in the drama club. Senior year, junior year... I think sophomore year, too, but that first year, I only did set design. I didn't get the guts to audition for any parts. I didn't actually audition for anything until senior year."

"You were a great Nurse," I said. "I went to go see that play that year."

"Yeah?" she said. She smiled a little, but still looked sad out of the eyes. "Huh. I guess you had to. Teachers *had* to come, right?"

I could remember that as a novice teacher, I had made it a priority to attend as many extracurricular activities as I could in order to support my students—show them I was there for them both inside and outside of the classroom. I had sat through football games, orchestra concerts, and student musicals. After Matthew was born, I took a break from attending events outside of school, since Sophia and I were so overwhelmed with all the duties that accompanied new parenthood. But we were finally emerging from that world when *Romeo and Juliet* was chosen, so Sophia had encouraged me to go.

I shook my head. "Nope. That's not true. I went of my own volition, on a Sunday afternoon, as I recall. And you were great."

She smiled again, but this time with a lot of added warmth. She closed her eyes. "I can kind of still remember some of the lines," she said. "If I think hard enough about them."

"Oh, the nurse has some of the best lines," I said. My enthusiasm was genuine, and I was glad for it. It felt like the most sincere thing I had said in a few days—at least the most sincere thing that hadn't been me borderline begging my wife to let me return home.

"The part where she comes back from meeting with Romeo and plays like she doesn't understand what Juliet is really asking? Juliet is dying to hear what Nurse has learned from Romeo about his intentions, and Nurse is complaining about her aching bones. Remember?" I said.

Lila smiled at the memory. "Yeah, I loved that part. I have to admit, I did enjoy watching Rosemary's face almost explode during that scene."

"The nurse is such a great character," I said. "I only teach that play with freshmen, so I haven't done it in a few years, but it's a good one. I'd rather do that than *Julius Caesar*, I think, but sometimes the curriculum is annoyingly specific with its requirements."

I realized that this was probably the most I'd ever said to Lila in one uninterrupted clip. I wasn't sure where it was all coming from. I was just so thrilled to have connected her to the past, to access a memory I had of her from a decade ago.

Her phone buzzed in her lap, and she jumped a little, turning her eyes to it.

"Oh, I can let you go," I said quickly, leaning back to give her some privacy. "I just wanted to make sure you were okay."

"No," she said quickly, turning the phone face down in her lap, shaking her head a little. "It isn't important." She hesitated. "Hey. The beach—maybe that was a bit much, you know," she said. "That was a little ambitious. It's like a half-hour drive. Can we do—do you wanna do something more low-key? With me? Like, around here?"

"Like, get a cup of coffee?" I joked. "I think I've had enough today. My brain is buzzing. I feel like I could run a marathon. And I'm not that big on running. It can't be healthy to drink this much coffee."

She laughed. "To be honest, maybe we could get a real drink. I think I could use one. Say yes."

It wasn't a question. It wasn't a plea.

I could see Lila had started to roll up her window and in the next moment, she cut the engine to the Jeep.

Nope. This wasn't an invitation.

This was an order.

* * *

Ten minutes later, I was sitting across from Lila at the faux-Mexican restaurant that I frequently made fun of—Excelencia Fronteriza.

This wasn't a bar, I wanted to say. It was technically a restaurant.

But maybe that was a good thing. Maybe this was a little more innocent than had we actually gone to a bar together, which I couldn't even imagine doing.

This was a restaurant, I told myself. I did not go to the bar with a young and beautiful woman.

As a married man.

As her old teacher.

Her former teacher who, yes, was also old.

Not a bar, not a bar, not a bar, my brain repeated.

I was already justifying the distinction in my mind, which let me know that yes, I was aware of the fact that I was probably doing something wrong by agreeing to get a drink with Lila, at 1:53 p.m. on a Thursday, but not wrong enough to put a halt to it, especially after seeing her crying in her Jeep, obviously very upset about something.

There was something about how far away she'd looked when she was crying. I was still thinking about it.

Inside the restaurant, the music was blaring, and terrible—cheerful, loud horns. I could barely hear the hostess, and I assumed she must have a headache. Her expression told me she hated working at Excelencia Fronteriza as much as it seemed like she would, but she gave us a nice booth with a high back in the corner, and gave us a courtesy smile as she walked away.

A lot of tables and booths to choose from at this hour, though.

Right after the hostess seated us, Lila asked me to get her ice water and told me she'd be right back. I figured she was checking on her face, her makeup, and judging by the way she looked when she came back to the table, a few minutes later, I wasn't wrong.

As she sat back down, I studied the plastic laminated menu with pictures of alcoholic drinks colored electric blue and lime green, trying my best to shut out the music, which was growing more obnoxious by the minute.

Elaborate beverages with crazy names.

Who comes here and orders these drinks, I wondered.

They were the boozy equivalent of the fancy coffee drinks we served up at JavaHut.

Just have one beer with her, my brain was saying. Domestic—not craft. Stay for thirty minutes—forty-five tops. Talk to her, but keep it light. Make sure she's okay and not still upset. That was the nice thing to do, right? And I had an obligation to do the nice thing for Lila.

Wrap this up as quickly and politely as you can, my brain said. *And then get your ass back home.*

Home, I thought.

Yeah, right.

This music was making me need a beer.

This week was making me need ten beers.

Lila looked over the drink menu, but gestured to me to order first when our waitress came.

"Just a Budweiser for me, please," I said.

She smiled as she jotted it on her pad with a black BIC pen. "Tall or short?"

"Tall," Lila answered for me. "You know what? Same for me."

"Great," our waitress said as she turned on her heels. I'd been tempted to joke about a happy hour, but then I thought better of it. It was too early to be happy hour. We just seemed like a couple of lushes, maybe.

Well...What did we seem like?

Father-daughter duo?

What father would let his daughter order a tall Bud for him this early in the day?

Surely, we didn't look like a real couple.

I hoped not, anyway.

Lila had picked the salt shaker up off the table and was sprinkling white grains onto a small white napkin.

She did it so expertly, and then she reached for a second napkin and did the same, pushing it toward me.

She looked up at me as she replaced the salt shaker back in its holster. "What?" she said. Then she smiled. "It's so the glass doesn't stick to the napkin."

I had to laugh. "I know what it is," I said. "I just haven't seen anyone do that in... a long time."

"It's a useful trick," she said, shrugging.

Alicia, our waitress, returned then with the two tall drafts, placing them neatly in the centers of our salted napkins. She knew the drill, I guessed.

"Anything else I can get for the two of you?" she asked, with more cheer than our hostess could muster.

"I think we're okay for now," I said, making a mental note to ask Alicia for the check the next time she passed our table.

Asking for it at this moment would be too much, too rude, but I wanted to make it clear to Lila this was going to be a one and done kind of thing.

Lila picked up her beer, a little foam spilling out over the top onto her fingers. I noticed she had a beautiful silver ring in the shape of a butterfly with two elaborate wings on her middle finger, and that her fingernails were a nice shape, and painted navy blue. Maybe black. Nope, navy.

"Cheers," she said.

I picked my beer up, clinking it gently against hers. She met my eye.

When in Rome, I thought, as I clinked my glass back at her.

This officially had to be the weirdest week of my life, I thought as I took a deep drink of the beer. It was a welcome relief as it entered my bloodstream, and I tried to picture it pushing out the effects of all the coffee.

Lila took a drink of her Budweiser, just as big, and I had to admit, it was impressive. She obviously knew her way around a beer.

One week ago, not one thing in my life was out of the ordinary—not one damn thing. The biggest issue on my mind was how the cable bill had jumped by another twenty bucks, so I'd made a mental note to ask Sophia to call about it. She was very good at getting customer service representatives to let us keep promotional rates long past their promised period.

A week ago, life was ordinary and normal and all of the boring things.

In the last week, my wife had kicked me out, my son had started dating—or wanting to date—a girl who kind of shared a name with a type of car, I had moved into the shittiest hotel Grand Rapids had to offer, and I had learned how to make something called a caramel macchiato, even if I didn't really understand its appeal.

And I was having a beer with a beautiful young woman, from ten years ago, who had done such a good job repairing her eye makeup, I couldn't even tell that she had been crying.

Although, I still did wonder what had upset her so much.

This was surreal.

"Thanks for getting a beer with me," Lila said, rotating her glass around in the salt pooled on her napkin.

"Sure thing," I said, nodding slowly. "What's summer vacation for," I teased lightly.

I was just thinking seriously about asking her what

was wrong, about why she was crying in her Jeep after work, when she piped up with a question.

"So tell me what else you remember about me. From back then, I mean."

I frowned, thinking for a moment, but not wanting to really tell her that so far, her performance as the nurse was the only thing I could associate her with, and not wanting to admit to the specific reason I couldn't look at an old yearbook to jog my aging memory.

I didn't exactly have one handy these days.

"I remember that you were a great student," I said.

"Ha," she said, letting out a jaunty laugh. "That's a lie."

I chuckled and took another drink.

She was outpacing me a little. I stared at the bubbles springing up from the clear glass.

"Why do you say that?" I asked.

"I think—well... I think I remember that I did okay, grade-wise. I liked English just fine. I think I got mostly Bs with you."

Makes sense, my brain said.

The *A* students and the *D* students were easy to re-member. It was those students who were always right in the middle that all blurred together for me, one paper on Dante's *Inferno* after the next, each one reaching the same conclusion after five painful pages: this was a terri-ble way to think about punishing your enemies, even your worst ones.

"Tell me what you've been up to since you graduat-ed," I said. "Did you always work at JavaHut?"

Lila practically snorted. She set her beer down. "No. I've only been there, like, a little less than a year... eight months, I think. Yeah."

"Ah," I said. "Okay. So. What else?"

She stared at me, leveling me with her eyes.

"I tried some classes at the community college," she said. "Well, wait. That's not true. The first thing I did was leave home to move to the other side of the state. I started at Eastern," she said.

"That's awesome," I said, even though it was obvious by the way she was unfolding the story that it did not wind up being particularly awesome.

"It sucked," she said. "I didn't like it. I was super lonely, super depressed. I went there because I thought I could be a stand-out in their drama department, but it was so crappy. I didn't like any of the professors there. I skipped classes all the time. I felt super homesick, I don't know. So I dropped out after one year."

"You transferred to CC," I said, trying to offer some optimism.

The Budweiser was kicking in and actually, I thought, it was nice not to be drinking alone, for once.

No way Sophia, my health-conscious wife, would ever approve of a tall draft beer this early in the day. She didn't like to drink until dinner, or after dinner. Said it made her too sleepy, and she always had too much she wanted to accomplish in the day.

Sophia was someone who was accustomed to accomplishing a lot each day.

"I tried that, but I never could decide on a major," Lila continued. "I took a class here and a class there. I did that for a bit. My parents kept pressuring me to pick something to study and stick with it. It drove them nuts I was so all over the place. Even though I know they meant well and were just, like, worried about me."

"What do you think you want to study?"

Lila sighed and then grinned. "Nothing," she said. "Everything."

I chuckled. Maybe I was kidding myself, but I was starting to think I could remember Lila from ten years ago.

Certainly, that frame of mind felt familiar.

"You love drama," I prodded. "Do you want to pursue that?"

"Yes and no," she said. She chuckled—probably realizing how contradictory she was being. "I love it, but I don't think I'm good enough, and it's like, it's kind of like—if you want to be serious about it, you have to move to a big city, like L.A., or New York. Or Chicago."

"Well," I offered. "We aren't too far from Chicago."

Lila had her fingertips on her glass, playing with the water and beer droplets on its side. I knew I wasn't allowed to tell her and barely allowed to think it, but she looked—in one word—kissable right then. The expression on her face was so gorgeous. I was building a picture of her as a young actress in Chicago, practicing her scenes in a small apartment, hustling to a show in the first heavy snow of a Midwest winter.

"Yeah," she said. "I—well, I did try that," she admitted. "A few years ago."

"You did some acting there?" I asked.

"I tried," she said. "It was—"

Alicia came back to check on us, ask us if we had given any more thought to some appetizers. I surprised myself again by not saying anything right away, but rather looking at Lila.

I did not ask, as I had planned, to get the check.

"We're okay, thanks," Lila said, offering her a smile.

From working in the restaurant industry, Lila seemed to know how to be exceedingly gracious to someone bringing you food and drink. I knew that even though I had only a week or so of experience at JavaHut, I was going to change the way I addressed every waiter and waitress for the rest of my life. I had vowed never to be even remotely rude to waitstaff ever again.

Not that I thought I was a particularly rude customer, but there was a way of being extra polite—I had just witnessed Lila doing it. I was going to be that way going forward, too.

Lila took a drink and shifted in her seat. She seemed to hesitate. "The truth is, I moved there, with a guy. To Chicago. A boyfriend. A Derek, to be exact," she said.

"Okay," I said. "But the acting thing didn't work?"

She sighed. "I don't know why, but I just—I couldn't go for stuff, not the way I had planned to. Derek is a musician—a guitarist—and he was trying to make it, too, but he took a job as a bartender, and then I did too, and then—I don't know. That all kind of took over, I guess. We were always working, but yet we were always broke. It felt like as soon as we paid the rent, and a few other bills, it was like—bam, the first of the month was here again, and it was time to pay rent. Derek didn't really spend much time practicing, and he would start to go for gigs and then stop, and I think I did the same. Like they have improv groups, and they have open mic—"

Lila stopped herself suddenly, staring at me.

"What?" I asked, not understanding.

I looked behind me, wondering if someone had just

walked in that she didn't want to see, or something. But no one had.

No one really seemed to notice us, as the place was pretty empty.

She grinned. "I just told a secret on myself. I usually don't tell anyone this."

"What?" I said again, but I was smiling. I could feel my grin. And the beer.

She sighed. "Well. I wasn't going to—like I said, I don't tell many people this, but... I secretly want to be a singer."

"Oh," I said, sitting back in the booth. "I think that's great."

She let out a long breath and took another pull from her beer. "Yeah. Maybe. I don't know. I don't know if I'm good enough, you know. So... I told—like, what I tell people is that I had wanted to pursue acting, and it's not a lie. I kind of did, but there is a bigger part of me that wanted to pursue singing. I just don't like to tell people that. Because... I don't know, then they ask me to sing on the spot."

I grinned at her. I realized I probably hadn't had this much fun in weeks. Maybe even months.

I took another sip. "I won't ask you to sing."

"Good," Lila said. "I'm not that great."

"I'm sure you're great."

She stared at her beer. "You have to say that," she said. But she let the rest of the sentence hang there in the air.

I had to say that because I was her teacher. I had to say something supportive because at one point in time, she sat in my English class and took notes on my lectures and wrote papers for me.

I was her teacher.

Her former teacher.

My whole job was to be supportive, encouraging.

"Did you do choir or anything in high school?" I said, combing my memory and also desperate to change the subject.

She shook her head. "Nope. I was too shy back then. I could only manage the courage to be the nurse."

"You were the best nurse," I said. I was grinning again.

Which made her smile. "Thanks," she said. "Anyway, Derek was supposedly trying to get gigs, and I was going to open mic nights or whatever, and trying to sing, but—I don't know. I would chicken out, or I wouldn't go. I just kept waiting for *something* to happen, I guess, but nothing ever did. And then, we just—the two of us ran out of money and we fought a bunch, over money, and like, six months went by, when I realized neither one of us had done anything creative. We just tended the bar together and then got drunk with friends after, and then would go to bed at 4:00 a.m., wake up at noon, and do it all again the next day."

"Sounds sort of wonderful," I said, taking a drink.

I realized I only had a few sips left and then my glass would be empty.

I realized we were going to have to make a decision here soon, and I realized I wasn't that happy to have to do that.

To order another beer was decidedly a mistake. We both had to drive home. Plus, this was a tall beer, which was closer to two beers than one. I felt fine to drive, but she was so much tinier than me, and I didn't want to make her feel like she had to get another one if I did. I didn't want to be a bad influence.

Then again, maybe Lila was a more experienced drinker than I was giving her credit for. She had been a bartender, I'd just learned. That would explain why she seemed so comfortable here, and maybe why she was such a good barista.

"It was fun," she said with a shrug. "But trust me, you get over the whole bar scene pretty fast."

"I can see that," I said.

"You get in this pattern, and you just—I don't know, you do the same thing day after day," she said. "You fill those spaces in your day with drinking with friends, which is fun, but if you're not careful, like a year goes by, and what do you have to show for it? I don't know. You wanna know what the worst part is?"

I did. I felt like I was hanging on her lips, or at least staring at them.

"The worst part is," she said, "I feel like such a cli-ché... moving to a big city to pursue my dream, or what-ever, and then just not. And moving there with a boy... my parents telling me it was a mistake, and then having to face them again and tell them, they were right, of course, it didn't work out. It was never going to work out."

I didn't say anything, not sure of what to say to ad-dress her failed romantic relationship.

"Are you pursuing singing now?" I said, bringing the subject back to something safer.

She sighed. "I took a few music classes at CC," she said. "I did like them. I was thinking about taking another one this fall, but it just feels like August is coming up so fast. Maybe I could be a vocal coach. That would be a fun job."

"Yeah," I said. "Teach people how to sing?"

She laughed. "You get the irony," she said. "I'm delighted."

She picked up her beer and finished it in four gulps. I raised my eyebrows like I was impressed, and tossed mine back, too, to keep following suit.

Yup. She was not the sixteen-year-old who once sat in my English class.

This was a beautiful, twenty-something-year-old woman with the whole world in front of her, and if I wasn't careful, I was going to get myself into some serious trouble.

"Those who can, do," I said, with mock solemnity.

"And those who can't, teach," she finished.

I wondered what she thought it was I couldn't do. As an English teacher, the answer was, probably a hell of a lot.

We both laughed, and thankfully, Alicia came by again, and she had the check with her in the front pocket of her black apron. I slipped my Visa from my wallet into the black book, shooing at Lila who had started to reach into her purse.

"Thanks, Holden," she said. The smile on her face nearly bowled me over.

Maybe Alicia had read my mind.

Maybe she didn't think we needed another tall beer.

Or maybe Alicia didn't think we needed any encouragement at all.

Lila and I walked back to our cars, slowly, in the

parking lot of JavaHut. I was hoping no one from JavaHut would see us—that no one from the rest of the world would see us, for that matter. I shuddered at the thought.

I felt a little lightheaded, but fine. I studied Lila walking, putting one foot in front of the other, to make sure she seemed steady. She seemed okay. And she thanked me again for the beer and for checking on her, cheering her up, which is when it occurred to me that I had never even asked her what was wrong in the first place.

She certainly hadn't offered.

So I just smiled at her, watched her get into her Jeep, saw her pull her cell phone from her purse and stare at it, although she hadn't taken it out once in our time together.

I gave her one more wave, turned the key in the ignition, and drove the old Camry very slowly to the Scenic View Hotel, Room 204, still hearing her laughter in my ear, her voice in my mind, and trying to put the two together to estimate how that voice would sound in song.

Ten

On Friday, I had my first day off since I'd been hired at JavaHut. The first order of business—the only order of business—was to sleep in. When I finally opened my eyes, I was beyond happy when I rolled over to see the clock in Room 204 blink 10:28 a.m. in its caustic red font.

My body thanked me for finally giving it some rest, and I decided to follow it up with giving it a decent meal—I'd go out to breakfast—after a hot shower and a shave.

On my way to find a diner, I stopped by the Scenic View Hotel office and paid for another week of rent. Geoffrey wasn't there. Instead, a short, overweight woman swiped my credit card and didn't look at me when she handed it back, nor did she bother to confirm the total amount I was even paying.

On a spur of the moment decision, I also stopped by the library on my way to Denny's. It would be good to get something to read. Give me something to do in Room 204 that wasn't watching cable or staring at the ceiling.

Or drinking.

I browsed the fiction section for a little bit, then grabbed a Tom Clancy novel I'd never read—or at least couldn't remember reading—checked it out, and found my way to Denny's, a place I remembered Sophia and I going to often in college. Near campus, at State, there was a 24-hour Denny's, and it was filled with young people sobering up or studying—roughly half of each kind.

Nothing unusual about an English teacher having brunch by himself on a Friday in the summer, I thought, especially with a mass-market paperback to keep him company. Anyone seeing me would understand I was a man on a well-deserved vacation, even if my choice in literature was a little low-brow.

After an omelet, a few good cups of coffee, and the first five chapters of the novel, I headed back to the Camry, feeling simultaneously proud of the fact that I hadn't thought about Lila at all that morning and absolutely crushed with boredom and confusion.

Only one place to go.

I drove to the Y on the north side of town, parked my car, and walked in, still holding the Clancy novel in my hand like it was some kind of prop, and I was in some kind of bad play.

A young woman greeted me at the desk with a big smile, her teeth enormous—and white. She asked for my membership card.

"Oh," I said. "I don't have one. I just wanted to see if Sophia Averett was working."

She frowned for a second, thinking. She brushed her bangs to the side. "I believe she is. Please hold on a second while I check."

She consulted her computer for a moment, click click click, and then looked back at me with a smile. "She *is* here. She should be in her office. Is she expecting you?"

"No," I said, smiling a little. "I'm her husband."

"Oh, great," the teen said, clearly relieved. Not a stalker. Kosher. "Go on up."

The young woman gestured to the upper floor of the building where I could make out a number of offices with windows for walls.

"Thanks," I said, a little surprised as she nodded again.

I'd never been to Sophia's office at the Y.

In fact, I realized I didn't even know she had an actual office. It made sense, I thought. Just not something that had occurred to me.

The Y was a big place with an aquatic center, basketball courts, tennis courts, and a play area for young children. Families were milling about, as were lots of young teens. I remembered they were on summer vacation, too, so probably part of some summer camps or leagues.

I spotted Sophia sitting at a desk in a large office with big windows. She was staring at her computer, dressed in black yoga pants and a sky-blue polo. Her hair was up in a small ponytail, all that her length would allow, and she was hunched over a little in her shoulders.

I knocked on the glass with the corner of the Clancy novel's spine and tried to smile when she met my expression with a look of not-too-happy surprise.

But she motioned for me to come in anyway, which I did, softly closing the glass door behind me.

"Hi there," I said.

"Hi," she said, looking a little flustered.

"I'm sorry to bug you at work," I said.

"It's okay," she said with a sigh. "I'm putting together some schedules for next month. No big deal." Her smile looked forced.

I nodded, waiting for her to ask me to sit down, which she did, pointing at one of the chairs opposite her.

Her desk was pretty and tidy, and I was happy to see two framed pictures: one of Matthew, his current school picture, and one of the three of us, Christmas from a few years ago. Matthew was missing a tooth, and I'd experimented with a mustache that year. We looked really happy, all of us touching each other's arms or waists in one way or another, Benny at my feet, that scrappy little mutt miraculously looking at the camera, too.

"What's up?" she asked.

"Oh," I said. "Well. You know." I shrugged and tried to laugh. "I just paid another week of rent," I offered.

She nodded her head. "Okay. That's probably good. Are you pretty comfortable there?"

I nodded. "It's okay. I'm staying at the Scenic View Hotel," I said, not remembering if I'd told her the name of the depressing hotel before. "Room 204."

"Okay," she said. "That's probably good to know, in case there's an emergency, or something. Although, I can just reach you on your cell."

I nodded and sighed.

God, this was so bizarre. She hadn't known where I was staying. She hadn't asked? I hadn't offered?

Standing there, I could feel that it was a huge mistake to make this my first appearance at her place of work. She was pissed at me for every time I had never visited her at work, it seemed, and pissed at me for showing up now, uninvited into her perfect and neat little office, her tidy little work world.

That was Sophia, I thought. She'd always been this tidy package. A perfectionist who wanted things just so, who did everything around the house and in our relationship because she knew how she wanted it done, and she knew no one else would do things up to her standards.

All I had managed to do was become the loaf who stood back, shrugging, and now she'd decided to relegate me to the background for the summer, with the thought that the summer might turn into the rest of our lives. Because somehow, a decision she'd made nearly two decades ago didn't fit anymore, and it wasn't the same decision she saw herself making for the next two or three or even four decades.

The sum of all these realizations, seeing her face and skin look so perfect, so put together, whereas I—even after my shower and shave, still looked a little worse for the wear in wrinkled clothes, the smell of coffee permanently emanating from inside me—made me feel like total shit.

All I could think at that moment was *lady, just give me the steps to getting our relationship back on track so that I can start working on them.*

Because it occurred to me standing there that Sophia probably already knew exactly what she wanted from me. She just wasn't saying.

Which is why I wound up blurting out a moment later, a little more hysterically than I had wanted to, "Just tell me what you want me to do, here."

I was glad there weren't any people in the office next to Sophia's.

She sighed. "Holden, look, I know... I know this is weird, or whatever, but I feel really good about the last week or so. I feel like I've had some time and space to do some thinking. About us."

"Well, what do you think?" I asked.

Even though I hadn't meant it to be funny, she'd laughed softly. She ran her fingers through her ponytail, and if I wasn't wrong, she made a quick glance at the clock on her office wall.

"I think," she said. She sighed again. "I think if I had a trained therapist here, a conversation like this might go better... I don't know if I can always articulate my thoughts."

"Well, there isn't," I said dumbly. "No therapist. And you're my wife, and I just want you to tell me what's going on with you, how I can fix it, and when I can come home."

She shook her head, putting both hands on her desk. "That's where it starts, Holden," she said. "Don't you get it? It isn't just something that's going on with *me*. It's what's going on with *us*."

"Okay," I said, slowly, waiting for her to continue.

"I don't think we're that happy anymore," she said, almost whispering. "I don't think I'm happy being married to you anymore. That's what all this is about."

"Okay," I repeated. "God, Sophia, I just wish in any way I'd seen this coming."

"I know," she said. Her voice seemed genuine. "That's part of the problem. With me, I mean. I am really good at hiding how I'm feeling. I know it's a problem. I'm sorry. I really am... I let this build and build, and then the feelings just spill over and explode, and the downside is, you're left feeling maybe a little blindsided... and I've already processed a lot of this."

"Yeah," I said. I wanted to reach out and put my hands on top of hers, but I was too afraid that if she pulled them away at my touch, I would die on the spot.

Her phone rang then, at her desk, and she glanced at it, seemingly to decipher the number and decide whether or not to answer.

"Hold on, Holden," she said. She picked up the receiver and held it to her ear. "Hi, this is Sophia," she said plainly.

I waited, staring at her, concentrating on the sound of the breaths coming in and out of my body, one at a time. I flipped the Clancy novel over in my hands, skimming the plot description on the back, staring at the glossy color photo of his face. I ran my thumb along the smooth edges of the pages. Then I cracked the book and flipped through the pages wildly, just to hear something else for a moment.

"Okay, thanks." She hung up the receiver.

"Look," she said. "I'm sorry. I just need more time."

"What is more time going to do?" I said. "If you truly think our marriage is over—"

"I don't think it's *over*," she said quickly. "I don't know, though. I really don't. I think I just need this summer to decide," she said.

"And I get no say," I said.

This is how all these conversations were going to go, I was starting to realize. This fit the pattern of all our arguments. I was so angry at her for singularly deciding to go against and outright abandon something that the two of us had promised each other a long time ago.

She wasn't allowed just to quit, was she?

She took a deep breath in and closed her eyes. "Maybe."

"*Maybe*," I repeated. "The hell does *that* mean?"

She let the breath out, opened her eyes. "Look, I think if we do stay married, then we have some things to work on."

"Okay, I agree with that," I said, trying to settle my anger down. If I squeezed the mass-market paperback any harder in my hands, I was going to owe the library a fine.

Neither of us said anything for a moment.

"I'm willing to do the work, Soph," I offered. "Really. I am. You just have to tell me what to do."

Sophia let out an exasperated sound. "That's another layer of the problem," she said. "I don't want to have to tell my husband what to do. See? No woman wants that."

I rubbed my forehead. "You're not making any sense," I said. "No offense."

"That's why maybe we should see someone," she said. "A mediator, or whatever. A therapist. Someone to help us talk about our issues."

"Okay," I said. "I'll do that. My schedule is pretty open in the afternoons. You know I am out of work at like, 1:30 p.m. most of the time."

"Okay," she said, and suddenly it felt like we had reached the conclusion of this bizarre exchange, and that now she'd like to edge me to the door, get back to her phone call and her spreadsheets and her schedules, forget about me for a few more days while I waited like a dog to be told it was okay to come back inside.

"Do you want me to set something up?" I asked.

"That's okay," she said. "I'll do it. I'll text you, okay?"

"Okay," I said. She stood up from her chair.

"That's it?" I asked.

"Well," she said, kind of shrugging. "I mean, I am at work. I should get back to it."

I stood up too, tucking the book under my left elbow, pressing it tightly to my side. "This is so messed up. I hope you know that," I said.

She nodded, sadly. "I get it. I really do. I'm sad, Holden," she said.

And then her voice cracked a little, and when I searched for tears in her eyes, I saw one in each blue eye, and I believed her. "I miss you—at home, I mean. The house is so quiet. Matthew is gone all the time, at practice, hanging out with his friends," she said. "I think he has a new girlfriend. I *do* miss you. I just think this is healthy, and I think we're doing the right thing by taking some time apart."

I didn't know what to say, so I just kept clinging to the idea that she missed me around the house. Which suggested she wasn't actually sleeping with someone else—something I wasn't ready to bring up until I had more proof.

Any proof, really.

Best to end on a high note, my brain said.

Best to assume the only other male in her bed was Benny, the terrier who liked to burrow deep under our ivory duvet.

"Okay," I said. "Take care. Can we talk tomorrow?"

"Yes," Sophia said. "I'll call you. I'll try to set something up. With a therapist, I mean. I'll see what's in our network. Make a few calls."

"Okay," I said. I walked to the door of her office. "I think I'm going to try to take Matthew to the movies soon," I said. "I think he's inviting a girl. I think you're right—he might have a girlfriend."

Sophia smiled. "That sounds great," she said.

I nodded again. "Hey," I said. "Nice office."

"Thanks," she said. "It is."

Then I left her office, walked down the long hallway back to the lobby of the Y, looking like any other dad there—a middle-aged man who'd come to watch his son play basketball, or to take his daughter to a swim lesson, instead of a man in the middle of a crisis over which he clearly had absolutely not one iota of control.

Eleven

"You can come in. Mom's not home," Matthew said, opening the front door for me and addressing my unspoken concern with enough ease to make me feel incredibly guilty.

I had no clear idea why I'd chosen to enter the house through the front door, except to say that since I hadn't pulled into the garage, as I had done thousands of times before, I hadn't used the door that led from the garage into the hallway.

And it felt so weird to enter the house the way guests and solicitors did.

"Thanks," I said, stepping into the landing. "I just wanted to grab some more clothes."

I still hadn't solved my laundry conundrum, so until I found a laundromat and a few rolls of quarters, it was time to get another duffel bag and fill it with socks, underwear, pants, and clean shirts.

JavaHut's dress code was pretty casual, but we were not allowed to wear jeans. I'd been wearing the hell out of an old pair of khakis, and it was time to see what else I owned that was somewhat expendable. Despite my best efforts, I seemed to be getting dark espresso stains on everything I wore to work.

"Give me just a couple of minutes," I told Matthew. "Then we'll go. And we're picking Portia up?"

"Yup," Matthew said. He was staring at his cell phone, standing in the doorway to the kitchen.

I forced a smile. "You eat yet?"

"Yeah," he said. "Mom made lasagna."

"Good lasagna? Or the veggie stuff?"

He considered. "Uh... The one with sausage. And Parm."

"Good enough," I said. "Warm up a plate for me, will you?" My stomach was already growling at the idea of a hot meal that hadn't come in a greasy brown paper sack.

Upstairs, I grabbed my navy duffel from the closet and packed some clothes. I could hear the insistent beep of the microwave—a familiar and welcome sound— coming from the kitchen. I could smell the Parmesan from the stairs, and it was heavenly.

Everything was familiar. It was so odd.

Of course, it was familiar, though.

This was still my house. This was still my stuff. And if we split up, I guess we'd be splitting all of it in half somehow.

I couldn't imagine going item by item to decide who got to keep what. The couch? The lamp? The ottoman in which we stored extra blankets for the winter months?

Jesus.

I did resist the urge to look for any clues in our bedroom that anything had changed with Sophia.

I didn't, for instance, open her underwear drawer, or the drawer in which she kept her pajamas. In the early years, there had been lingerie, but more and more, it was gradually replaced with sensible cotton tops with matching bottoms. After Matthew, it was more about comfort than sensuality. Now, the sexiest thing she slept in was an old nighty that was only see-through because it was so old.

Not that I much minded.

Sophia would never know how disciplined I was, that I hadn't looked in our bedside table for anything that would suggest she was entertaining a new man.

Not that she would, in our bed. No way. Not in front of Matthew.

That would be too weird. Wouldn't it?

But to not snoop around on my wife seemed like an important step, a key part of the equation.

Show her I trusted her.

Besides, if I did find condoms or something in her bedside table, I'd never be able to tell her. I'd never be able to tell anyone. I'd only be able to be angry about it.

If she were going to sleep with another man, it would be somewhere else.

Somewhere I would never know about.

I shuddered.

Stop thinking about this, I thought, zipping the duffel hard and going back downstairs for the best meal I'd had in a week.

* * *

Small talk in the car was my job, it seemed.

Otherwise, the three of us would have driven to the movies in complete and awkward silence.

"So, Portia," I said, trying to sound cheerful. "Are you doing anything fun this summer?"

"Just working," she said shyly.

She was very pretty, I thought. Freckles decorated her face, gathering in high frequency near her nose. I liked the height of her forehead, the gentle slope of her chin. She carried a quality that made her seem easy to talk to.

"Oh, that's great," I said. "What are you doing?"

"I'm working at Adventure Place," she said. "They have a day camp."

"Sounds fun," I said.

"Yeah," Portia answered, and glancing in the rear-view mirror, I saw her tuck some of her hair behind her ears. "It's cool. I play with little kids all day. They're so crazy. Some are even potty-trained," she giggled, and I caught Matthew's hand inching toward hers on the middle seat between them.

They seemed more than ready to bid me goodbye at the door of the movie theater, and before he shut his car door, Matthew thanked me for the ride and told me he'd text me when they were ready to get picked up.

I opened my wallet to give him a twenty, which he accepted with a grin.

At least this felt normal. I could convince myself that a little routine like this was all part of business as usual.

What to do with two hours, I thought, realizing I hadn't given it any consideration and now it was time for a decision. I felt far too restless to sit through a movie myself.

I remembered that there were a few restaurants within walking distance of the theater where I could definitely scare up a beer, but Matthew might not approve if I drove Portia home and smelled of alcohol.

I wouldn't really approve of that either.

A break for one night would be nice.

Or at least, I could commit to taking a break for now, for the next few hours.

Maybe it's time for a long drive, my brain said.

The thought entered my mind and before I gave it too much time, I was headed west, into the sun—despite the sun—the radio on classic rock, blissfully not thinking about anything until thirty minutes passed, and I was standing on the shore of Lake Michigan, my shoes off, staring at the waves and thinking that even though I had been to this exact beach a hundred times, living in West Michigan, I wouldn't be here tonight if I hadn't loosely been thinking about a woman who had recently extended an invitation to me to come here.

And how that woman had made it sound like it was the best place in the world anyone could possibly be.

Twelve

"What we're here to do is establish some boundaries for a healthy conversation," said Dr. Garrett.

I wasn't sure what to expect from a certified family therapist, but Dr. William Garrett made a good first impression: a middle-aged African-American man with a full beard and a friendly, firm handshake.

We'd entered his office after a few minutes in the waiting room, which was the awkward part—sitting there and not talking to each other, because we knew that at 4:00 p.m., we would be talking to someone professional.

Then we were led down a dimly-lit hallway inside a building next to the physical therapy place Sophia had visited a few times when she was having ongoing pain with her IT band.

And here we were now, years later, sitting stiffly next to each other in two blonde wood chairs with ugly purple upholstery, ready to throw all of our problems out for a stranger to judge and dissect.

Which was the point, I knew, logically.

Objective third party. A disinterested third party, even.

UNBIASED, Sophia had corrected me over text.

She was correcting me before our first session even started.

"My goal is to open up this space for dialogue, and hopefully guide you both through some questions to get you thinking," he continued.

He had a charming smile. Reassuring, probably. I wondered if it was in bad taste to ask him how many marriages he'd saved in his career.

It felt relevant.

People often asked me how many students I'd failed while teaching my classes at St. Bridget's.

It was like some kind of a yardstick to prove I was a good teacher—one who would give ample opportunities, but who also wasn't afraid to fail a kid who just refused to do any of the work.

Dr. Garrett looked relaxed in his leather maroon chair, leaning forward just a little, a yellow legal pad and pen in his lap.

Didn't look like, from where I was sitting, he'd written anything more than the date, maybe our names. Perhaps he had written, *session number one.*

Maybe he could already tell we'd need dozens of sessions.

Maybe just by looking at us, he could already tell if we were going to make it.

Maybe as soon as we walked into his office, he had sized us up and—perhaps judging by the way we had sat down or how we had interacted with each other—he'd already decided if we were going to be in his success column as a family therapist, or become a tick mark in his failure column.

"A good place to start, I have found, is with each of you expressing what your goals are," he said.

I examined his office, hoping Sophia would take the bait first. There were degrees on his wall, as well as framed paintings of nature scenes, but not a lot by way of personal effects.

A box of tissues was perched on every available surface, it seemed.

I checked his finger for a wedding ring and found one—a thick, gold band.

Okay, I thought. *That's one marriage Dr. Garrett has saved, has kept saving.*

Immediately, I looked over at Sophia's left hand and breathed a little easier when I saw she was still wearing her wedding ring. A small gold ring, but we'd added an anniversary band with diamonds around it on our tenth anniversary, because she had told me that's what she wanted to do, and I thought it had made her happy.

It had seemed to, at the time.

Sophia said nothing.

"I'll start," I said. "My goal is to get my marriage back on track."

"Okay," Dr. Garrett said. He wrote something down, although I couldn't possibly imagine what. Did he need to jot that down to remember it?

The husband wants in. Check.

"And what about you, Sophia?" Dr. Garrett asked.

"My answer is a little more complicated," she said softly, with a smile. When she wanted to be, Sophia could be utterly charming.

"Go on," Dr. Garrett said. "We're off to a great start."

"I—I just... I think my goal is to decide *if* this is what we want. What we *truly* want. This marriage. You know, for the foreseeable future, or the next—oh, I don't know, thirty years? However long we live?"

"I see," Dr. Garrett said, writing again.

Yeah, I thought. I'm dying to know how he parsed

that one out.

The wife isn't sure she still wants to choose this dude.

"How many years have you been together?"

"Eighteen," I said quickly.

Write that down, Doc, I thought.

Quiz me on something harder.

Eighteen years is a pretty substantial accomplishment. The divorce rate is fifty percent in the United States—higher, right? That statistic is touted all the time in the news. All things considered, Sophia and I were doing pretty well.

"Married for eighteen," Sophia said, looking at me with a small smile. "We dated for a few years, before that. Four years? Almost four and a half, I think. We met when we were... I was twenty-one. We were in college."

"Okay," Dr. Garrett said. "Good. Good."

I wondered if he wanted the whole backstory, but he didn't seem to care about how we met or how we fell in love. Then again, there wasn't too much of a story to tell. We did not have a love story fit for a Nicholas Sparks novel or a Hallmark made-for-TV movie.

We met the usual way, at Michigan State. Junior year. Through mutual friends. We fell in love the usual way: gradually, and then all at once, when it was clear we were a great pair, and we didn't want to be without one another.

At least, that was my recollection.

Ours was always a relationship without a lot of dramatics, without many problems. We spent time together and it was just—in one word—easy. I had always thought it was right because it was easy, that I hadn't ever had to give it too much thought because our love was so natural.

Had I been wrong about that the whole time?

"And so... Why do you think you two are where you find yourselves today?" Dr. Garrett asked.

He'd recrossed his left leg over his right, at the knee, his pen poised over the pad for the answer.

I looked at Sophia.

Seems like your domain, I said inside my head.

"I don't know," she said, and her voice started to break a little.

Dr. Garrett gestured to the box of tissues next to her. She laughed the laugh she usually mustered when she was embarrassed.

"I don't—it's so hard to explain," she said. "I think just the day to day, you know how it is. We have a son. Matthew. He's fourteen. He's wonderful, of course, and we love him. And I don't think he made us grow apart, but it's like, between both of us having careers, and caring for Matthew, we just—Holden and I have *completely* grown apart. We're completely different people sharing a house. We're roommates. We are nothing more than roommates. And there's no romance," she said. Tears were coming down her face now as her words started to spill out, one after the other.

I realized I had been holding my breath. Sophia continued, "Which is why we're here... I'm thinking, like, is this all there is? And should we make a choice now while we're still young enough if we want to move on, you know, either alone or to pursue other relationships..."

Bingo.

"Do *you* want to pursue another relationship?" I interrupted, not able to conceal the anger in my tone.

Dr. Garrett raised his right hand gently. "Holden,

trust me. I know it's going to be tempting to ask for clarification all along the way here, but it's important to the process that we let Sophia express herself first, and then we can discuss and break down her thinking together, okay?"

I nodded, but she seemed bewildered. "Umm. I don't know," she said. "Sorry," came out next, as a whisper.

"It's okay," Dr. Garrett said. "You did great, Sophia, thanks. This is a very productive place to start. Holden, why do *you* think you two are where you find yourselves today?"

I was still thinking about Sophia wanting another relationship, still remembering what Matthew had said about listening to her on the phone, giggling to someone who wasn't me.

Flirting.

I sucked in my breath, pushed my lips together. "I don't know," I said. "Sophia kicked me out of the house about a week ago, and told me she needed time to think. She blindsided me. I moved into a hotel room. I'm doing everything she's asking. I even got a crappy job, but I just want to get this thing solved so I can get back to normal. So we can get back to our normal lives."

"Okay," Dr. Garrett said. "Good. Okay. Thanks, Holden." He looked down at his legal pad. He sighed, and then smiled.

"If it's a comfort to you, you should know, this is what many people come in feeling and saying. They realize they're on different pages, but it's hard to say exactly how they got there. It happens slowly over time, and often there isn't one divisive moment. It's not like in the movies, let's say, where a breakdown in communication has a precise or traceable moment. It's far more ambiguous, which can make working through it more difficult."

I looked over at Sophia, who was nodding and quietly crying, the knuckles of her right hand pressed against her lips.

I realized at that moment that there was a fifty percent chance my marriage was ending in a divorce, just like the statistic I'd been thinking of a few moments earlier. I'd never truly thought that I might be included in that statistic.

Regardless, here we were.

Like it could be the toss of a coin.

"I'm going to give the two of you some homework," he said. "Some questions I want the two of you to consider, and write the answers out, and then we'll talk about your answers in our next session."

"We're *done*?" I asked, unable to conceal the incredulity edging my voice. Our session must have only been seven minutes, eight minutes tops.

Dr. Garrett chuckled a little. "No, I'm sorry for the miscommunication, Holden. I just like to mention the homework thing upfront, so you aren't caught off guard later. I find that to be especially important as we begin to delve deeper into a few of these issues, and things may start to feel more emotional. It can be hard to remember things when we're emotional, so I'm putting my plug in now, as they say."

He smiled and handed us each a piece of paper, which had been tucked into the pages of his legal pad, telling us to put them away and look at them later, when we weren't in session.

"Sophia, are you able to continue?" he asked, looking

at her.

"Yes," she said. "I'm sorry to cry, like, immediately."

"It's natural. These are tough moments," Dr. Garrett said. "Let's unpack some of the things you said, Sophia, about when you started to feel this way."

What Dr. Garrett said about not being able to think when feeling emotional held true. The rest of the hour—the fifty-minute session that I wasn't one hundred percent sure would be covered by our health insurance, but told Sophia it didn't matter if it was, if therapy was what we needed—was a blur of hurt feelings, strange comments, unfair things Sophia said, peppered by incidents I couldn't believe she was bringing up. Things I couldn't believe she even remembered. Things I had said and hadn't thought twice about. Stuff I had done or not done that had caused her great pain—things that would have been nice to know about years ago.

It was like getting attacked by a toddler, who seemed harmless, but was barreling at me with steak knives in his fists. I felt punctured, and it was all I could do to keep myself from crying, too.

As it was, I teared up a few times, but managed to knuckle the tears away before Sophia or Dr. Garrett could notice them, or worse—offer me a damn tissue.

Sophia and I said nothing to one another on the way out, setting up our appointment for the same time on Thursday, which felt like a relief to me. I couldn't imagine having to have to wait an entire week to sit back down and keep talking to my wife. To keep working through this stuff.

If we could talk Thursday, again, I just had to get through Tuesday and Wednesday, and we'd get another chance to make some progress.

All of these thoughts buoyed me in the moment, taking the small business card with Dr. Garrett's name embossed importantly on it in blue ink with our appointment time scribbled on it underneath by the same receptionist who had checked us in.

But that feeling dissipated as Sophia was stone-cold silent in the elevator ride to the lobby.

For a moment, I wondered if we should take separate trips in the elevator, but the only thing stranger than riding the elevator with her would have been *not* taking the elevator with her, considering we were headed to the exact same place.

Stepping out of the building, I finally felt like I could breathe all the way in again. Sophia looked drained.

"You work tonight?" I asked her. She shook her head. "You know, I still don't actually understand your work schedule," I admitted.

"I know you don't," she said. She sounded sad. "You never did. You never bothered to learn it when I took on Lead Supervisor."

"Hey," I said, trying to produce a chuckle, because it felt unfair. I held my hands up like a boxer who'd just seen his last round. "Therapy is over for today. Can you save your attacks for Thursday?"

"I don't know, Holden," she said. "I feel—I feel different right now. Like once the therapist got me started talking, a lot of stuff started coming up. I'm not even sure I realized it was there, you know?"

I nodded, but I didn't know. I didn't have a clue.

I could look at my wife's face, a face I'd seen consistently for more than two decades, and realize I had absolutely no idea what was going on in that head of hers. Or where the hell any of this was coming from, honestly. She'd been holding on to stuff from years ago. Stuff I'd more or less forgotten.

She was holding on to a lot of stuff that I sure as hell wasn't.

"Can I call you tomorrow?" I asked.

She nodded. "I'll see you."

"Wait," I said. She turned to look at me, pushing her purse back behind her left hip. I said, "What are you telling people? About us, I mean?"

"What am I *telling* people?" She looked confused.

"Yeah," I said. "Like your sister, and your parents. Your friends."

Your co-workers, my brain said.

"I'm telling them the truth," she said, looking at me like I had two heads. "I expect you're doing the same."

I'd asked because the truth was, I'd skirted a phone call from my mother a few days ago, and although I had texted her back that everything was fine, we were just busy, I knew I needed to return that call soon.

And as soon as I talked to her, my sister and my brother would be in the know, and whether or not it was obvious to Sophia, I was kind of hoping we would get all this settled before I would be forced to say anything to any member of my family, or to any of our friends.

"Okay," I said simply.

One more sucky conversation I would be having that evening.

It would help to stop at the store on the way home for another twenty-four pack before I got on the horn with anyone to whom I was related.

"Thanks," I said, as she turned to get into the minivan, although I had absolutely no idea for what I was thanking her.

* * *

Inside the Scenic View Hotel, I had a beer before I called my mother, who made me wait five minutes while she got my father from outside—he had been mowing—and then I had a beer while I explained to them what was going on, and then I had two beers after we hung up the phone, to recover.

Room 204 was blurry and familiar, but less depressing after my fourth beer.

Something about detailing the ways in which I had completely failed my wife without my knowledge evoked little sympathy from my parents, and made me feel like a kid again. Like I was being lectured. Like I was seventeen and had just crashed the family car.

I had also been avoiding telling my mother because I knew she would immediately tell my sister Judy, and then I'd get an earful from her.

Then again, maybe I wouldn't. She was more into texting than phone calls.

Still. I could picture her face when my mom told her. Awful. My brother on the other hand—he was divorced. He would leave me alone. Or at least he would offer some sympathy, which would be the next best thing to being left alone.

All of which made my head feel like a lead balloon on Tuesday morning when the alarm on my bedside table went off at 4:30 a.m., and it was time to choke down a cup of shitty coffee from the single-brew Keurig machine I'd brought over from the house and outfitted into Room 204.

We'd received that Keurig as a gift at Christmas from Judy and her family, but after it sat unused on our kitchen counter for many months, it eventually migrated to the purgatory that was the storage shelving in the basement.

We were two appliances that no longer seemed to have a place at home.

At least it now had a place to be useful in Room 204.

And I liked to think the Keurig provided a small semblance of class, but I didn't like the taste of the coffee that came out of those little pods. It wasn't as good as Java-Hut's.

I sipped it anyway, and pulled on some navy slacks and a clean shirt, ready to sling shots for eight hours, interrupted by an unpaid thirty-minute lunch break and one fifteen-minute break.

Carmen started me at the register, which is where I was standing when I felt Lila come up behind me.

It was as though I could sense her before I could hear her, and I had to admit that I'd thought of her that morning in the car, buckling my seat belt and starting the drive to the most depressing strip mall plaza in all of Michigan.

I'd actually thought seeing her face was something I could look forward to.

"Good morning," she said softly, almost in a singsong voice.

I turned to look at her, and all I could think was how unfair it was that she looked so lovely. Her long hair hung loosely around her face. She had replaced her black choker with a long silver necklace that carried a heart pendant. The top she wore under her JavaHut apron was a simple, clean white shirt, cut into a slight V-neck at the top. Bold for a coffee shop, I thought, where I couldn't go more than half a shift without getting something dark spilled on me. She also wore a black skirt that reached her knees over tall brown boots.

There was no way this girl didn't have a boyfriend, my brain said.

She still hadn't revealed anything about dating anyone, though, and we hadn't spoken too much since we spent time together the other day at Excelencia Fronteriza. We'd shared several shifts, of course, and she'd been friendly and smiley, but whatever we'd shared over the Budweiser at the fake Mexican place next door felt like a book on a high shelf, and not something we were going to pull down and look at together.

Best not to even break that spine, I thought.

Except for one small thing.

Those text messages.

Since last Thursday, Lila had sent me two more text messages, a day or two apart, and like the first one, I had no idea what I was supposed to do with them.

So, I did what I had done with the first few, which was to stare at them on my phone, and think about what I would say back if I *were* to say something back. And then, say nothing. Then, read the text messages eighteen to twenty times, for some reason, unable to delete the conversation or to actually save her name in my cell phone as a contact.

The first message was actually a picture: it was a cup

of black coffee in a big white mug, sitting on what looked like a square coaster. It was kind of artsy, and I could see three of Lila's fingernails to the left inside the frame.

Underneath the photo, she had written, THIS MADE ME THINK OF YOU.

That one had stirred something up in me. There was no doubt about it, and no use in denying it.

It was like the picture had been of some intimate part of her body, but it wasn't. It was just her fingernails for crying out loud. The tips of her fingers were slender, and her fingernails were painted a deep color of red.

But why in God's name was she sending it to me?

Why was she thinking about me?

The second text was just as damning or just as innocent, depending on your perspective, I guessed. It was a simple quote from a song. I knew because she had attributed it with the artist and the name of the song, and I had gone online on my phone to hear the full thing. I found a video for it pretty quickly on YouTube. Matthew had teased me so mercilessly for not having the YouTube app on my phone that he had installed it months ago, but I thought he would be impressed with how it hadn't taken me long to locate a video to watch through the cracked screen of my cell phone.

It was a pretty song. Very pretty, actually. The artist was Maya Harrison. Not really my usual taste, but dreamy and a little moody.

Lila had texted the lyric from the song, I WISH FOR YOU A DAY LIKE MINE/A DAY THAT HAS NO WALLS...

Those ellipses...

I had to admit, that was the part of her message that confounded me the most.

What the hell was that supposed to mean? And what did she mean about a day not having walls?

She had texted me that on a day I had worked with her, and as I recalled, that day hadn't been a day without walls. That day had been a day with an eight-and-a-half-hour shift, interrupted by one fifteen-minute break and an unpaid lunch break.

All of my days felt like they had walls.

All of my days were boxed in with the heavy feeling that my wife might be cheating on me, that I might be getting a divorce, and that I might soon discover bedbugs in Room 204, or a cockroach climbing up the drain of the shower that hadn't been updated since the 1970s.

All of my days had the walls of a constant hangover that no amount of JavaHut coffee or extra-strength ibuprofen seemed to mitigate fully.

I thought it was maybe time to address the texting thing with Lila, but I was looking for the right way and the right time.

Certainly not when Charlie or Carmen were around, or the new hire, a young African-American girl named Stacy. I liked Stacy immediately. She was a recent State graduate herself, contemplating grad school options. She said that her shifts at JavaHut would keep her occupied when she wasn't studying for the GRE and researching the country's top linguistics programs.

There was never quite a right time, though, and part of me wondered, if I never responded to Lila's texts—if I never said anything—how long would Lila keep it up?

Not for too much longer. Right?

Would she just wonder if she had gotten my number wrong from Carmen, and think maybe the text messages she was sending were going off into thin air? Or—weirder—to some stranger who wasn't saying a thing about them?

Come to think of it that way, it was pretty weird she had texted me so many times, and we'd never actually talked about it.

"Hi," I said to Lila. Cautious.

Today wasn't the day to bring up the texting.

"How are you?" she said.

"Good," I said. "You?"

I tried not to stare at her for too long, but every time I looked at her, I just saw the picture of her black coffee. I lingered in this idea that she was abstractly thinking about me in the morning. I imagined her singing that Maya Harrison song, dreamily, about the beauty of a day without walls. I kept picturing her the way she'd looked sitting across from me last week in front of her tall draft, talking about how she rarely told anyone she wanted to be a singer. Talking about love, about failing, about coming home defeated, and feeling far away. Talking about big dreams, about Chicago.

Whatever this was—this thing with Lila—it was confusing as hell.

But not addressing it meant it could keep going, I supposed.

And considering all I did when I wasn't serving customers at JavaHut was drink beer in Room 204, feeling bored with all the extra time I had on my hands and all the things I no longer had to do with that time, maybe it was okay.

Finishing the Clancy novel was the only thing I had to show for the week, really, other than taking Matthew to visit Portia at Adventure Place. He told me she had a sweet tooth and a predilection for Frappuccino. I had beamed at his vocabulary.

All I did, when I wasn't thinking about Lila or working, was drink beer in Room 204, or feel exhausted, or run all the stuff Sophia had said in Dr. Garrett's office over in my mind, my eyes bouncing around among his many framed degrees on the wall. She kept saying how things had changed so much, and that she couldn't really explain it, but things just felt *different*. Sophia wasn't sure if this relationship had legs anymore.

Whatever that meant.

How does a relationship lose its legs?

"I'm good," Lila said with a sigh. "A little tired. I'm jumping right in with my favorite drink this morning, because... why not? Life's short. Right?"

And then she winked at me and I stared, dumbfounded, first at her, and then when I felt like I had done that long enough, into the air in front of me, until a customer finally walked in and ordered something I had just recently—thanks to Lila and her patient teaching—fully understood how to make.

Thirteen

Now I had to think about Lila winking at me when I closed my eyes in Room 204 that night, my head spinning from how many Budweisers I'd put away.

Seven? Eight?

Hard to say.

Hard to keep count.

Without exercising, without eating much other than muffins from JavaHut and fast food, I was probably gaining a little in the belly. I felt soft around the middle, sunken around the eyes.

In short, I felt like shit.

I was trying to fall asleep to an old movie—*The Shawshank Redemption*. It was one of those movies Sophia and I would stop and watch on TV every time we came across it, flipping through channels with the remote, even though I was pretty sure we owned it—albeit on VHS—somewhere in the basement.

But that movie never failed to suck the two of us in. It made me think that the next time I taught a short story unit, I should come back to the original piece by Stephen King. Like all of his short stories, it's very, very good.

When the movie first came on, and I was probably a little tipsier than I should have been for what I was about to do, I called Sophia.

She didn't answer.

It was after ten, so she very well might have been asleep. But I suddenly felt completely desperate to talk to her, to tell her our movie was on TV, to ask her if she remembered that one time we watched it, and that had led to one of the more memorable nights of making love. Matthew had still been a baby, but he'd finally gotten to a point where he consistently slept through the night. We were well-rested and we'd had a wonderful pasta dinner, and we hadn't even made it upstairs, since we had a fire going in the living room. All I had to do to make it perfect was lay a blanket down on the floor, and then it was one of those rare times where everything just felt right with us, with the world.

Because she didn't answer her cell phone, I called her again.

She didn't answer again, and because I couldn't possibly leave all of that romantic stuff on a voicemail, I called again.

Then again.

Then a fifth time.

Then, I called again because I was surprised she hadn't even texted me. What if there was some kind of an emergency with Matthew?

Didn't she need to be reachable at all times for the sake of our son?

Then I remembered that Matthew was with *her*—at her house, rather—our house, depending on how you looked at it, and that she didn't need to answer a phone call from me for any reason at all. It was a thought that made two tears come to my eyes and slide down my cheek before I finally willed myself to put the phone down.

First, though, I sent her a text message as a way to do a little bit of damage control.

Hopefully, she wouldn't think I looked too pathetic.

Not as pathetic as I felt, anyway.

I AM SORRY FOR CALLING YOU SO MANY TIMES, I wrote. I'LL TALK TO YOU SOON. DON'T WORRY. THERE IS NO EMERGENCY.

I must have fallen asleep after the part where Red and the men drink beer on the roof in the sunshine, because the next thing I was aware of was my cell phone buzzing loudly on the bedside table next to me, jolting me out of half-sleep.

The movie was still playing. I sighed and awakened my cell phone, remembering with dread my terrible showing of calling Sophia six times in five minutes. I fully expected a text from my recently-estranged wife calling me a complete psychopath, but it wasn't there.

My phone said it was 11:29 p.m. now, and that I had a new text from a number that hadn't yet been assigned a real contact.

Lila.

Of course.

HEY, it said.

I was groggy and still buzzed, I realized, my head spinning, and everything I'd thought earlier about letting this silence as Lila texted me drag on ad infinitum felt like total bullshit. Andy Dufresne was extending his arms in triumph in the rain when I wrote back simply, YEAH?

Immediately, the little dialogue bubbles popped up, so I knew she was saying something back.

GOOD, she wrote. YOU'RE THERE. SORRY IT'S SO LATE.

Then she didn't say anything else. I considered teasing her about still being awake this late because she had had too much coffee during our shift that day.

When another five minutes passed and she hadn't

said anything else, I felt myself drifting back to sleep with the phone in my hand. I finally thought just to ask, LILA, ARE YOU OKAY?

It was, after all, late on a Tuesday night.

It was so late on Tuesday, it was almost Wednesday morning.

YEAH, she wrote. I'M OKAY. I WAS JUST—TO BE HONEST, JUST KIND OF WANTED SOMEONE TO TALK TO. I WAS BEGINNING TO THINK YOU DIDN'T KNOW HOW TO TEXT.

I laughed out loud then, even though all of this felt like a big mindfuck. What did she want? What did she need?

And why did she need anything from me?

I just sent her a smiley face emoji.

I JUST WONDERED IF YOU WERE UP, she said.

YUP, I said. WATCHING AN OLD MOVIE.

She didn't say anything for a minute or two, so I added, I DO KNOW HOW TO TEXT, YOU KNOW. THEY LET US OLD MEN TEXT.

OH YEAH? WHICH OLD MOVIE?

I told her, and she immediately wrote back saying she loved *The Shawshank Redemption*, that she'd seen it a hundred times.

IMPROBABLE, I said.

YOU'D BE SURPRISED, she said. A LOT OF LONELY NIGHTS FOR ME OVER HERE.

Whoa, I thought.

What was the right answer to that?

Probably to say nothing, and stare at the screen to see if those little dialogue bubbles were going to pop up again.

I half-wished they wouldn't, but I also knew I was dying to see them on my cell phone screen.

She didn't say anything for a long time, though, and I was just beyond the point of good judgment—just enough to say the following to her, which, in retrospect, was not the right thing to say.

I HIGHLY DOUBT THAT.

YOU CAN DOUBT IT ALL YOU WANT, she wrote back quickly. DOESN'T CHANGE THE TRUTH.

More silence on her end, more silence on mine.

I should go to bed, I thought. For real. What were we even talking for?

The night was a blur, and I wondered now if I'd ever be able to watch this movie the same way again.

I SHOULD PROBABLY GO, I said. IT'S LATE. GOODNIGHT.

GOODNIGHT, she said back. HEY, THANKS SO MUCH FOR LISTENING.

I laughed out loud in Room 204, for the second time that night. Not a lot of joy to be had in this hotel room. YOU DIDN'T REALLY SAY ANYTHING.

SOMETIMES, IT'S JUST NICE TO KNOW SOMEONE'S OUT THERE, she said.

OKAY, I said.

I plugged my phone into the charger next to my bed and was setting it down right as it buzzed one more time.

BY THE WAY, AND FOR THE RECORD, I DON'T THINK OF YOU AS AN OLD MAN.

Jesus, I thought.

The question was right there—in my mind, and the answer was probably on the tip of her tongue, if I had asked, but she didn't say anything else, and I didn't say anything else, and the whole thing felt—in a word—dangerous.

The question kept me awake for maybe another hour, though: if she didn't think of me as an old man, what exactly did she think of me as?

* * *

Not a question I was ready to put in front of Dr. Garrett that Thursday, whom I concluded I did like: he was fair and he seemed to listen well. He had a firm but kind way of cutting straight through some of the things Sophia said that didn't make sense to me, and I thought if they had been things she'd hissed at me in the kitchen, or in the bathroom, for instance, I would have just gotten angry, assumed she was in a pissy mood, that it was unacknowledged PMS, and we would never have come back to it.

Which, since I had done that for so many months, apparently, was how we got ourselves here.

Inside the quiet space that was Dr. Garrett's office, I didn't feel the urge to run away; I felt like I had someone in my corner.

Not at every moment, though. Dr. Garrett pressed me, too, although it didn't make me outwardly emotional the way it made Sophia, who seemed to be crying just as much in the second session as she had during the first.

For the next appointment—assuming we would have one—I should ask Dr. Garrett if I could bring him a latte. Was he a black coffee kind of guy, too? Or did he indulge in something sweet from time to time?

Or Sophia. She was more of a tea person, though.

I had been surprised that Dr. Garrett hadn't asked us for our homework when we first sat down.

What also surprised me was that he hadn't made any jokes about collecting homework from a teacher, since as far as jokes went, that would have been some low-hanging fruit.

"I'd rather hear you articulate feelings from your written answers," he'd told us. "The act of writing answers forces us to consider the questions and put thoughtful words around our most honest responses, after reflection."

Whatever you say, Doc, I thought.

"Start us off, please, Holden," Dr. Garrett was saying. "What did you write under the question about your top three needs in a relationship?"

I pulled the paper out of my back pocket, where it'd been tucked all day during my JavaHut shift.

Carmen hadn't put me on the schedule for Wednesday, so I had been able to avoid Lila, and Lila got put on a half-day shift later on Thursday, to help cover Charlie and train Stacy. Which had honestly been miracle manna straight from heaven. I wasn't sure if I was ready to face Lila after the series of confusing texts from late Tuesday night.

I cleared my throat. "My top three needs from a partner, in no particular order," I said, trying to smile: "loyalty, trust, and honesty."

"Okay," Dr. Garrett said. "Good. That's great. Those are good words, and there are elements there that we can certainly unpack. Can you say a little more about any one of them, or perhaps the three of them together?"

I shrugged.

Glancing at the piece of paper Sophia had laid neatly on her lap, she'd taken the question as more of an essay prompt than a short answer. It made me look like a dummy for just writing three words down.

But the question had seemed pretty straightforward to me.

You want a partner to be loyal.

You want to trust them.

You want them to be honest.

"I guess—I'm not sure how to expand, I guess. But I've always valued that Sophia is honest and I can trust her. Not just—you know, not just in the sense of fidelity, but I trust her with money, our finances, our son, Matthew."

"Good," Dr. Garrett said. He seemed genuinely pleased. "What I'm hearing is throughout your long relationship, you've found Sophia to be a partner who is trustworthy and loyal, and someone who is honest, and that's been important to you. You'd say she's proven that to you many times over, and in many different ways. Do you feel like you've communicated that to her, let her know how much you appreciate that she's been consistently trustworthy?"

I shrugged. "I think so? I mean, part of it is, of course, there's an expectation of loyalty, or whatever, so some of that goes unsaid, when you take your vows. But no, I mean, part of the reason why we're sitting here is maybe I haven't always done a great job of communicating with her that I really value how honest she is. You know one time, the cashier at Lowe's forgot to ring up a plastic shovel we had in our cart, and it was like twenty bucks or something, and I told her not to worry about it, but she made us turn around and go back inside the store to pay."

I was smiling a little at the memory, and as soon as I finished, Dr. Garrett broke eye contact with me and looked at Sophia, gesturing for her to take a tissue. I looked over at her and realized she was and probably had been during my monologue wordlessly sobbing—like sobbing hard.

"I didn't want to cut you off," Dr. Garrett said. "Sophia, it seems like something about what Holden is saying is making you feel something. What can you tell us about how you're feeling right now?"

Sophia had a wad of white tissues at her eyes, and it took her a few moments to stop heaving and say something.

"I'm so sorry," she whispered.

"There's no need to apologize," Dr. Garrett said. "This is good. This is why we're here, to get at these tough emotions. Let's talk about your reaction to what Holden just told you."

"Guilt," she said. She was still whispering and wiping snot from her nose.

Dr. Garrett just nodded, silently, and my eyes went from her to him, him to her.

Guilt? That meant...

Did that mean what I thought it did?

"I'm feeling *so* incredibly guilty," she blurted out. "Because all that nice stuff he said isn't even true anymore."

"Okay," Dr. Garrett said. I could see him taking in a deep breath. "What do you mean by that? Can you tell us when you're ready?"

"I'm not honest, loyal, or trustworthy," she blurted, and started sobbing again, this time straight into her hands. Dr. Garrett looked at her, and then back at me.

"Sophia, if there's something else germane to our time together, it would behoove you to let Holden and I both know. Anything we leave on the table, as they say, isn't helping me help you reach solutions to the issues that brought you here."

She was leaning forward now, sobbing. I didn't know if I should put a hand on her back, or just keep both hands in my lap, lamely holding my sheet of wrinkled paper with my shitty short answers on them.

"I think I have feelings for someone else!" she blurted out.

Dr. Garrett was a true professional. He kept his face neutral.

And if I hadn't had Matthew's warning at Old Chicago in my head, I might have been a little more off the chain.

It was quiet for a long moment. I frowned and studied Sophia, then my shoes.

Your move, Doc, I thought.

"Is that something you feel safe exploring here?" Dr. Garrett said. "One option we have is, you and I could meet one-on-one, in addition to this therapy."

Great, I thought. We could spend more money on therapy. Every penny I was earning this summer slinging espresso shots was going into Dr. Garrett's bank account. We could spend more money padding the college funds of our therapist's kids so that my wife could sit here and talk more about having feelings for someone else.

What a great way to spend my paychecks.

But I knew I was deflecting, building a layer around me, grasping at the wrong thing to think so that I didn't have to sit in a room with a strange man and let the words really sink in.

My wife liked someone else.

My wife had feelings for someone else.

My wife had feelings for another man.

I bet it was that scotch-guzzling lank of a man, Ian, from the Y. Wasn't he one of the aquatics guys?

Sophia nodded. "I think that's a good idea," she said. "I just—I can't do this exercise when he answered that way, and I feel so terrible," she said.

Dr. Garrett nodded. "Totally understandable, and I am still hoping to guide you two through this, because whatever your issues are, I can help you to achieve your common goal—"

"But we *don't* have a common goal," I interrupted. Then I apologized for it. "I'm sorry, but the whole premise here is pretty messed up—what we started with during the last session was that I wanted to get back together, and she wanted to think about it. Is that even true now? You just want out? So you can go be with some other dude?"

I looked over at Sophia, who had her eyes closed, and tears were rolling down her cheeks. She looked exhausted, and I felt bad, a little, for making her cry.

But not that bad.

Dr. Garrett sighed. "It *is* true that initially, Sophia articulated a less firm goal, or should I say, Sophia maybe left the door open a little more, comparatively, for what other options are out there, other than reconciliation. But remember, my goal as a family counselor isn't to magically glue married couples back together," he said, spreading his hands apart and smiling.

I wanted to pick up his pad of legal paper and smash

it into his face.

"My goal is to help people—in this case, a married couple, move forward in whatever way they decide is best. It's important that you two take care of yourselves and your emotions during this time—regardless of what the outcome is. I'm a mediator for conversations that may be too difficult to have without some external guidance. It can be especially difficult when a child is involved. You two are navigating the waters of your relationship while trying to be fair to your son, and that's important as well."

I should have become a family counselor, I thought cynically.

He doesn't even have to answer to a success rate, a track record. He just has to listen and talk, and barely give a shit if anyone he consults recommits to a marriage.

It sounded easier than teaching, that was for sure.

I would probably make more money.

And get all the fancy-looking diplomas on my wall.

Hell, I spent so many hours listening to my students vent about their problems in my classroom, I could probably just start working as a family therapist. If I had desired a summer job that would have used my brain, I could have sat in for Dr. Garrett.

"Sophia," he said, looking at her. "What do you want to do here. We have a couple of options. One is that we can complete our session here... We have about twenty minutes left, and we can go over your answers to the homework. Another option, though, is to end it, or excuse Holden, and you and I can chat, and I can plan on seeing the two of you again next week."

"Do I get a say?" I asked.

I couldn't help it. I was just pissed now, and this was the most recent thing in a long list of events I seemed to get absolutely no say in. I felt like I kept having no choice other than to keep letting things happen to me.

Dr. Garrett held up a hand. "Yes," he said. "You are an equal part of this, Holden, but I do want to defer at this moment to Sophia—for a few reasons. For one thing, she may be quite raw at the moment with her emotions, considering the revelation."

Sophia just nodded, and then she looked at me. "Holden, I'm sorry," she said. "I do think we should meet again. I just need to talk this out. I'm sorry."

I just stared at her. "If she's cheated, that changes everything, right?" I asked.

My mind was spinning.

Sophia shook her head. "I didn't cheat on you, Holden!" she said sharply.

I started to fire something back, and Dr. Garrett stopped me, putting his hand on my forearm.

"Okay, whoa there. Let's stop, please. This is why I suggested we consider a course forward together. Emotions are running a little high right now. They're all sitting right there under the surface—for both of you. Holden," he said, taking his arm away. "Of course they are. I want you to know that just because Sophia is the one crying and expressing her emotions that way, and you're not—I don't discount that you are experiencing extreme emotion right now."

I took a breath in and out, and felt my body calm down. And in that moment, Lila's face flashed in my mind, for whatever insane reason.

Dr. Garrett continued. "Marriage is a complex thing,

you guys," he said. I realized it was the first time I'd heard Dr. Garrett say something that didn't sound formal.

"As my mentor used to say—and I'm paraphrasing here—marriage is some dark and deep water, and there are many ways in which expectations are not met. Infidelity can look like a lot of things to a lot of people, depending on culture, experience, and so on," he said, rattling the ideas off on his fingers.

"We agreed earlier this week together to approach conversations with respect, love, and empathy," he said, "and I'm just holding you to that. So, Sophia, it sounds like maybe the best thing to do is you and I continue for a bit, and let's all meet again next week. Okay, Holden? Would you allow us to excuse you?"

I stood up and nodded.

It didn't exactly seem like I had a choice, and it also seemed like I would yell some more if I continued the conversation with Sophia and Dr. Garrett.

All I could think about was getting back to Room 204 and getting a beer, or two, or three, and not having to listen to this anymore. I couldn't wait to not think about this anymore.

My wife had feelings for another man. What did that even mean? Everyone had a wandering eye sometimes, I thought, and I thought of Lila again, her red fingernails on that coffee cup, her bare feet padding around a hardwood floor.

Her many text messages to me.

Her legs. Her laugh.

Her beautiful face.

The way she looked at me.

God, I did love the way she looked at me.

Lila looked at me like she could hang on my every word, like she wanted nothing more than to know everything about me. It had been a long time since I had felt like that, I realized.

Those feelings that you get in the beginning of a relationship—they are intoxicating.

But Sophia feeling like her crush on someone else was serious or severe enough to kick me out for the summer to decide if she liked some other man better than me?

What the actual fuck?

I was speechless, so I just nodded again, and then Sophia reached up and grabbed my hand, squeezing it hard before I left Dr. Garrett's office, as though she was offering me some kind of outrageously lame consolation prize.

Fourteen

Except for one thing.

I couldn't do it.

I couldn't bring myself to drive back to that depressing hotel, especially when I realized that rent would soon be due for another week. I had put off paying it yesterday. Why? Because I had been hoping I would hear from Sophia last night, or I was hoping that today in therapy, she'd finally indicate that she was finished with—well, whatever nonsense this was.

I had been entertaining some kind of a fantasy that we'd leave Dr. Garrett's office holding hands and that she'd tell me to come home sooner rather than later, and in that case, I would just suck up the small late fee I'd incur by switching to paying by the day and not by the week. The pay-by-the-day option was more expensive, but I only needed a half-hour—hell, ten quiet minutes—to pack up all my stuff, leave Room 204, and it would be like I had never set foot in that room.

After I left Dr. Garrett's office, closing the door behind me and leaving our therapist to talk with Sophia one-on-one for another twenty minutes about how she felt about some other guy, after eighteen years of marriage to me, the last place in the world I thought I could go was Room 204 at the Hellscape Hotel, located in one of the inner circles of a hell so demented, Dante probably couldn't have even dreamed it up.

Back in the Camry, I drove too fast without bothering

with a seatbelt or the radio, and somehow found myself back in the parking lot of the JavaHut, where I'd left roughly an hour and a half prior.

And I realized for no real reason that I could articulate, I was scanning the parking lot for Lila's green Jeep.

I spotted it, and let out a breath I hadn't realized I had been holding.

But I didn't go into JavaHut.

I didn't want to go in.

I just wanted to sit there, breathing, staring at my car's steering wheel and Lila's parked Jeep. It felt oddly comforting to have her car near mine.

I wasn't really aware of how much time passed with me sitting there, running everything over in my head, wishing I had a six-pack in my console, watching people park their cars, go get coffee, come back with drinks, get back in their cars, and drive off.

God, JavaHut really did need a drive-thru.

I stared at the door to JavaHut, holding my phone in my hand, hoping to get a call or text message from Sophia, but she stayed silent. There was a chance she'd call or text me and tell me how the rest of the session with Dr. Garrett went.

Or at least tell me if we had another therapy session on the books.

We hadn't made a follow-up appointment before going in for today's, so for all I knew, this was the end of the line, the last stop. We may never meet with Dr. Garrett again. It was all on my wife to decide, I guessed. I seemed to have no say.

Then something expected and unexpected happened as I sat there, tired and sober, staring at Lila's Jeep: my phone rang, but it was Judy.

What was worse, I had to deliberate: letting it go to voicemail so I could ignore her, or getting it out of the way now, and allowing all her verbal shit to enter my ears on what was already a shitty day.

I went with the latter.

Bring it on, I thought. *I'm bulletproof.*

Obviously, I had nothing better to do than sit in the parking lot of this strip mall, and nowhere more critical to be, either.

"Hi, Judy," I said, trying to sound normal.

"Hi there," she said.

She sounded startled I'd picked up the phone, and part of me was, too.

"I know why you're calling," I said.

"Oh, you do, do you?" she said, a little playfully.

At least she was in a good mood. Her kids must not be driving her nuts, as they usually were. Especially in this late afternoon hour, when the time grew thin, and I knew she was counting down the minutes until her husband Stewart would come home.

"How do you know I'm not calling you to tell you your adorable nephew has lost his first tooth?" she asked.

"Bush league," I teased. "Call me when he needs braces, like Matthew will soon."

"You're in quite a mood," she said, laughing softly. "I'm calling because Mom talked my ear off about you recently. You and Sophia."

"I figured," I said.

"You better come visit us," she said. "I'm serious. Even if it's just, you know, you. Although it would be better if you brought Sophia and Matthew. Or at least Matthew. Don't touch that, honey," she said. The last comment was obviously not directed at me.

"I'll see what I can do," I said. "Things are a little fragile around here."

"I surmise," she said. "So, what the hell did you do wrong?"

"I don't know," I said with a sigh.

I could picture Judy in her kitchen, her smart brown bob almost to her shoulders, probably holding a glass of red wine and stirring something on the stove. She lived an hour south—Kalamazoo. It was close enough for a day trip, but the truth was, we were both so busy, we didn't make the effort nearly enough.

I was thinking about trying to remember, in fact, the last time I had seen Judy and Stewart and their kids, when I realized that what I was also doing was still staring at the door to JavaHut and hoping to see Lila.

And I realized that I was no longer hoping Soph would call or text me, just hoping I would see Lila.

I realized she was the only person I wanted to see or talk to right then, and I wondered what I was supposed to make of that.

"You must have done something," my sister said.

"How do you know *Sophia* didn't do something?" I asked.

She was my younger sibling, so obviously had many years of experience believing that she knew more than me about just about everything. Truth be told, though, she usually did.

"Because," she said. "I know these things."

"Yeah," I said. "I don't know anything right now."

I wasn't ready to tell my sister what Sophia had just

told Dr. Garrett and me.

Judy sighed. "I'm sorry, you know."

"Yeah," I said. "Thanks. It sucks. All of this just sucks."

"Mom said you're at a hotel," she added.

"Yeah," I said. "Hotel. Weekly rates. It's a shithole."

"Spring for somewhere nicer," she suggested gently.

"Not unless you want to bankroll it."

"Speaking of money—or just—not even money, but will you please let me know if there's anything Stewart and I can do?"

"I will," I said.

We talked for a few more minutes about the kids and the stress of Stewart's new project at work. She liked to buck the typical dictum of birth order and openly boss me around as though she were the older sibling. She always had. And actually, it was a little comforting to have my little sister firmly boss me around for a few minutes. She told me I should eat better. She told me to take better care of myself. Her voice in her goodbye sounded so tender, I felt tears welling up in my eyes and ended the call before she could hear them catch in my voice.

After we spoke, I texted with Matthew about his day, about how basketball was going, so I could feel a little more normal. Every once in a while, I asked myself when I would be ready to leave this damn parking lot, but the answer kept being an unrelenting *not yet*.

Finally, I spotted Lila walking out the door, shoving her phone into her purse and fishing her keys out with her slender hand.

She stopped in her tracks when she saw me, sitting with my elbow out the window of the Camry, sweating because it was pretty hot out, but I hadn't wanted to run the engine for the AC. I had lost all concept of how long I'd been sitting there.

Which felt fitting.

Apparently, this was the summer I didn't know how long I'd be sitting, waiting.

If I'd been running the engine, I probably would have run the car all the way out of gas and then, I would have been stranded at JavaHut.

"Hey, Lila," I said, to her puzzled look.

Oh, you're doing great, my brain said.

"Holden," she said. "I—I thought you left like hours ago. I took—Carmen had me change my hours a bit today," she said, pointing back at JavaHut.

"Yeah," I said. "I think it's my turn to ask you if you'd like to hang out for a bit."

A slow smile spread across her face, and I felt like the air had finally entered all the way into my lungs.

"Sure," she said. "But you're going to have to follow me to my place. I've got a very cute, very impatient dog with a small bladder."

She winked at me, and without waiting for me to answer, slid smoothly into her Jeep, started the engine, and gave me a little wave as she put on her seat belt and pulled away from the parking lot.

And then I was staring at her brake lights and turn signals as she led me away from the JavaHut parking lot, and I happily followed, feeling not too unlike a dog myself.

Fifteen

I had expected an apartment complex, but Lila led me just east of downtown to the oldest historic district of the city. That area had many older homes that were built in the late 1800s and early 1900s. Many of the city's affluent business leaders and influencers at the turn of the century had lived in these ornate homes. I always thought it would be cool to live in one of them. A fair number of the homes had since been converted to apartments, and Lila's, on a broad north-south street lined with old oak trees and cracked sidewalks, was no exception.

Finding a spot to park on the street was a little challenging, though. I was not in the suburbs anymore.

My awkward parallel parking job gave Lila something to tease me about when I finally settled into a spot, clicking the car fob after I slammed the door, almost tripping on the uneven curb to the sidewalk.

"Easy there," she said, laughing lightly, holding out her arm for me. "Do you need an elbow?"

"No," I said. "I'm just an old man."

"I told you," she said softly, "I don't think of you as an old man."

"Well, I am an old man," I said lamely.

But her back was to me, and she was already walking up a flight of outdoor stairs on the side of the large brown home to a door on the second floor.

I was surprised any city inspector worth his salt would approve a staircase like this, but evidently, at one point, one had. I couldn't imagine negotiating those stairs in the snow and ice that marked our Michigan winters.

Lila slid her key into the lock above the doorknob, and in the next moment, a very hyper corgi bounded out, jumping onto Lila's legs, and then onto my legs, when she spotted me halfway up the staircase.

"You need a leash for this thing?" I called to Lila.

"Nah," Lila said. She chuckled. "Zen is fine. Just let her go by you so she can pee on the lawn."

"Okay," I said as the corgi ran around the three trees in the side yard before settling in on a place to pee. Lila was still standing at her door, calling out encouragement, telling her she was a good girl. Zen bounded back up to see Lila the second she was done squatting.

Lila looked at me. I was still standing awkwardly in the middle of her rickety staircase. She smiled.

"You want to come in?" she asked.

"Okay," I said again, dumbly.

It was hard to process what was even happening. Evidently, though, this was.

Her place was more or less what I had expected, given the style with which she dressed and presented herself, even somewhere as banal as JavaHut. It was decorated in much the way Lila decorated herself.

I spotted a lovely couch with teal and salmon throw pillows. A framed black and white picture of the Eiffel Tower hung on the wall, next to one depicting a river scene. Scarves hung from wooden hooks on one wall, and jarred candles sat on nearly every flat surface. It was cozy and warm.

I recognized one corner of her place, near the couch, and I realized it was because of that picture she had texted me where she was drinking the black coffee, and thinking of me. It was weird to be so familiar with part of her home.

Three weeks ago, she was a virtual stranger to me, and now here I was in her living room, having a seat on her couch, her dog bounding onto my lap to give me a better sniff.

The weirdest part of all of it may have been the fact that Lila seemed not in the least surprised I was sitting there, as though somehow, maybe all of this had been bound to happen if given enough time.

Or like she was used to this kind of thing happening.

Perhaps she was.

She struck me as the type of woman who was more or less accustomed to getting what she wanted, eventually.

Lila had pulled off her brown purse and placed it on the table with two chairs just next to the small kitchen.

I wondered how many people lived in this building. I had counted three apartments carved from the large house. It had its own complex history, this house—one so different from the home Soph and I had purchased in the suburbs. Unlike our house, this one held a hundred years of history.

And now this old house was where this gorgeous young woman slept every night.

Seemingly alone.

Not unlike me.

I felt as though I had no control over the part of my brain that had already scanned the room for a framed picture of Lila with someone. I couldn't help but look around for evidence that there was a man in her life.

A pair of men's shoes on the floor.

A man's jacket on a chair.

But there was nothing.

"I'm pouring some wine for myself," Lila said, grabbing a goblet from the cupboard. "Would you like a glass?"

"Uh... sure," I said.

She returned a few moments later with a glass of red wine in each hand, and to my relief, sat down in the wingback chair directly across from the couch, instead of choosing to sit directly next to me. Which was her only other option, except for the floor or in one of the chairs pulled up to the small dining table.

Lila took a big sip from her wine glass and started chatting with me about Stacy, and training her, and cracking jokes about Carmen's sassy comments, and how nice it must be for me not to be the newest JavaHut employee anymore.

"You've got more seniority than Stacy," Lila said, smiling, running her fingers through her hair. "But I mean, other than Carmen and me, there's so much turnover, don't let it go to your head. Although, Charlie has stuck around longer than I thought he would. Poor guy. Starbucks just won't give him a chance."

She smiled playfully at me, and I felt a skip in my chest.

So I took a big drink, and I rallied my mind about what should and should not happen in this very charming little apartment.

"You have a nice place," I said finally. It was the first thing I'd managed, other than easily and perhaps too passively acquiescing to that glass of red wine.

She smiled at me.

Zen had lost interest in me and jumped off the couch to the wingback chair to cuddle up on Lila's lap.

"Thanks," she said. "I was lucky to find it. These apartments go so fast, but when I was coming back from Chicago, one of my friends gave me the lead, and introduced me to the landlord, so she never even put it up for rent. If she had, someone else would have snatched it in a heartbeat. It's kind of perfect," she said. "Just the right size for one person, and just the right price, too."

Okay, my brain said. *Did you clock that? She just said, "for one person."*

Just Lila.

She scratched Zen thoughtfully. She'd worn her long blonde hair down that day, and she tilted her head to the side so it fell behind her shoulder.

"This is actually the first apartment I've ever lived in by myself, come to think of it," she added. "I moved out of my parents' house for college with a roommate, you know, and then there was Chicago," she said, rolling her eyes a little. "It's a bit of an experiment, living by yourself, isn't it? You really get to know yourself."

She studied me and took another drink of her wine. "Have you ever lived alone?"

"Uh," I said. "Let me think." I let my brain swirl around what to say next for a second or two. "In college, I roomed with a couple of guys, you know—as an undergraduate. Then I was actually in a fraternity my junior and senior years—"

She interrupted me with a big grin. "No way! I *cannot* picture you as a frat bro."

I chuckled. "Not—it was not like that. I mean, it

wasn't *that* kind of fraternity. We were nerdy," I said. I couldn't help chuckling more. It felt good to laugh, though. "It was more like an academic residential program than a fraternity. I think we only had two parties—around the holidays. I promise you, it was all very PG."

She was still amused. "My old English teacher—a frat bro." She shook her head at me, teasing me. "To be honest, I can't picture any of the teachers at St. Bridget's as frat brothers—or like, being sorority girls."

"Well, listen—don't spread that tidbit around," I said. "That is some pretty privileged information. There are not that many people in my adult life who know that. Certainly no one at St. Bridget's."

Lila made a motion like she was zipping her lips, swearing herself to secrecy.

I had to smile.

I had to take another deep drink of wine.

She laughed. "Don't worry, your secret's safe with me. Besides, I don't keep up too much with people from—you know, people from high school. A few friends, here and there, you know. But really, when I moved back here, after Chicago didn't work out... I guess I kind of decided specifically not to reconnect with old friends. I wanted a fresh start. You know what I mean?"

"Sure," I said. I took another large sip of wine. It was starting to do its job.

I loved that Lila wasn't pressing me, wasn't asking me why the hell I was here. She knew I had a son, so Lila could safely infer that there had been a woman at some point, but she hadn't pressed me on that, either.

Talking to Lila felt so easy, and I felt easy, and the chair felt comfortable, and my day started to feel like maybe it had no walls after all, just like they did in that song of hers.

Something was drawing me to her, then, even if I couldn't say what the hell it was.

Lila sighed and sat back in her chair. Zen looked as though she was in heaven, and seemed to be just a few more strokes from falling completely asleep.

"So, I haven't asked you how you're liking JavaHut," she said. "At least not outside the confines of the building, I mean," she giggled. "You *have* to say you like it when you're around Carmen."

"I like it," I said. "It's fun. I mean, it's really short-term, for me," I said, thinking about her comment from earlier about all the turnover at JavaHut. "I'll start teaching again at the end of August. Really, in the middle of August, when you count all the teacher professional development days the district makes us get in..." I let my voice trail off.

"Will you be sad to leave us?" Lila said.

She was smiling, baiting me.

"Sure," I said slowly. "You guys—you guys are great. It's fun. It's nice to have—I mean, it's nice to have a job where your brain can kind of turn off. Not that every drink is easy to make," I joked. "But you know—it's not breaking down Homer. It's not trying to get sixteen-year-olds to get their eyes off their phone and care about the plight of Hamlet. Would you believe me if I told you most teenagers don't give an actual shit about iambic pentameter?"

She chuckled, almost coughing a little on the sip of wine she was taking. I felt inordinately proud of myself for making this beautiful woman laugh so hard she struggled with her wine.

"I get it. It *is* kind of mindless. Sometimes I kind of zone out when I'm at work. Not at the register so much, but when I'm just standing there, steaming milk and pulling shots. I will tell you, though, I'll take slaving away at JavaHut over working at the bar any day of the week. Coffee drinks are easier than alcoholic drinks," she said. "And coffee customers are a lot more pleasant than drunks. I like not having to worry about over-serving anyone."

She smiled.

I felt like I could keep listening to her all night.

I felt like I was already dreading the moment I was going to have to leave.

"Don't get me wrong, the tips were way better at the bar. But it was awful, sometimes. And cutting people off at the bar is the absolute worst," she added. "You like to think, oh, I am cutting that guy off because he's getting a little wild, and having too much fun—usually at the bar with all his frat bros," she said, grinning.

"Residential program partners," I corrected, not being able to help but grin back.

"But the truth is, usually when I had to cut someone off, it was not for being too rowdy, but because they were sad-drunk. Like crying-drunk—like, in a bad way drunk. Like grown men wailing into their drinks, belligerent. It was very depressing," she said, staring at her wine glass, which was growing emptier and emptier as we talked. "And then I'd try to be kind and ask them if there was someone I could call for them, and half the time the answer was like, *No, I don't have anyone you can call for me.* And I'd just have to call them a cab. Try to do it in a subtle way to save them some embarrassment, you know. Once, I had to help a guy into a cab who had literally pissed himself."

"I can imagine," I said. "I mean, I can't really imagine. That sounds horrible."

No doubt, I had reached some low lows in Room 204, but at least I hadn't gotten myself shit-faced in some bar and taken all my problems out on a beautiful young bartender. I had that going for me, at least.

I felt like I was choking on all the things I wanted to say to Lila, but now that I was sitting across from her, in her place, my wine glass nearly empty, I couldn't get any words out.

What was behind all the texting?

I was so angry at Sophia. And Lila would listen, if I wanted to bare my soul to her—which I realized I did.

You could do that, my brain said.

But then what?

Then what?

Does Lila become my best friend and confidant?

Shouldn't I be careful not to burden my former student—and current coworker—with the emotional intricacies of my marital problems? She wasn't my peer. She had never been married.

No offense to Lila, but only people who have been married—and married for a long time—know about the kinds of things that go on in a marriage. Only people who have been married for a long time know that it gets complicated at times. No matter how strong of a couple you are, there are times it just feels lonely.

She might comprehend because Lila was turning out to be as smart as she was beautiful, but that didn't make delving into my situation with her a good idea.

"Well, we'll miss you when you leave us in August," she said. "I'm sure if you like the work, Carmen would gladly keep you on for Saturdays and Sundays, if you want to be part-time. Not that you would. I'm sure you have better things to do on the weekends. Kelsey's gonna leave us in August, too," she said.

"Right," I said. "More new faces at JavaHut."

She hesitated. "I—well, I'll still be there, but I think I'm going to cut back. Drop down to part-time, if I can afford to."

"Yeah?" I asked.

She nodded and sighed. "Well, I gotta get back on that horse. School, you know? Get moving? I can't work as a barista forever. I'm sure I don't have to tell you that. I have to—I have to start with classes again, or something. Do *something*. Maybe look more seriously at degrees, vocal coaching, take a job or an internship at a... I don't even know, at a church or some music place, I don't know. The music society. The point is, I gotta use this summer to get my shit together," she said. "I have to."

I bit my tongue so I wouldn't tell her that we had more in common than was appropriate for me to say.

If she only knew.

I simply nodded, sipped the last of my wine, which actually was very, very good.

"Hey, are you hungry at all?" she said, switching gears. "It's probably the time when adults eat dinner." I looked at my watch. It was already almost eight. It didn't seem possible, but the clock wasn't lying.

"I'm okay," I said. "Thanks. I should get going soon."

"I feel like you just got here," she said gently, her

head cocked a little, like she was baiting me again.

I studied her face, her slender hands.

Maybe I didn't remember her from ten years ago, but it didn't matter. I was meeting Lila for the first time now.

Maybe I could be honest with myself, and admit that when Sophia confirmed what Matthew had told me—that she cared for someone else—well... It wasn't the most insane thing to hear.

It wasn't as insane as I wanted it to be to hear.

Perhaps that was the real reason I was so upset.

Because it wasn't crazy to care about someone you weren't married to.

It happened.

It happened all the time. Right?

It started with moments like this, when another human reaches out to you, offers you warmth and listens to you, and talks to you, and connects with you, and makes you feel like the rest of the world with its disappointments and troubles lived outside of the space you two created when you were together, when you were just talking together.

Maybe I could be honest with myself and admit I was doing the exact same thing Sophia had very likely done to me, apparently.

I also hadn't cheated, because this wasn't exactly cheating.

But this was certainly something.

I would be lying to myself if I said this wasn't something.

Idiot, my brain said. *This is something.*

I studied Lila's face as she studied mine, and then said finally, quietly, something I knew she would not like me for saying, but in the moment, I couldn't help the words from spilling out of my mouth.

"I'll stay longer if you sing for me."

She laughed out loud, the last of her wine sloshing around her goblet. "Not a chance, buddy," she said. "I don't sing for people. That only happens after a full bottle of wine, not just one measly glass."

She raised an eyebrow, and I knew this was an invitation.

A very dangerous invitation.

But I smiled, and stood up.

"No, wait!" she said, standing too.

Zen grumbled as she took over the cushion of the chair where Lila had been sitting.

"I have an idea," she said. "Stay right there."

She disappeared into a room I could only assume was her bedroom, and came back out with a CD in her hand, inside a clear jewel case. It was unlabeled.

"I made this when I was in Chicago," she said. "Like a few years ago. You can—you can *borrow* it," she said slyly. "Only if you promise to tell me what you think. But you can only tell me what you think if you like it. If you hate it, you just have to give it back to me and not say a word about it for the rest of your natural life. Pinky swear?"

Then she actually held out her pinky to me and made me shake it with mine.

I could tell I liked the feel of her skin on mine, and I doubled down on my resolve to leave, even as I couldn't help but laugh at her, staring down at the blank CD now occupying the space in my hands.

I set my empty wine glass down on the kitchen counter, and I resisted what I realized was my strongest urge of the moment, which was to wrap her in a hug, and kiss her wide, smooth forehead.

She looked at me, expectantly.

"Thanks," I said. "I will listen to this tonight. And I'll give it back to you and tell you that I like it tomorrow, at work."

She grinned again.

"And thanks for the wine," I said, heading toward her door. "You have very good taste."

"I should hope so," she laughed. "I was a bartender for so long. I would have been a bad one if I couldn't pick out a good bottle of Merlot."

I thought she sounded a little sad, so I closed the door behind me before I could change my mind, and waited until I heard her latch the lock behind me before I took a step. Walking down her staircase, I could picture her staring at my back through the peephole in the door as I began to make my way down to the street. I forced myself to take in a deep breath when I got to my car, my body aching for another glass of that red wine—and, I realized, if I was honest with myself—aching for something much deeper, too.

Sixteen

I saw, when I buckled myself into the Camry and started its engine, pulling my phone out of my back pocket, that I had an unread text from Sophia. I forced myself to wait until I was home to read it, unsure of what it would say.

It could say anything from "I'm sorry" to "it's over, when do you want to come and get your things, I've got a good divorce lawyer on retainer ready to go."

I used the unread text as motivation to keep me driving home.

Not home, but rather the Scenic View Hotel.

Room 204 was not home.

Once inside, though, I was greeted by the same mess I'd left that morning. My clothes—both clean and dirty—were everywhere. My pathetic bed was still unmade. The whole room smelled like coffee to me. The lines between being at work and being home were weirdly starting to blur.

I took a deep breath, went to the mini-fridge to chase the red wine with a cold beer, which I felt I desperately and absolutely needed, and finally allowed myself to read it—the text from Sophia.

It was just a text asking me if I was free to meet with Dr. Garrett next Thursday afternoon—the fifth. It was his next available appointment, she'd said, considering the holiday.

SURE THING, I wrote back, then clicked my cell phone off, watching the screen go dark.

Immediately, I woke it back up again, dialing Sophia's number before I knew what I was doing.

She answered the call right before it went to voicemail.

"Hi, Holden," she said softly.

It sounded like she'd been crying some more. "Does that date not work for you after all?"

"Hi," I said. "No. It works. I just wanted to hear your voice."

She laughed softly. "I can't believe that for one second."

"Well, it's the truth."

"I texted you actually because I didn't feel too much like talking," Sophia said.

"I figured," I said. "So why don't you let me do all the talking."

"Holden..."

"Remember that time we stayed up until five in the morning? We'd gotten home from that party, the one at the Stivers' house, and we made love, but then we just got another bottle of wine and drank it in bed under the covers? And we just—talked? For like—just for hours?"

Sophia didn't say anything.

"And you remember that time when Matthew was a baby? I think he was probably seventeen or eighteen months old. We put our comforter in the middle of the living room and sat in our pajamas all day, watching movies? Just one movie after another, giving Matthew his naps and changing his diapers or whatever, feeding him, and he crawled around everywhere, babbling, playing with his toys, but just—we ordered a pizza. We just spent the *whole* day that way? Like we didn't want to move off that blanket? Like that blanket was a boat, and the carpet was an ocean, and the only way we could stay safe was to stay on it together, as a family?"

I could hear her starting to cry quietly again, and even though I didn't want to be the reason she was crying, it felt oddly enjoyable, like I was finally breaking through a layer of ice.

"Another time. I think early on when we were dating, we'd been together for only like four months, you came over—"

"Holden, stop it," she said. She was sobbing. "You're making me very sad."

"Damnit, Soph," I said. "This is our life. Together. This is our marriage and two decades of history. More than two decades. I get that you're going through something, but I'm your husband and I'm Matthew's father, and that's not just going to change overnight, and you can't erase all these memories just because you have a fucking crush on someone else."

I heard her take in a sharp breath.

I already hated myself for what I was about to ask next, but the words were out of my mouth before my brain could clamp my lips shut.

My brain said, *Don't say it.*

Don't say it.

Don't say it.

"Is it Ian?" I asked.

"Goodbye, Holden," she said, and in my ear, I heard the soft tone signifying that she had abruptly ended the call.

And then I taught myself a lesson I probably didn't need to learn: chasing red wine with a six-pack of beer does not for a good night of sleep make.

* * *

Thankfully, Carmen didn't put me on for a few days, and on Sunday, she put me on the late watch with Stacy.

This was good for two reasons.

One: because I had a chance to actually get some sleep. And I had a chance to brave the laundry room at the hotel and feed my shiny quarters to the washing machine and dryer.

Two: because my shifts would overlap less with Lila's.

I hadn't bothered to look closely at Lila's schedule, but since we were both the only full-time employees, other than Carmen, it was hard to find pockets of time when I wasn't working with Lila.

And a third reason, I realized when I woke up at just after 9:00 a.m. on that Sunday: I could see if Matthew wanted to get brunch with me. When I called him and he didn't pick up, I texted him. He responded to my text right away with a request to go to iHop.

Sophia's car wasn't in the driveway when I arrived at the house to pick Matthew up, and as though reading my gaze, Matthew assured me she wasn't home as he slid into the car, shutting the passenger door behind him.

"That's fine," I tried to say evenly. "Seems like her schedule is all over the place these days."

"Yeah," he said. "It is. She says summer's so busy. She leaves me a lot of notes."

He had his phone in his lap, and it looked like he was texting with someone.

I let it go.

"Is everything going okay?" I asked as I started driving.

Something about sitting side by side in the car, maybe, made it a little easier to talk. I was hoping Matthew would open up to me a little bit. His parents were showing him no signs that things were going to go back to normal before the start of the school year.

Although, I could remember being fourteen and feeling like the summers used to go on forever. I remember July feeling like one listless day after another. I missed the way time used to crawl like that.

"Sure, Dad," he said. "Everything's fine. No big deal."

Which made me chuckle—not from humor, though. "Well, I think it *is* a big deal," I said. "This summer, I mean. Obviously, your mom and I are both upset and sorry that this is happening, but we're committed to trying to figure it out, you know. We're in therapy."

"I know," he said. "Mom comes home crying."

"Yeah," I said. "She cries there, too."

He didn't say anything, so I glanced at him. He was back to texting, giving that tiny device all his energy, all his attention.

"I know I've said this before," I said, "but this doesn't have anything to do with you—this thing that your mom and I are going through. That we're working through. *Trying* to work through."

I wasn't sure, but I thought I saw him nod his head.

"Is that Portia you're chatting with?" I asked.

He smiled. "Yeah. It's all good."

"Good," I said. "I'm available to chauffeur you two again, anytime," I said, remembering that time I dropped them off at the movies, then stared at the shoreline of Lake Michigan for an hour, thinking, even if abstractly, about Lila, and how the darker sand by the waves wasn't unlike the color of her eyes when she looked at me. Actually, when Lila looked right at me, she absolutely leveled me with those eyes.

"Thanks," he said. "Hey, Dad?"

"Yeah?" I said.

"Can we not talk about girls anymore?" Matthew asked.

I laughed. "Okay," I said. "That sounds good to me. No girl talk."

We rode the rest of the way to the iHop in silence, and I congratulated myself for not pumping my son for any new information about any women at all.

* * *

JavaHut was pretty quiet that evening. Charlie worked with me for a bit, and Carmen left just after 6:00 p.m., after carefully going over the closing procedures with me.

Twice.

Her trust in my intelligence seemed to me to be at a low point, but perhaps she wanted to put on a united front for the newbie. Stacy raised an eyebrow when Carmen told her it would be my first time closing, too. Carmen left her cell number and instructed us to call if we ran into any problems, which it seemed like she was half-expecting.

When we hit a slow point at around 7:30 p.m., Stacy surreptitiously pulled her iPad out of her bag and asked if I minded if she did some online research if there was nothing else to do.

A gamble, I thought. There was a large camera, hidden in one of those ominous-looking black domes in the ceiling. However, from studying it, my guess was that it was mostly pointed at the register. If you stood toward the back counter, it seemed a safe bet you were more or less off camera.

I guess JavaHut Corporate was only concerned with employees making off with money, not extra chocolate sprinkles.

"Sure," I said. "I mean, there's only so much cleaning one can do."

"Thanks," she said, smiling. "I am deep into research, and I hate wasting time like this. Every one of these grad programs wants you to write a slightly different essay on a slightly different topic, you know? But it's mostly the same question over and over again. It's so obnoxious."

I smiled. I admired her dedication, but did not tell her I was an English teacher who'd been through grad school, nor did I tell her that I would be more than happy to help her refine any essay answer she was crafting. I did not tell her that I was far better at editing than I was at making elaborate drinks with marshmallows and cold shots.

"Good idea," I said. "I actually have something I should be working on tonight, too."

She nodded but didn't ask me what.

God bless these Millennials, I thought. Or whatever the generation that came after Millennials called themselves.

My students were the same way. They were very adept and practiced at minding their own business—

although Soph would say they were a little on the self-absorbed side, that they spent a little too much time taking selfies and posting them to social media. A little navel-gazey, she said once of some of her younger coworkers at the Y.

I pulled from my back pocket the latest homework Dr. Garrett had assigned for our next session—a piece of white paper I had folded twice into a fat, quarter-sized chunk.

This time, for the homework from Dr. Garrett, there were five questions with space in between them to write. I had read all the questions earlier, but hadn't yet really considered them or written anything down.

I couldn't imagine that Dr. Garrett had pulled these from any kind of workbook; the questions felt catered specifically to Sophia and me.

Good on him, I thought. He was certainly earning our money—in-network or not.

I grabbed a pen sticking out from the cup of espresso beans by the register and leaned against the counter, holding the paper in my hand.

There were only six or seven customers inside Java-Hut at that point, and they were all equally engaged with their laptops or cell phones, white earbuds providing the soundtrack to their work or their separate distractions. Only one couple seemed to be there actually to talk to each other—a middle-aged man and a middle-aged woman. He seemed to be smiling far more than she was.

Perhaps they were on a date.

Question One, from Dr. Garrett: If the relationship is to feel fully repaired, what is necessary for you to receive from your partner?

Question Two: In what ways will you communicate to your partner these needs, and in what ways will you know if you are getting your needs met?

Where should I start?

These questions presupposed I wanted the relationship to be repaired, I thought.

Maybe.

The word *if* was in there, plain as day.

I remembered what Dr. Garrett had said about not rooting either way, for reconciliation or separation, just that his goal was to get us through this tricky time in life.

Tricky. He used that word a lot.

Rewiring circuitry in the basement while hoping to avoid calling an electrician last fall had been tricky.

This was a mess.

I sighed, glancing over at Stacy. She was in the other corner, opposite me, her pointer finger gently touching the surface of her iPad as she scrolled and scrolled.

What did I want?

It was a good question.

It was a *great* question.

The last few weeks had been such a haze of exhaustion and alcohol and the depressing ceiling of Room 204, and the curves of Lila's face, I thought, if I was honest. As well as calling my wife every day, or at least every other day, to see if it was time to come home yet. And learning how to make a cappuccino with light foam.

Had I even really considered if that was still what *I* wanted?

Maybe I was approaching this all wrong. Maybe assuming we needed to find our way back to each other was all wrong.

Maybe I should be meeting with Dr. Garrett by myself and having him help me figure out what it was I wanted.

Especially, I thought, without letting my brain fully articulate the answer, because in these past few weeks, it felt like what I wanted wasn't a *what*, but rather, it was a *who*.

Lila.

I took a breath, gave another glance to the customers who didn't care Stacy and I were paying them no attention, and read the third question from Dr. Garrett.

Question Three: What obstacles (from your perspective) stand in the way of achieving an improved connection?

What did that even mean?

I jotted down *being interested in someone else*, since it was obvious from our last appointment Sophia was interested in someone else, even if she hadn't acted on it, according to her.

Yeah. That was a huge obstacle.

If I moved back home to work on our marriage, that would mean she would have to stop interacting with this guy, right? Whoever he was.

Some guy who I assumed worked with her, because I didn't know how else she would be in a situation to get to know a man who wasn't me. Unless she was a hell of a lot sneakier than I thought.

Which I genuinely didn't think.

Sophia was a very honest person, my brain reminded me. It wasn't like she was going out of her way to sneak around or meet someone. This crush had to be the result of getting too close to someone at work, which wasn't all that uncommon. Right?

Hell—shouldn't I now be in a position to understand that, for crying out loud?

Question Four—the last question: What steps could I take to ensure the improved connection was sustainable?

I jotted, *start fresh, forget about past with her*—

I was about to write down the word *indiscretion* when a couple of customers came in asking for decaf iced mochas with extra whipped cream. I rang them up, and Stacy went to the espresso machine to make them. Then, we were sort of steady until it was time to start the closing procedures, which prompted a lot of jokes about the blind leading the blind. We didn't, however, have to call or text Carmen, even though setting the building alarm took us a few tries to do correctly.

I said goodnight to Stacy in the parking lot. Overall, I decided I liked the closing shift at JavaHut. It was much more relaxing than the opening shift. The customers we served had seemed more relaxed as well. No one was in a hurry to get to work. No one was ordering extra shots in drinks that frankly already contained plenty of caffeine.

I also resolved that for once, I was going to go home—back to the Scenic View Hotel—eat something, and then go to sleep, after texting Matthew goodnight, after asking him how his day was. And after texting Sophia too, with the same message. I was going to not drink. I was going to give my liver a break. I was going to get a full night of sleep, and everything was going to look better in the morning.

Seventeen

Which it didn't.

Decidedly, things did *not* look better in the morning.

My alarm on my cell phone went off at 4:30 a.m., as usual. Suddenly, it was Monday morning, and an entire week was about to start again. I dragged myself out of bed and into the shower, cursing the "turn and burn" shift, as Carmen had called it. That was when a barista had to close JavaHut one night and open it the next day.

I'd have to think twice about agreeing to another turn and burn.

It seemed like something the young kids should be doing—not the resident old man.

Lila was donning her apron when I walked into the area behind the counter at JavaHut. If I had followed through on the mental note I'd made to check the schedule posted on the back of the door in the staff room, I wouldn't have felt knocked off my ass at the sight of her.

"Morning," I said simply.

"Good morning," she said. She gave me a wide smile. Her teeth were impossibly white.

My brain picked that moment to remind me that I had failed to listen to the music she had given me at her apartment the other night.

"Your CD," I said suddenly. Despite a cup of crappy Keurig coffee in Room 204, it was possible I wasn't fully awake yet.

She looked at me expectantly, and I thought about

how we'd be unlocking the door for customers in just a minute or two, and we still needed to brew a third carafe of coffee before then.

"I'm so sorry," I said. "Lila, I haven't listened to it yet."

That wasn't even a lie. I'd tucked the CD in the sun visor above my seat the night she had given it to me—the night we had shared that wine—and had somehow forgotten all about it.

Which I realized sounded totally lame and a little insane, but it was true.

I'd just had a few full days with nothing to do, and I'd filled them with nothing, when I could have been listening to her CD.

Her shoulders sank a little, but I could see she was trying to smile. "It's okay, Holden," she said.

But it wasn't convincing.

"I'm sorry," I said again. "I wanted to, I just—I closed last night, with Stacy, for the first time, and before that, I spent some time with my son, and it slipped—"

"It's okay," she said, interrupting me and chuckling. But her voice sounded a little sharp. "You don't have to explain yourself to me. There's no pressure. I'd like your feedback, whenever you're ready to give it. Maybe you can take me out for a drink, or something, and tell me that you like it."

I wasn't sure what to say to that, but I didn't get much of a chance to respond anyway. Lila had already squeezed by me, and I couldn't help but catch her scent—vanilla and cherries and something else insatiably sweet, as she turned the sign in the window over from CLOSED to OPEN.

* * *

But Lila had been acting a little strange around me during our time together, not really looking me in the eye.

When Kelsey arrived for her shift, Lila practically hugged her. It was weird. I wasn't sure what was going on with the two of us, but this was something new.

She was mad, I thought, *because I hadn't made the time to listen to her music.*

Which, in a way, I thought, *she had the right to be.*

It only would have taken me twenty minutes, right?

And to tell someone that you hadn't been able to find that short amount of time within a few days was kind of bullshit, especially considering listening to a CD is something I ostensibly could have done while driving my car.

I recalled that Sophia had told me more than once not to use the *I had no time* thing as an excuse. It really seemed to rile her up.

"You always have *time*," she would say. "It's that you didn't make it a *priority*. Unloading the dishwasher takes about five minutes, and you had five minutes this morning," she'd say.

She was right. I had to admit it.

I could see that I had hurt Soph when I hadn't made helping with chores a priority. There were so many times when I hadn't made things with Sophia a priority. There were so many days and nights and weekends I just—I didn't make time. I didn't make the things that were important to my wife important to me.

I should have been honest with Sophia about that stuff.

And I should have just been honest with Lila.

I should have told her I hadn't listened to her CD because I hadn't made it a priority.

I could leave out the part where the reason I wasn't able to make it a priority is because I felt so fucked up in the head over my wife and over her, too, that when I got into the car and when I got into Room 204, I just wanted to not think about either of them. I just wanted a beer, two beers, four beers, six—I just wanted to be buzzed, and I just wanted to pass out, or sleep, or do whatever I could in order to escape my reality for a few hours before I had to go put on a professional face and be the middle-aged white man in a sea of young people asking if the customer wanted to add an extra shot for free on Free Shot Fridays.

No.

I'd let Lila down, and she knew it.

I'd hurt her feelings, even if she wasn't being honest with me about it.

But because we started our shifts at the same time, we were done at the same time, and there was no avoiding walking to our cars together, and no avoiding the fact that we'd managed to park our cars near each other.

Lila felt awkward next to me, and when I was close enough to my car to pull my keys out and hit the fob, I felt relieved.

It was just after 1:30 p.m., and I had planned to head back to Room 204 and take a nap before getting some dinner and getting on the horn with Sophia, even though my recent experiences let me know not much fruitful would come out of the conversation—just frustration.

The last time Sophia had talked to me for more than

ten minutes, she had said she was sorry, but that she wasn't really ready to talk about the whole having feelings for someone else thing. She did say—she did promise me—that she would be soon, that she would let me know when she was ready to talk, and that we could talk whether or not it was in Dr. Garrett's office.

Right as I was about to open my mouth to utter at least a polite goodbye to Lila, to see if there was any way I could end this day with her on a high note, she put her hand on my forearm.

"Holden," she started.

"Yeah?" I said.

I had my fingers on the handle of the car door, ready to pull it open, and the feel of her hand on my skin utterly disarmed me.

"I, um," she said. She looked down. "I don't know what *this* means," she said.

That's when I looked down and saw that in her hands, she had a piece of white paper that had been folded into a fat chunk.

A piece of paper that was small enough to fit into the back pocket of someone's pants.

"But I would like to know if we could talk about it," she said.

She unfolded the paper, and sure enough, it was my homework from Dr. Garrett. It must have fallen out of my pocket Sunday night when I had closed with Stacy, and I hadn't noticed.

"I found it this morning on the floor in the staff room," she explained. "First thing. I mean, I assume it's yours. You closed last night, and it's just been you and me here this morning. I mean... I don't think this is Stacy's."

Jesus H. Christ.

"I—" I didn't even know what to say.

"It's clear that you are working something out," she said. "I just wanted to give this back to you," she said, "and ask if you'd like to go somewhere and talk about this. Because I don't...Like I don't know what's going on here, with you and me, but...I think we should talk. Yeah. We should talk."

This was becoming quite a pattern, I thought.

Talking to Lila.

Alone.

And alcohol seemed always to be involved.

I looked down at the paper and focused my eyes, which were quite tired. But my answers glared up at me just the same:

being interested in someone else

start fresh

forget about past with her

"Oh," I said. I suddenly read it the way Lila must have—that this all had something to do with *her*, although it was probably very confusing as to in what ways.

I looked up at her and searched her face for what to say, like the answers could be written on her pale skin.

"Lila," I said. "I—this is— I—," and then I just started to laugh.

Because I was so tired, and this was insane.

This was beyond insane.

She thought I had written these answers about her. Lila thought this paper was proof that I had feelings for her, and that in some way, those feelings were an impediment to another relationship in my life.

Of course she did.

There was some kind of a thing going on between us, and she knew it, and I knew it, and of course she thought she was a part of these answers, even though she didn't know that this was homework my family therapist had given to me because my wife liked someone else.

Even though now it was possible I had an overwhelming crush on someone else, so I would be the last person to tell Sophia she was a hypocrite.

And then I realized I was crying. It was 1:38 p.m. on a Monday, and I was standing in the parking lot of JavaHut in the strip mall between the place that did dry cleaning and Excelencia Fronteriza with Lila, and I was actually crying.

I felt broken.

"Holden," she said, and she leaned into me to wrap me in what I soon realized was a hug.

I could feel how slim she felt. Her breasts pressed into my chest, and I took in a deep breath of her hair, her perfume, before I knew I needed to get my body pulled away from hers.

Immediately.

"It's okay," she said. She reached up, put her hands on my shoulders, squaring up to me like she had the first day I worked with her at JavaHut.

"It's okay. I'm here for you. Tell me what you need," she said.

I read a lot of essays from students about romantic moments in novels, and my reaction was usually to cringe.

It wasn't as though I didn't remember what it had felt like to fall in love with Sophia. I still did.

I was just never able to reckon all the phrases with her, exactly.

All the clichés, all the old adages: my heart stopped, my breath caught, my pulse raced. All of it. Even though it was probably true at one point, when we were young, I couldn't remember feeling those moments with Sophia.

Not really.

But right at that moment, in the most godforsaken parking lot in all of the Midwest, standing close to Lila—so close I could smell her lip balm—looking at her smooth skin and deep hazel eyes, I did feel it.

I felt like my heart was falling down a mountainside, and it was all I could do to watch it slide.

I leaned in and kissed her, but somehow—and thank Jesus for this—I had the restraint to let it land on her forehead. It was easy to do, because I was just about three inches taller than she was, and it felt like a natural journey for my feet to take. I closed my eyes. I could feel her take a breath in and a breath out. I held my lips there for a long second and finally broke away. She had her eyes closed too, and she kind of smiled at me.

She raised her hand like she was going to put it on my chest, but I stopped her.

"I'm sorry," I said. "I have to go."

And before she could stop me or say anything, I was in my Camry, not bothering to take the piece of paper that had gotten us into this mess out of her hand, not even bothering to buckle my seatbelt before I put the car in drive and pushed that old red hunk of metal to speeds it was only accustomed to seeing on the highway.

Eighteen

I pulled up to the house and wasn't sure if I was relieved or disappointed that Sophia's minivan wasn't in the driveway.

I wondered if Matthew was home.

Feeling a little like an oaf, I parked on the street a few yards down from our driveway and walked up to the house. I let myself in the front door and called out a very loud hello.

No answer.

The house was so quiet.

Too quiet, I thought. There was no one home at all.

Not even Benny.

Maybe Matthew had taken him out for a walk or something.

I went to the fridge in the kitchen and pulled out an IPA, opening it without thinking. I drank about half of it, then grabbed another, opened it, and headed down to the basement.

A few bookshelves lined the walls of the basement, which was only partially finished. There was a nice den area with a big TV, where I sometimes retreated to watch something if Sophia was into a movie I didn't feel like watching, and where Matthew and his friends had hooked up the PlayStation. Recently, he'd gotten a gaming chair for the corner; his headphones and a half-full bag of Doritos sat on the coffee table.

Sophia would not approve of those Doritos. I could

almost hear her asking our son, "Do you think it's natural to eat something coated in artificial orange powder?"

I smiled at the thought, and then took another swig of the IPA. My eyes found the lower shelves of the leftmost bookcase—the one that held the yearbooks.

2008, I was looking for. Or maybe I was looking for 2007.

I found Lila immediately in the former. It was as though my thumb somehow knew what page to open to.

There she was.

Lila Elizabeth Parks.

I was staring at Lila's senior picture. I had been kneeling by the bookshelf and at the sight of her, eased myself off my knees and to my ass, sitting cross-legged on the basement floor.

She was pretty, but not nearly as pretty as the woman she had grown into. In her senior picture, she looked like a younger version of herself. A few other names and faces popped off the page, sparking my memory, but I tried to stay focused on the task at hand.

I looked her name up in the index in the back of the yearbook and smiled when I saw her in the photo of the drama club. There she was, smiling in the back of the group cast photo: *Romeo and Juliet.*

I flipped through the senior section listlessly, looking to see if there were any other candid shots of Lila.

Only one: a funny picture of her and another girl sticking their tongues out in front of the trophy case by the main office. I finished my first beer and set the empty longneck on the bookshelf, next to the yearbooks, and started in on my second.

I had no idea what I was trying to find, really, but

searching felt right.

I finished the second beer while flipping through some even earlier yearbooks—some from the 1990s.

Undeniably, I was better looking in those early volumes. I had more hair, less of a beer belly.

As evidenced by last year's picture, I was nothing to write home about now. If Lila actually found me attractive—and judging by the look on her face when I'd leaned in and kissed her on the forehead, she wasn't exactly repulsed by me, even though I probably smelled of beer and coffee—what the hell was going on?

Maybe she wasn't looking at me and seeing me as I look today.

Maybe when she looked at me, she got caught up in the past, in some kind of weird wave of nostalgia for something from a decade ago. Maybe when she looked at me, she was just thinking about what I looked like back then, when she would have seen me every day—well, an hour or so every Monday through Friday.

Added up over the course of a semester, that was a lot of time.

Maybe she had a blind spot when it came to my appearance, just as she'd been a blank slate to me until I remembered her as the nurse.

If she had some kind of crush on me—if she had real feelings for me—I had no honest-to-God idea what she saw in a mess like me.

Idly, I left the yearbooks in their place on the bottom shelf and started to touch the spines of the nearby novels with my fingertips, like they could give me comfort. I was probably already a little buzzed. The IPAs were heavy.

My library used to live upstairs in our house, but Sophia and I moved my books to the basement when Matthew was a toddler wanting to gum up everything with his stickiness. No matter what we did, he wouldn't leave the paperbacks alone. So, down to the basement shelves they went.

They'd been weeded over the years, too—my personal library. When I first started teaching English, I had hundreds of books. Now, maybe it was a stretch to say I had triple digits. That was fine, I thought, although sometimes I missed the gluttony that was my bookshelf overrun with paperbacks. Part of me missed the version of myself that stacked books on every flat surface of the house. There was a time, in my twenties, when I was never *not* in the middle of three books at once.

I kind of missed that guy.

Perhaps it was my buzz talking, or the feeling I had now that I was back at my house for the first time in a while. I wanted to stay in this house. I wanted this to keep being my home.

All my memories were in this house. This was where we lived when Matthew came home from the hospital. Upstairs was where he took his first steps. His bedroom— it had started out as a nursery, painted a pale shade of yellow because Sophia had wanted to be surprised by the gender of our first baby, and yellow meant ready for anything.

Seeing all these old yearbooks and all my books down here—I was overcome with nostalgia. And it had to be more than the IPA talking. I couldn't give all this up.

I saw a complete Shakespeare volume that I had kept from my undergraduate years. It was pretty beat-up and dog-eared. It wasn't the copy I used while teaching plays in my classroom. This copy always stayed home. I didn't want anyone—any of my students, anyway—to see the parts I'd underlined, to see the kinds of things I had written in the margins when I was eighteen and trying to make sense of things that felt above my head.

I opened the large tome to *Romeo and Juliet*. It didn't take me too much reading in Act One to get to the good scenes featuring the nurse. Some of the lines I was starting to forget. Some of them made me smile, picturing Lila saying them. Once or twice, I even chuckled out loud.

Oh, this part, my brain said as I got to Scene Three.

Nurse and Lady Capulet are talking. Lady Capulet is ready to marry off her daughter, even though she is only thirteen. Almost fourteen, but only thirteen. God, how my students freak out at that fact.

Lady Capulet asks Nurse to leave when Juliet enters the scene—she wants to talk to her daughter privately. Then without skipping a beat, or without anyone interjecting, Lady Capulet immediately rethinks the directive and says, "Nurse, come back again, I have remembered me."

That line had always stuck out to me.

Nurse knows all of their secrets since she's helped raise Juliet—why should she have to leave the room now that the mother-daughter duo is discussing marriage?

It isn't exactly an apology. It's a moment of clarity for Lady Capulet—not incredibly significant to the overall plot, but nonetheless, a moment that shows Lady Capulet doing one of the most human things there is to do: making a mistake, realizing it, and immediately correcting it.

And a realization she came to all on her own, as soon as the words were out of her mouth. It was like a *what was I thinking?* kind of moment—certainly something that stood out in a play that was largely about impulsive desires and impatience.

She doesn't say, "I made a mistake."

She says, "I have remembered me."

I have remembered me.

God, I should teach this, I thought. Maybe this fall I could ask to teach freshmen again. Why not? I'd grown lazy and complacent with my teaching the last few years, if I was honest with myself. I'd told myself I'd perfected my lesson plans—honed them to perfection.

But wasn't that another way to recognize I'd grown a little lazy as a teacher?

Perhaps it was time to change things up.

Perhaps I'd been coasting through teaching, just like I'd been coasting through my life with Sophia and Matthew. Sophia made it so easy to sit back and just be—I don't know... complacent, I guess? Somehow content to settle for the status quo.

The longer I sat there, the more I was convincing myself.

I needed to stop living in this kind of comfort zone. I needed to push myself to do better—in my career, in my marriage, as a father, and in my life.

I should teach this play again, just as I had in my first years at St. Bridget's—when I looked like this young teacher in these early yearbooks. When I was all drive and passion—when I worked hard every day to be the best teacher I could. When I went back to get my master's degree when Matthew was still young, even though I didn't necessarily need to in order to keep my position. I had *wanted* to—I had wanted the challenge. It hadn't been about moving up to the next pay bracket, since that step was modest at best.

I'd wanted to be—I don't know. I'd wanted to dive deep and prove I could do it, or just—live with resolve.

Although now, would I ever be able to teach *The Most Excellent and Lamentable Tragedy of Romeo and Juliet* without Lila hanging around the quiet corners of my mind?

Wouldn't I, for the rest of my life, picture her beautiful face every single time Nurse has a line?

* * *

Finally, I heard the garage door open. I set my second empty beer on the bottom shelf next to my first one and stood up to stretch, realizing I had gotten a little stiff sitting on the floor for so long.

I was an old man, no matter what Lila said.

Speak of the devil, my brain said. I felt my phone buzzing in my pocket and pulled it out. Opening it, I saw I had three new texts from Lila.

She'd been texting me as I'd been sitting in my basement getting buzzed and looking at black and white photos of her face.

HOLDEN, the first one said. I WISH YOU HADN'T DRIVEN AWAY SO FAST.

The second one, a few minutes later said, I REALLY CAN'T WAIT TO TALK TO YOU.

The third one, about another hour after the first, made me glad I was two beers in before I read it.

I CAN'T STOP THINKING ABOUT YOU. HOLDEN, PLEASE SAY SOMETHING. PLEASE.

I shoved the phone back in my pocket and went upstairs, trying to be as casual as I could.

I can't deal with this now.

I can't deal with this potentially ever.

The basement stairs led into the hall adjacent to the living room, and as I opened the door at the top of the stairs, three things happened at approximately the same time.

The first thing that happened was Sophia screamed, and then yelled "Jesus! Holden!"

Hadn't she seen my Camry parked on the street? Judging by the look on her face and her outburst, she hadn't.

The second thing that happened was I realized she was crying—that she had been crying.

The third thing I observed was that Soph had cut her hair short. It was in a pixie cut now—what I'd heard her call the look on celebrities before. And I saw that there was a streak of color in it, too—lilac undertones. Interesting. Not *unattractive*, but I'd never seen her color her hair before, only get highlights from time to time, as she called them. She hadn't yet started going that gray.

The short hair looked great on her, but it was going to take some getting used to.

Maybe, I thought. Assuming she wanted to keep me around long enough to get used to her new hairstyle.

Then, my slow, exhausted, slightly inebriated brain noticed one more thing about my wife: there was blood streaked on the white Colombia zip-up shirt she often wore to the Y.

"Wait—what's going on, Soph?" I asked.

Sophia was still standing in the middle of the living

room. She pushed by me, not really looking at me, wiping her face with her hands. I heard her breath come in as a shudder. She walked into the kitchen, and I followed her numbly.

She put her purse and keys down on the kitchen counter.

"It's Benny," she said, her voice breaking. "He—he got hit by a car," she said.

She looked down at the blood on her white shirt—a stark contrast.

"I grabbed him, you know, right after it happened and we—Matthew came with me, we went to the Pet ER. The one up on Plainwell. They couldn't do anything for him. They just gave him something to speed it up." She shook her head. "Matthew just went upstairs. He's devastated." She whispered the last part.

"Oh, my God, Soph," I said, and walked to her without thinking, wrapping her up in a hug.

I felt her start to cry against my chest, and I kissed her forehead, hating myself for having kissed Lila's an hour or so before, hating myself even more for not knowing which one felt better. They both felt good. It wasn't surprising to feel stirred by my wife, who I hadn't touched in weeks; it was only surprising not to be sure if it was her or Lila doing it to me.

I eased out of the hug a little.

"What happened? Are you okay?" I asked.

She laughed dryly into my chest. "I'm fine, Holden, it's the dog who died. He got out—the door was open. Matthew had opened the door and hadn't realized, you know, and—and Benny ran across the street..."

She pulled away from me and wiped her face with

her hands again, as though her skin had absorbent properties. I reached over to the counter and tore a paper towel off the roll, handing it to her.

"You should go talk to Matthew," she said, wiping the rough towel across her face. "He's upstairs," she repeated. "There's blood in the Honda."

"Okay," I said. "Don't worry about that right now. We'll clean it. Are you sure you're okay?"

She shrugged, tearing at the paper towel in her fingers. She had blood on her blue jeans, too, I noticed.

Benny. I was going to miss that dog.

"Everything is so fucked up right now," she said. She put her fingers to her temple. "The dog might as well die, too."

It was an uncharacteristically bitter and negative thing for her to say, and it caught me a little off guard.

"Now's as good a time as any to tell you that I slept with Ian last night. So, there you go."

I stared at her and the blood on her clothes. I took a deep breath in and let it out slowly.

Would it be rude to get a third IPA?

They were my beers, right? I had purchased them, and I was the only one drinking them.

I pictured Lila staring at her phone, refreshing her text messages, waiting to hear from me, wondering where I went and why I wasn't texting her back.

Her last message had felt particularly stirring.

I CAN'T STOP THINKING ABOUT YOU.

PLEASE SAY SOMETHING.

PLEASE.

It made me feel shitty to ignore her.

"So," I said finally, quietly. I was thankful Matthew

was upstairs, although I felt a pull to go check on him and make sure he was okay. "I was right, huh? It was Ian."

She buried her face in the paper towel. "What the hell is wrong with you?" she yelled. "I just told you I slept with someone else, and you just care that you were right about *who*?"

I shrugged. "Honestly, Sophia—"

"It's my fault the dog died," she said, crying loudly again. "This is what I get. This is what I deserve, you know. *I* did this. This is the universe punishing me for being unfaithful."

"You think the universe killed our dog because you had sex with another man?" I said. It wasn't really funny, but I still felt a little like laughing.

I thought about how that actually was a common literary device, but not one that typically happened in real life. Narratives often punished a character's wrongdoing, but it didn't seem like the right time to say that to my wife. I could give her examples, but I thought to put the literary lecture on the backburner for the time being.

She sobbed and leaned against the counter, bracing herself with her palms on the Formica. "I don't know what else this is," she said dryly, "other than what I deserve. You tell me."

I considered. I felt my phone vibrating in my pocket again with a new text.

"I'm thinking a lot of things right now," I told her. "But I can sincerely tell you that the universe didn't kill Benny because you slept with Ian. It was an accident, right? The Benny part, I mean. Benny was incredibly good at sneaking out of the house. We knew one of these times, his luck was bound to run out. Something like this was bound to happen."

She closed her eyes. "I don't even know what to say right now," she said. "You don't even seem angry."

"I'm not angry about the dog," I said. "I'll miss Benny. But he had a nice life with us."

"Not about the dog, oh my God, Holden," she said. "You're so crazy! Why aren't you mad about what I just told you? About Ian? Why aren't you screaming and like, why aren't you—yelling at me and—"

Good question.

I knew someday I would want all the details.

Well, I thought. *Maybe someday I would want all the details.*

Maybe that day would never come. Perhaps the less I knew, the easier it would be to push past it and move on.

What the hell did I know?

But for some reason, right then, I just didn't—I didn't want to know anything else. I just wanted to stand in the clean, familiar kitchen of my beautiful house and just be there. Next to Sophia.

A woman I had loved for half my life.

A woman without whom I couldn't really picture living the rest of my life.

The haircut was already growing on me.

"I think I'm in shock," I said, honestly. "I think I'm buzzed, too. I think I am going to go check on Matthew. I also think I need another beer."

She nodded. "Okay. I'm going to take a shower. Get out of these clothes." I saw fresh tears well up in her eyes and sincerely, my heart ached.

"Okay," I said. "Good plan."

Then I followed my wife up the stairs, to the second floor of our house, as I had done a thousand times before, resisting the urge to smack her lightly on the butt as she walked in front of me, because one time I had done it, early on in our marriage, back when we'd first moved in, and it had really made her laugh.

Nineteen

I knocked on the door to Matthew's bedroom, but turned the knob before he could say anything. The knock was just a warning shot.

I found him face-down on his bed, his head on his pillow. I couldn't remember the last time I had seen him cry. A year ago, maybe, when he broke his arm skateboarding.

"Hey," I said. "It's your dad. Can I sit on your bed?"

He nodded, his face still deep in his blue sheets, and then sobbed some more. Part of me felt glad he wasn't embarrassed to sob in front of his old man. I wasn't sure, even as a young teen, I would have been able to cry in front of my old man. He was a tough guy, ex-military. It was a tough enough blow for him to hear his oldest son was interested in literature more than any other thing.

Inside the pocket of my pants, my phone vibrated again, and I used my thumb to silence the button on the side, even as it made me sad to think of Lila's disappointment. What if she was somewhere crying, too? In her bedroom?

"I'm so sorry about Benny," I said. "Mom just told me."

I took a pull from the beer in my hand, cold in my palm. My body was beginning to get so accustomed to the feeling of being buzzed, it was hardly even registering the fact that this was the third beer I'd opened.

Solve that problem later, I thought.

"It was all my fault," he sobbed. "I let him out."

"It's okay," I said, reaching my free hand out to put between his shoulder blades. "It isn't your fault."

"Yes, it is, Dad," he groaned. "I know it is." He sobbed again. Snot trailed from his nose on his pillow.

I sighed. "Something isn't your fault if it's an accident, and this was an accident. You didn't mean for this to happen. The driver of that car I'm sure didn't mean for this to happen."

He covered his face with a pillow. "Fuck!" he yelled.

"Yeah," I said. "Fuck. Fuck this whole day. This month. This summer."

He was still crying, but he pulled his face out of the pillow and looked at me, probably surprised I'd dropped the F-bomb—twice.

My phone buzzed again in my pocket. "Sorry," I said. "It's a coworker of mine. She wants to switch shifts with me. Really bad. Getting really annoying," I chuckled.

I took another drink of the IPA.

"What are we going to do?" Matthew asked, and it was like he was five years old again, when he would ask me to fix every toy that broke, even the ones that were beyond the scope of my repair. Sometimes, he would be playing with a toy and he'd bend or break a component so far out of shape, there was no way to bring it back to life. Those were the toys Sophia and I had to secretly throw away when he wasn't looking and pray he forgot about.

I always hated telling Matthew when something was broken beyond repair. It was hard to explain when he was young. Now he was old enough to know his dog was out of repair, and he was probably wondering if his family was going to go the same way, too.

"I don't know," I said. "All I care about—honest-to-God, Matthew, all I care about is you, and that you're okay. This sucks, that Benny died. I totally get why you're sad. And I wish—to be honest, man, I wish I had been here. This might not have happened if I had been here, like I had planned to be this summer. I was supposed to be home all summer."

"So, it's Mom's fault," he said.

I had to chuckle. "Don't say that," I said. "Mom feels horrible."

"I know," he said. Fresh tears fell down his cheeks.

"Matthew, there just aren't any words right now to make you feel better about this, and that's the truth. It sucks, there's no way around it. It's just going to hurt for a while. But then it'll get better, over time. Trust me. You remember when Grandpa John died?"

He shook his head. "Not really."

"Yeah," I said, "you were kind of young when he passed away. We were all sad then, too, but now we just think about him and smile."

"Mom's still sad he's gone."

I nodded. "Yeah. You never quite get over that. Bad example, maybe. A dog isn't like a dad. That was her dad. Sorry—I'm bad at all this kind of stuff, buddy," I joked, pulling him into me. I took another sip of my beer, not caring that he was watching me. "Do me a favor, okay? Don't tell your mom that in my attempt to make you feel better, I compared the dog dying to her dad dying? She just wouldn't—it was—yeah, I'm sorry."

"I won't," Matthew said.

"I'm really sorry," I said again.

"I know," Matthew said.

"I am really sorry I wasn't here, Matthew."

He took a deep breath. "It's not your fault. You took that job to pay for your apartment," he said. "I get it."

I chuckled. "You think I live in an *apartment*? God, I wish it were an apartment. It's a shithole. It's a hotel room."

"Really?" he asked. It occurred to me he didn't know exactly where I'd been staying. I guess Sophia had been trying to spare him that detail as well. It was arguably better that he never Google it.

"Yeah," I said. "Why do you think I haven't invited you to come over? It's depressing as hell."

"How long are you going to be there?" he asked.

I hesitated. "I don't know. If your mom and I decide we want to make this separation permanent, I'm going to have to get a nicer place, that's for sure. An actual apartment. Then you'd have your own room, and you'd stay with me sometimes."

"That sounds kind of okay," he said.

I took for granted that as an only child, Matthew was pretty expert at hanging out by himself, although that didn't mean he wasn't sometimes lonely, I guessed. No siblings, but Benny had been his friend for years.

I wasn't quite sure why Sophia and I hadn't had more kids. We were just fascinated with Matthew, then we didn't really think seriously about having another one until Matthew was in kindergarten, and then we just decided that he was enough. That our life together was enough.

Who knew nearly a decade later, she would suddenly decide that I wasn't enough?

That there was a man out there who understood her better, I guessed, or—Fuck. A man she liked more. A man she wanted more.

Maybe a man she wanted to be married to more.

And now that man had a name, and a face, and I had to accept the fact that they worked together and had probably been flirting for many months. Late meetings. Long looks. Giggles in the hallway. All that shit.

I took another swig of my IPA. Matthew sat up in the bed, next to me.

"I'm not saying that that's going to happen," I said. "We do need some more time, your mom and me."

"You guys are still in therapy," he said.

"Yeah," I said. "We are. And it was good of your mom to work this out with me over the summer, you know, so—so we kind of have some space to think. I'm sure by the time the school year starts, we'll have a decision."

"What if you need more time than that?" he asked.

I considered. "I'd probably have to go ahead with getting a nicer place to stay," I said. "I'm getting pretty bored in that place, and I hate not spending more time with you. It's just that Room 204 of the Scenic View Hotel is not a place I would bring my worst enemy, so it's definitely not where I'm bringing my son."

He smiled at me then.

Finally, I'd said something to cheer him up.

"Come here," I said, wrapping him up in a big hug, awkward as it was sitting next to him on his full-size bed. "Nobody blames you. Not for any of this. Our marriage problems or for Benny, who had a wonderful life with us." I felt him nodding in my shoulder.

"Okay, Dad," he said. "Okay."

I patted his back and sat back a little, polishing off my beer.

"You hungry?" I asked. It was probably around dinner time.

My body was asking either for food or for a fourth beer. It was hard to tell.

In the master bathroom, I heard the shower turn off, and I pictured Sophia stepping out all wet, wrapping herself in a big fluffy towel. But I couldn't conjure her face in my mind anymore without picturing the deep circles that had taken residence under her eyes from crying. Probably from lack of sleep, too.

Or a guilty conscience, I thought.

Or, worse, from staying up too late last night with a man named Ian.

How had she even had sex with him? Not how but... What had she told Matthew? And where? I wasn't sure if I wanted to know, but I was growing more certain that if I stayed here ten more minutes, and if I was going to continue to ignore the vibrating phone in my pocket, a fourth IPA was certainly in order.

* * *

Sophia came downstairs and into the kitchen dressed in what I knew for a fact to be her comfiest comfort clothes: gray sweatpants and a worn-out white fleece she had stolen from me five years ago. Her hair was wet, combed back. I offered her a glass of red wine and she took it from me, taking a big sip from the goblet.

"Are you making me dinner?" she asked.

"I'm making us spaghetti," I said.

"That was the one thing you were always good at making," Matthew yelled from the living room. I hadn't realized he was listening in on us, but of course he was. He was watching every move we made around each other, every word we exchanged. Poor guy. I hated that he was wrapped up in all this mess.

Sophia smiled weakly, taking another sip of wine.

"Go sit on the couch with that," I told her. "Relax. Take some deep breaths. We'll eat in about twenty minutes."

"Okay," she said. It was as much a concession as it was a relief for her, it seemed, one decision she didn't have to make right then, because I was there.

And just that easily, it became totally normal that I was at the house, making dinner for my family, swerving a little clumsily in the kitchen. I already knew we were going to eat in front of the television, which was usually something we only reserved for parties or when someone was very sick.

But this was weirdly a special occasion of its own: a wake for Benny, whom I learned Sophia had left at the Pet ER to have cremated. They were going to call Sophia later in the week to ask what she'd like to do with the ashes.

She could pick the ashes up, or they would spread them on her behalf. They liked to give families a few days not to worry about logistics, not to have to make any decisions on the spot. It was terribly kind.

And so, this was Benny's celebration of life, I supposed.

Beer and wine, spaghetti with marinara, and the movie *Anchorman* on TV.

I sat in my usual seat on the couch on the left—Sophia next to me, closer than I would have expected. Matthew sat next to her, a throw pillow in between them. But I couldn't help but notice that Matthew was leaning pretty hard to the left tonight, his head on the pillow, just a few inches from Sophia's shoulder.

I realized it was also nice to see Matthew's face so much this evening. He wasn't glued to his cell phone for once. In fact, I hadn't seen it out all evening. No staring at that little screen, no texting girls. He was fully present, and we were all fully present with each other, and I realized that I could spend the rest of the night combing my memory for the last time something like that occurred, and I'd never be able to find it.

Once my plate was clean, I had my arm draped across the back of the couch—not exactly on Sophia's shoulder, but behind her, nonetheless. The only thing missing from the picture was Benny, who liked to sit on the armchair next to me when I sat on the couch.

After *Anchorman*, we started watching *Austin Powers*. I knew for a fact Sophia hated that movie, but it was one of Matthew's favorites, and since he was the one we were there to cheer up, it was understood we would watch the whole damn thing. I was on beer five or six, and I was realizing it was past the point where I should be driving myself back to Room 204, and Sophia wasn't shy about her third generous glass of wine, either, so I did not think she cared.

Halfway through *Austin Powers*, Sophia announced softly she was heading to bed. She went into the kitchen with some dishes and I excused myself from Matthew to join her.

"Hey," I said.

She set down the plates and glasses, reached around and gave me a huge hug. She felt so familiar, so warm. I wrapped my arms around her and held her like that for what was probably a full minute.

"I'm a little drunk," she whispered. I smiled and whispered back to her, "It's okay. I think I am, too."

"I have to work early tomorrow," she said, groaning. "I think I'm going to be in trouble."

"Take a couple of ibuprofen, drink some water before you go to bed. You'll be okay," I coached her. "I will tell you, Soph, I shouldn't drive home. Do you want me to take an Uber?"

She shook her head quickly. "No, that's ridiculous. Just stay here."

"I can sleep in the spare room," I offered.

She shook her head. "I have stuff all over that bed. Cleaning out my closet. Decided to go all Marie Kondo on my wardrobe, for some reason. I guess the truth is, I've been on a bit of a crazy tear lately, taking everything apart and trying to figure out what still makes sense to me."

She chuckled wryly.

We stood there together for a long moment in silence.

"I can sleep on the couch, Soph," I said, more softly. "I'd be more than happy to."

Even the couch sounded better than Room 204, and not just because the idea of leaving the house totally exhausted me. Everything in my bones told me I needed to be here, in this house, for my son, for my wife. For their pain.

She hesitated. "If it isn't too weird, I think you should

sleep in the bed. But you know, it's just sleeping. Just for sleep. Okay?"

I considered. "Okay," I said.

I was practically drooling at the thought of a night in my own bed, and a hot shower in my own bathroom to-morrow.

"I'll be up when it's over," I said. "The movie, I mean."

"I knew what you meant," she said, smiling at me and stumbling a little as she left the kitchen. She was a little tipsy.

If everything wasn't turned upside down, this would be the kind of night on which we would make sure the bedroom door was locked and make the quietest love possible.

Although, we hadn't done that in.... a very long time. Too long. A big part of me wished that tonight was the night I could turn all that around, but given everything, it probably wasn't.

Not if she just slept with Ian. Last night.

Not since the dog died. Hours ago.

Not since I kissed another woman, on the face. That afternoon.

It was probably time to make one right move for the day, and that move was to rejoin my son on the couch and listen to him chuckle at Mike Myers as he made his asinine impressions with his terrible teeth, until my son told me he was ready to go to bed, that he was ready for this shitshow of a day to be over.

Twenty

The ring of Sophia's alarm on her cell phone brought me out of a deep sleep—and a dream, I realized, about Lila. Nothing sexual, which was a relief. I'd had a few less-than-innocent dreams about Lila since she had come back into my life, but in this one, she was just there, wearing a simple summer dress, sandals, her hair down and flowing. In my dream, we were in a crowd somewhere, and she kept pulling at my arm to follow her, but I didn't understand where we were going, or why.

I looked over at Sophia, holding her cell phone in her hand, her eyes closed.

"Hi," I said softly, aware of her likely predicament. She had less experience than I did with hangovers, particularly as of late.

It was just starting to get light in our bedroom. The light was coming in through the blinds covering the window near our bed. I could see her pixie cut was quite disheveled. Her eyelids I could tell looked a little puffy from all the crying she had done yesterday, but otherwise, she was beautiful. Her face was so familiar to me. *This* was so familiar to me—this act of waking up next to Sophia and letting my eyes drift gradually from her face to the rest of her, half-covered under the tangled sheets and duvet.

I let my eyes travel downward and noticed that her comfy white fleece had ridden up and exposed her stomach and the bottom part of both breasts, and that it was so loose in the neck that it was falling off, showing her collarbone, which I had always found to be incredibly sexy.

"Good morning," she said finally, her eyes still closed.

"Good morning," I said.

"You're here," she said. "Oh, Lord," quickly followed. "God, Holden, I have the worst headache I think I've ever had," she moaned.

"This isn't your worst," I reminded her, smiling. "Remember Judy's wedding?"

She rolled over, buried her face in the pillow so I could barely understand what she said next. But I got the gist of it. "I drank too much last night. I'm too old for this."

"I know the feeling," I said. My head was pounding, too, but in a way that felt comforting in its familiarity. I picked up my phone off the nightstand: 6:01 a.m.

Eight new texts from Lila.

Jesus H.

I put my phone back down on the nightstand, face down. It was going to die soon anyway, considering I hadn't charged it last night. It had less than ten percent battery life left.

I felt like I knew that feeling, too.

"It's okay," I said. "It was a special occasion."

She moaned into her pillow and said something that sounded like, "why the hell do you say that?"

"We had to celebrate the life of Benny," I said.

Feeling brave, I reached out and stroked her back, gently, on top of the fleece. I wasn't going to push my luck.

"Oh, God, Benny," she said. "I forgot."

"Shh," I said. "It's okay."

"Matthew's crushed," she said. I could tell it was all coming back to her in a flood of memories, everything about yesterday: me sleeping there, Benny getting killed, Matthew's devastation. I had to get out of the bed before she started to think about Ian, or overthink the fact that I had slept next to her all night as though nothing at all had happened.

I reached out and wrapped her in a hug, and she leaned into my torso in the familiar way we had perfected over the years. My chin was resting on her scalp, and I could feel the tips of her fingers barely digging into the skin of my back.

"I wonder if he'll skip basketball. He can if he wants," she finally said.

I let her words hang in the air for a minute. Even hungover and exhausted, I had what felt like a million things rattling around in my brain that I wanted to tell her.

I think you're right, Soph, I wanted to say.

We got way off track.

I'm sorry I made you feel so alone for so long.

Let's start rebuilding. Okay?

From where we are today.

Let's not just throw away all the years we had together because the last few have been tough. We care too much for each other to do that.

Then, I thought about what I wanted to hear *her* say.

First and foremost, I wanted Sophia to tell me that the sex with Ian was lousy. It was petty to want to hear that, I recognized, but I still did. I thought it would make me feel better.

Then she could tell me that being with him in that way was a one-time thing, and she hadn't really loved him, didn't love him now, and didn't want to ever see or talk to the guy again.

I wanted her to say she was just confused, and things with us weren't or hadn't been going great, and that's why and how she got close to Ian.

I wanted her to say that her feelings for him were nothing but a mirage.

I wanted her to say she wanted nothing more than to keep lying here with me, or that later this week, or even today, she wanted to go back to Dr. Garrett and sit in his office and start to try to work on our relationship.

I had a fantasy of us sitting in his office, and me winking at him and telling him this was going to be one of the marriages he could put down on his list of "saved" marriages.

Get ready to win one, Doc, I pictured myself saying.

I wanted to tell all of that to Sophia, who had her eyes closed now and her hand on her forehead as though she could massage her hangover away.

But I couldn't find a way to get the words from my brain to my mouth.

"I'll get you a cup of coffee," I said instead, finally, extracting myself from our cozy bed.

I kicked myself mentally the whole time the coffee was brewing in front of me.

Once there was a full pot, I brought a cup to Sophia, who hadn't made it very far. "I'll put this in the bathroom," I teased her. "That way, you will be forced to get your ass out of bed to get it."

"You're a terrible, terrible man," she said.

But she was smiling at me.

I closed the bedroom door and went down into the kitchen to refill my mug.

Then I sat at the kitchen table, aware that there was no Benny who needed to be let out. I sighed. And then I woke up my dying phone.

These were all the text messages from Lila:

SERIOUSLY, WHERE ARE YOU, THOUGH?

Shit, I thought. That was the most recent one. That one was from an hour ago.

I was supposed to work at 5:00 a.m. today, wasn't I?

Obviously, I had not cared last night, nor had I cared to think about my schedule at JavaHut.

I scrolled back through the older unread messages in reverse chronological order on my phone.

I WISH YOU'D SAY SOMETHING TO ME RIGHT NOW.

I THINK I LIKED THAT MORE THAN I SHOULD HAVE.

I HOPE YOU'RE OKAY, WHEREVER YOU ARE.

I'M REALLY LOOKING FORWARD TO SEEING YOU TOMORROW.

WISHING YOU WERE HERE.

That one came with a picture of her couch in her apartment, two glasses of red wine poured and sitting in the foreground of the photo, on her coffee table.

Jesus H. Christ.

Another said, I'D LIKE TO TALK TO YOU ABOUT WHAT JUST HAPPENED.

And the last couple—well, the oldest couple—may have been the worst:

YOU HAVE NO IDEA HOW MUCH I'VE BEEN WISHING FOR THAT.

What an honest-to-God mess.

Eight percent battery left. I had better make this call

before my cell dies.

I opened up my contacts. Under "Carmen JavaHut" was the number for JavaHut, and I hit the "call" button, feeling glad I'd had the foresight to store the number at all, and also quite thankful Carmen picked up—not Lila.

What the hell was I going to say to Lila?

The worst part, perhaps: I hadn't even listened to her CD yet, which seemed to make everything worse.

Or maybe better. I couldn't decide.

Worse.

Definitely worse.

Like insult to injury, that I hadn't made time to do this one simple thing that obviously meant a ton to her. That she had shared something deeply personal to her, and I'd basically sent her a message that it meant nothing to me, by ignoring it.

But better... maybe... because... Her voice stirred me a little—more than a little—and I couldn't tell her that, but it was probably best that I avoid situations where I was stirred by Lila.

I should avoid from now on any situation that made me think of her as anything other than a former student and current coworker. Although maybe Carmen would just fire me for pulling a no call, no show today.

Lila had told me that was one reason JavaHut's turn-over rate was so high.

Three no call, no shows, and Carmen considered that your voluntary self-termination.

What if they were love songs on that CD from Lila?

For God's sake.

If they were songs about desire, or longing, or want-ing, or love in any way, I was in trouble.

More than trouble.

I was in deep, deep shit.

And even with a hangover the size of Texas, I knew that much for certain.

"Hi, Carmen," I said after she picked up and gave me her standard greeting, "Thank you for calling JavaHut, how can I help you?"

"It's me. Holden Averett."

"Holden," she said. Her voice had morphed from friendly to arctic. "We were just wondering about you." She sounded pissed, but she also sounded like she was trying not to sound pissed. Classic Carmen.

"I know my shift started at five. I'm so sorry. I had a family emergency. My dog Benny was hit by a car and killed. I've been helping my wife and my son deal with it."

"Oh," she said.

This was probably legitimately the first time I'd ever talked about having any kind of personal life, like having a family—a dog, or a wife, or a kid. I'd been so tight-lipped about anything personal, just as I was when I was in full-on teacher mode.

Carmen was probably in shock.

Or just happy I hadn't quit and planned to never come into JavaHut again, which Charlie told me Aiden, my immediate predecessor, had done to Carmen as soon as June hit. He'd gotten the chance to be a lifeguard at the country club, and he couldn't turn it down. "Too many skimpy bikinis," Charlie had said, wagging his eyebrows at me.

"Jeez. I'm sorry to hear that, Holden." Carmen's voice sounded sympathetic in my ear. "That sounds terrible. Is everything—I don't mean to sound insensitive but... Are you able to come in for your shift today? We do still need you."

"Yeah," I said. "I can be there in an hour. Maybe forty-five minutes."

"Okay," she said. "Let's talk more when you get in."

Which definitely meant this was strike one on my attendance.

Whatever. Carmen could fire me if she wanted. I hadn't been reprimanded in a job since college, and certainly this one didn't matter the way my real career did.

I was way more concerned about Lila, and what the hell I was going to say when I saw her beautiful face in an hour.

* * *

Never had I been so thankful to see a line in JavaHut consistently stay three-people deep, even as I knew the admission to myself amounted to me being a bit of a coward.

Carmen had me at the espresso machine, slinging drink after drink, after she'd given me a lecture about not being a no call, no show.

I surmised that indeed, many JavaHut employees had burned Carmen. Perhaps it was the hangover or having slept next to Sophia all night, or the reality that my dog had died and my son was still sad, but my heart softened for Carmen. In fact, I realized it made me almost feel sorry for her, and I told her it was completely fine to dock my pay the two hours I'd missed that morning. I mustered my warmest smile for Carmen when she told me once again that she was sorry to hear about my dog.

Even though she intimated that she was more of a cat person.

That figured.

"It's okay," I told her. "I think my son is taking it the hardest."

She raised her eyebrow again and nodded.

She'd learned more about me this morning than she had in my previous three weeks. I couldn't tell if she liked it or not.

For the first hour or so, Lila stayed at the cash register and shot me looks I couldn't begin to decipher.

Angry? Curious?

She looked tired, but at this point, I had been tired more days than not in my time at JavaHut, so the regular customers probably thought it was part of my normal visage. I hadn't taken the time to shave, so I was working with some serious salt and pepper stubble.

But a lull was inevitable.

Carmen went to lunch, and Charlie wasn't due to arrive for another half hour. Lila spun on her heels and walked over to me as I was wiping down the milk wands and steeling myself to face her.

"Holden," she said. "You never texted me back last night," she said.

"Sorry about that," I said. I hesitated.

She knew what I had told Carmen, but I still wasn't sure what to say about it. "My dog got hit by a car last night, and Matthew was pretty upset about it. I overslept this morning, not really thinking."

I knew if I was honest with myself, I was leaving out mention of Sophia in a way that wasn't exactly deceitful, but certainly was deliberate.

"I totally get it," she said. Her big eyes were sympathetic. I thought she might hug me right there.

I didn't hate the thought. I would have welcomed the feel of her body against mine right then, offering me comfort. I realized I wanted it from her in a very deep and undeniable way.

"I'm sure we do need to talk," I chuckled. "I just think, probably not here."

She nodded quickly. "No. You're absolutely right. Come over tonight. I'll make us some dinner. Or—like lunch, or whatever meal you eat in the middle of the afternoon."

My answer caught in my throat, and what had started out as a "no thank you" somewhere in the middle of my esophagus had turned into an "okay."

She smiled broadly.

My head hurt so bad I thought about pouring hot espresso shots onto it.

What the hell. My body had betrayed me once again.

My body wanted something, that was for sure—something that my brain and my heart weren't so sure about.

My body had let me know it wanted something from Lila the first time we got beers together, at the bar that wasn't really even a bar but a terrible faux-Mexican restaurant.

And it had made it even more clear to me when I'd stepped in to kiss her on the forehead, unable to resist the few feet that separated us in the parking lot after she'd found that damn piece of paper I'd let fall onto the floor.

She turned back to the cash register to help the next customer, obviously pleased that I had agreed. I shook my head, feeling a little dizzy, hungover, trying to tell myself that maybe this was a good thing because I could work this all out with her and clear the air once and for all, and wondering when everything in my life was going to get back to its ordinary, boring normal.

Twenty-One

And part of me was tempted to bail, following Lila to her place.

Now that I knew where it was, unlike the first time, I could take my eyes off her Jeep as I followed her, and I could think about what I was doing.

I thought about what Dr. Garrett had said the first time we met with him—that we needed to be very intentional about our thoughts, our conversations, our interactions. Sophia had nodded profusely to that.

I thought about Sophia and how she looked this morning and how it would feel never to get to wake up next to her again.

I thought about Ian. Weird looking guy. Tall. Skinny. Wasn't he married too? I thought I remembered a wedding band on him. Maybe not.

My thoughts were swirling together and getting harder to understand the farther we got from the strip mall, and the closer we got to the historic district, to her place.

Finally, we were there, and I parked my car on the side street with a sense of confidence that did not match my mood.

She waited for me on the sidewalk and was smiling at me as I followed her up to her apartment via her rickety, unsafe stairs. Zen gave her the same excited greeting, and breezed past her for some clearly needed relief. Zen greeted me and let me have a seat on Lila's couch with not a lot of fanfare.

This is maybe the weirdest part, I thought. This was only the second time I had come over to Lila's place, and yet this felt normal, natural.

Lila pulled her bag off and hung it on a hook on the wall and proceeded to use her phone to put on some music. Something I didn't recognize, but something nice. Moody. A little soulful.

"Would you like something to drink?" she called out from the kitchen.

No, my mind said. *For once, for the love of all things holy, say no.*

"Yes, please. That sounds great."

What is wrong with me, I thought.

Lila came into the living room and handed me a Heineken. Surprising.

"Do you like these?" she asked.

"It'll do fine," I said. "Thank you."

She opened it with a church key in front of me. "You're full of surprises," I said. "I wouldn't have pegged you as a Heineken girl."

She shrugged and smiled. "In Chicago, I drank them a lot," she said, after hesitating for a second. "Derek always bought them. They did kind of grow on me. Every once in a while, they sound appealing. Just like him," she said, chuckling at her own joke.

I took a long pull and smiled at her.

Spending time alone with her at her apartment was not something in my best interest, nor my wife's, nor my family's, nor my sanity's, nor my liver's, but I would be lying to myself and everyone else if I didn't admit it felt good.

"Is that why you were crying?" I asked, since she was still lingering near me, standing a few feet from where I was sitting. She was holding her own Heineken by its neck. She had taken one long pull already, a third of the bottle.

We could go toe to toe, I realized. It would be easy. Natural.

"Crying?" she asked with a frown.

"Yeah, the other day," I said. "In your car. The first time we got that beer."

"Oh," she said. "God, I'd forgotten about that."

"This summer feels like it's been going on for a long time," I agreed.

She slumped down in the chair across from her couch, looking thoughtful. "Yeah," she said. "I believe it was."

"You know, I did figure that it had something to do with a boy," I said, smiling at her.

She playfully threw a small throw pillow at my face. It almost knocked my beer out of my hand, so I made a great show of rescuing it and taking another big drink as some foam lifted to the top.

We sat for a few moments together in silence, and I couldn't help but think again how good I felt around her, all the way down to my bones.

"He still reaches out to me, from time to time," she said finally. "Derek, I mean. My ex. It's always a mixed bag when he does. It's nice to hear from him, you know, but. On the other hand..."

She let her sentence trail off, and patted her lap for Zen to come sit, which barely took any prodding.

"On the other hand, it sucks," I offered.

She nodded, pulling her Heineken away from Zen, who was trying to take a lick off the neck. "Yeah. I mean, there were a lot of reasons why we broke up. I don't know why he keeps reaching out to me every once in a while. It's... Honestly, it's been a confusing time."

"For *you*?" I asked.

I could have laughed.

She met my gaze and didn't look away for a long second. "Yeah," she said. "Hey, listen, can I change the subject?"

"Please," I said.

"I know I said I'd cook dinner for you, but I don't know, maybe we should just get really drunk together," she said.

I hesitated. "We work tomorrow, early," I said.

"No dummy," she said, "tomorrow's the 4th."

"Of *July*?" I asked. Somehow, it was the most incredible thing to date that had come out of her mouth.

"Yes," she said, laughing. "Did you forget? We're closed. There are signs everywhere in JavaHut. I think you helped me hang one in the window."

"I guess I did," I said, honestly baffled at my own ignorance. "I mean, I knew we were going to be closed on the 4th, but it still managed to sneak up on me."

"Yeah," Lila said. "Well, it's tomorrow. So, no work for us. And later tonight, some of my more boneheaded neighbors are going to start launching fireworks at like 11:00 p.m., right when I want to go to sleep. So, I have found that it's better in these situations just to get very drunk, and then you're in the right frame of mind to put up with it," she said. "Then, I'll sleep all day tomorrow and get drunk again tomorrow night, because if it's anything like the last few years, there will be even *more* fireworks," she said grinning. "I encourage you to do the same."

"Nah," I said. "I probably can't get drunk. I have some stuff I need to do tomorrow."

"Do you—sorry," she started.

"What?" I asked.

"I was about to ask if you're planning a dog funeral, but it sounded so crass in my head, I couldn't say it out loud. I didn't mean—of course I care," she said.

I smiled. "Of course I know you care," I said. "You've got Zen. You love dogs."

"I do love dogs," she repeated. "Boyfriends come and go, but dogs? Loyal to the end. Aren't you, Zen?" she said, leaning down to kiss her head.

I sighed. "I'm not sure what exactly I have to do tomorrow, but I feel like I shouldn't be hungover to do it."

"Oh," she said. "Okay. I get it. I have better beer I was thinking about bringing out for you, but I will just drink it all myself." She winked at me.

I laughed. "Lila," I said.

This was where I needed to find the balls, I thought to myself.

Find them somewhere.

Let her down easy, right?

This wasn't a real thing.

This was my twenty-six-year-old self living in some kind of a fantasy and frankly enjoying the fact that—well, a young and beautiful woman wanted to spend time with me, when my own wife didn't.

Or did.

Did she?

Sophia hadn't been in a huge hurry to kick me out this morning, other than that she had to get to work.

But regardless, my brain chimed in, *this is just a distraction.*

Not even a rebound, because you're not single, but it's a fun little tangent you've let yourself go down because it took the pressure off deciding if your longstanding marriage was going to come to an end, and you were going to have to start all over again with someone new. Spending time with Lila made you feel like maybe it's not so scary out there. All the other fish in the sea and all that.

If there are more women like Lila out there, going fishing again won't be the worst thing that's ever happened to you.

If your wife leaves you, for Ian, you won't break.

Not if there are people out there and connections out there and moments out there like the one you had in the parking lot, when she looked up at you, blinking, trying to understand, and this beautiful woman made everything feel less terrifying.

"You're ready for another one?" she asked, pushing Zen off her to stand up.

I reached out for her hand, by instinct, and I held it in mine. She glanced at me, a shocked look settling onto her face, and slowly sank back down into her chair.

I was so nervous I actually laughed, and then I did finish my beer because it seemed like she was not only kind and empathetic, but also prophetic.

"Yeah," I said. "I think I am."

Twenty-Two

Several hours later, we were sitting on her couch, and just as she told me, I could hear the fireworks out on the street, even though she had closed all the windows and it wasn't yet midnight.

We'd ordered a pizza, which had been a good idea, and I'd ignored two texts on my phone until I could excuse myself to Lila's bathroom.

One from Matthew: I WANT TO TAKE PORTIA OUT THIS WEEKEND. CAN YOU DRIVE US?

I wrote back immediately, SURE THING, and then added, I HOPE YOU HAVE A FUN 4TH OF JULY. BE SAFE.

The other one was from Sophia.

I took in a deep breath before reading it.

I had kind of expected it to be a long one—I wasn't sure exactly why.

But it was just a heart, and, HOLDEN, THANK YOU FOR LAST NIGHT.

Which had flooded me with relief.

Relief, I realized, that she wasn't asking me where I was—although, she had every reason to think I was just in Room 204.

Then again, I wasn't sure where *she* was. She could be home. She was probably home.

She was weirded out that I hadn't been too upset to learn that she'd slept with Ian, but at the same time, she hadn't really seemed that happy about having slept with Ian. She hadn't seemed happy. She had just seemed tired.

Of course, that's also because our dog had died while she was the parent on duty. Sophia was the one who had to take our sobbing adolescent son with her to the vet to put the dog down and be assured that there was nothing else that could have been done for Benny.

I looked in the mirror in Lila's bathroom and ran my hand through the stubble on my chin. I was in my head again, and I was drunk again, and all my crazy thoughts were blurring together, just as the days of the summer were blurring together. Independence Day already. Only five or six more weeks until the school year started again.

That had seemed forever away when Sophia had kicked me out of the house. Now, I was going to have to start organizing lessons and unit plans.

Quit JavaHut.

Quit all of this nonsense.

Quit drinking.

Well... quit drinking so much.

I gave myself a quick pep talk in the bathroom mirror and went back out. Lila was in the kitchen, putting the rest of the pizza away in gallon-size Ziploc bags and ordering empty Heineken bottles into a bin under the kitchen sink.

For a moment or two, I just watched her, admiring her beauty. She was graceful and relaxed. Her hair was falling all around her. Her feet were bare. She was quite possibly the most beautiful woman I'd ever seen in my life.

So after a moment or two longer, I blurted out, in true poetic fashion, "Lila, I'm sorry I haven't listened to your CD yet."

She closed the cabinet door and turned to face me.

She could slap me. She could kiss me. I had no idea.

"It's okay," she said. "That means you listened to it, but you didn't like it, and you just don't know how to tell me that you didn't like it. You don't want to hurt my feelings."

"No, I swear," I said. "I cannot tell a lie. Especially not right now. You've given me too much truth serum for me to be able to hide the truth from you."

She laughed, but she sounded convinced. "It's just Heineken, you know. Derek used to call them *Heinies*."

"What a prize he sounds like," I said, teasing her. "A real Romeo, huh?"

Which made her nearly double over laughing. She stumbled a little on her feet, losing her balance. She snorted. I started laughing too, but reached down to help her back up, afraid she was going to fall onto her kitchen floor.

Which she did, about a second later, and then I was laughing at the fact that she had fallen and I fell down on her kitchen floor too, making another heroic effort to keep the beer upright and not spill any on her floor.

Zen ran into the kitchen to see what was going on, wagging her tail, happy to be licking up Lila's face, which made Lila laugh harder.

"Oh. My. God," she said finally. "This is ridiculous. We are so ridiculous."

I laughed again and petted Zen. Outside, a bunch of fireworks went off in quick succession.

"Finale?" I asked.

Lila listened for a second, and then checked the clock on the stove. "Maybe," she said. There was still laughter in her voice. "It's still a little early to tell... you know... if it's really over or not."

She wiped at her face with the edge of her thumb, which was when I realized she had laughed so hard she'd made herself cry, and I felt my eyes welling up with tears, too.

Together we sat there for a second, on her kitchen floor, listening to the pattern of the fireworks outside.

We were wrong. It wasn't a finale of any kind.

To have a finale would suggest that this was some kind of choreographed, organized show. Nope. This was all just chaos—a random smattering of explosives outside on the street, and we were just two drunk people sitting on a kitchen floor of a hundred-year-old house, listening to the racket and trying to make sense of it all.

* * *

I told Lila three times I should take an Uber home, but each time I did, she protested so much, I dropped it.

I was starting to sober up, and on the one hand, I couldn't believe I had let this night slip by without talking to Lila about that damn piece of paper—my homework from Dr. Garrett—which had been the original point of me coming over. I had wanted to tell Lila that I was actively working on getting things back on track with my wife.

On the other hand, though, I didn't want to tell her that. For some reason, I thought it would hurt her feelings to hear that, although I couldn't articulate why.

It was easy to understand why I never said anything about that, though, despite my concern over her feelings: our conversation dipped back and forth, bouncing from

Chicago and life in Michigan, to JavaHut and books we love, and then into nothing of real consequence.

Lila wasn't one to dig into me with personal questions, and she didn't make demands of me in conversation. She offered up what she wanted to about herself, and I felt myself doing the same. It was different talking to her this way, at her place, than it was talking to her at work, though one big determining factor was, of course, the alcohol.

But I knew it was more than that.

She was even easier to talk to one-on-one without the threat of an uptight middle-aged woman walking in and asking how many calories she would save by getting non-fat milk, or asking three different times if something was really, truly decaffeinated.

"I'm getting you a glass of water," she said. "You're going to need it."

"It's not too late for me to leave," I said. "I probably should, Lila. This is weird—me staying is weird. Right?"

She laughed. "It *is* a little weird, I'll give you that, but I like having you here, and we can have breakfast in the morning." She looked at me after saying it, and I could tell she was trying to gauge if it had been a step too far, a thing too bold to say.

Perhaps it was.

Perhaps it wasn't.

"Plus, it may be hard to get an Uber this late. People are drunk out there," she said.

Lila had already brought me a pile of blankets and a pillow, but then she sat down in the wingback chair after handing me a tall glass of water, and hadn't made any kind of move toward going to bed herself, other than to let Zen out for her last break.

"Are you tired?" I asked.

She nodded. "I am," she said, "but honestly, there's no point in even trying to go to sleep until the last firework goes off."

"I should go," I said again.

"Please stay," she said. "I like having you here."

She'd said that before.

"Why?"

She smiled and took in a deep breath, closing her eyes. "I just do. I like being around you. I like talking to you. Do you not, like, get that?"

"I like being around *you*," I said. "It's just that—"

"Don't," she interrupted, in almost a whisper. "Stop. Right. There."

"Lila—"

"Please," she said. "Don't say it. I don't want you to say it."

"Oh," I said. I wished to be more sober.

Or perhaps, to be far, far more drunk.

"Don't say what?" I said softly.

"Don't say what I *know* you're going to say," she said.

She sounded sad. Maybe she was rethinking me leaving after all.

Zen was next to her on the chair, curled in her lap, probably wondering why Lila hadn't gone to bed yet. It was close to midnight.

"All right," I said. "I'll bite. What do you think I'm going to say?"

She sighed. She leaned down and kissed Zen on her head, as though for courage. "You're going to say, I'm amazing, and that you love spending time with me, but

I'm too young for you, and it's too weird that I used to be your student, even though that was literally eons ago."

I didn't say anything, just nodded. "Anything else?"

She sighed again, then chuckled. "You're obviously going through something—with a girlfriend, or a partner, or whatever, and you're also going to tell me it's complicated, and I wouldn't understand because I'm just a kid, you know, and so young, you're going to tell me I'm *so* young—way too young to understand."

"I wouldn't say that," I said, even though it was pretty safe to say I would.

She stared at me thoughtfully, and I realized that drunk or sober, there was never a moment I wanted more to reach out and kiss her fully on those soft lips, so that my body, which seemed to do what it wanted to do anyway, no matter the better ideas of my mind, could finally do something right, which was show this person how special she was, how much she had come to mean to me in such a short amount of time.

But I didn't.

I'm an idiot, but at least I didn't.

She sighed.

"You're going to tell me that you'd be just *so. Lucky.* To be with me," she said, punctuating her last words. "That's what they all say."

"They're all absolutely right, you know," I said. It had been maybe a full minute since we had heard any sound of fireworks outside. I continued to stare at Lila, and she stared back at me.

"Yeah, well," she said, a little distantly. "After you hear something a hundred times, it starts to lose its meaning."

"Lila," I said. "Jesus."

"What?" she said. Her voice had a new snap to it. I didn't like it.

But I just shook my head. "You have no idea—"

"Ack," she said, standing up so fast Zen raised her head in alarm. "Don't do that one either, please. I hate that one, too. The *you have no idea*... You know, that one might even be the worst one because it implies that I'm too stupid to hold an idea in my head."

"No, you're not stupid," I said. "Not at all. You're very bright. But you don't," I said, almost laughing. "Very sincerely, you don't have any idea. You're very—"

I stopped myself.

Which word was this English teacher reaching for? Lovely? Irresistible? Tempting?

Anything I would say would be wrong to say, right?

"You're very... You must know you're very beautiful. And I *would* be so lucky, honestly. I'm just not in a place where I can... and it wouldn't feel right, to me, and you know, it wouldn't be fair to you. Listen, I can just go home—I'm starting to think that that would be best."

"You're too scared to face me in the morning," she said. "That's what this is all about. You're a coward, after all this, huh."

Which was true. I was. It was amazing how she seemed to see right through me.

"No, of course not," I said.

She was still standing a few feet away from me. "Oh my God, you're going to be all awkward around me, at work now," she said. "Aren't you?"

I almost chuckled. She was worried about *that*?

"No," I whispered. I shook my head, wishing it wasn't

pounding quite as much as it was.

I felt like I'd been on a four-week bender—probably because I had been. My brain felt like it'd finally had enough—the alcohol, the loneliness, Room 204, the sexual confusion.

The mess I was making.

"It'll be fine. Lila," I said, still hoping the right words would find me if I kept talking long enough. "I think it's clear that we both like each other," I said slowly, carefully. "But you deserve—"

She scoffed before I could finish. She was still just standing there, and Zen was staring up at her.

"There—you said it all now. All the stuff I asked you *not* to say. The whole trifecta." She held her left hand out in front of her and ticked three fingers forward, starting with her thumb and moving to her index finger and then her middle finger, as she spoke. "I'd be so lucky. You have no idea. You deserve better," she said. "Textbook trifecta. You have no idea how many times I've heard it."

She looked so incredibly sad right then, I could hardly stand it.

I stood up. Zen looked at me, quizzically. "I can go," I said. "I shouldn't stay tonight."

But I didn't make a move toward the door.

When I looked back at Lila, I saw that there were tears on her cheeks.

"Oh, Lila," I said. I closed the distance between us and put my arms around her, hugging her. I held her like that for a long time until her breathing got slow and even, and her sniffling slowed down. I wanted to tell her so many things right then, but I didn't say a word. The silence between us felt perfect, and I could have honestly held her like that for the rest of the night.

She finally pulled away, and I lifted her left hand to my lips, kissing her on the knuckles. She laughed because it was an odd gesture of affection, an old-fashioned thing to do, but I was afraid if I let myself get near her face, I wouldn't land on her forehead this time. I'd land much lower, on her lips, and that would be the end of my resolve without a doubt.

"Goodnight, Lila," I told her.

"Goodnight," she said, sighing. "Happy Independence Day," she said, a little hint of irony in her voice.

I was pretty sure if I stayed even ten more minutes, I would just fall in love with her, so I squeezed her hand one more time, and by some miracle of the heavens, found the door, walked out of her apartment, and closed her door softly behind me. I made my way down her stairs and got into my car, but I didn't get into the front seat. I unlocked my car and crawled my tired old bones into the backseat, where I promptly curled up into the fetal position.

Just like last night, there was no way I should be driving.

Also, I was too tired to call an Uber back to Room 204. And also, if I was honest, there wasn't anywhere else I wanted to be. I wasn't ready to be far away from her yet because I knew that soon, I was going to be far away from her and would probably never see her again in my life, and the thought absolutely crushed me.

All I wanted was to lay there in the backseat of my Camry and fall asleep thinking about how good she felt to hold, how calm I felt breathing her in. I wanted that feeling to wash over me and if I could, I wanted to find a way to bottle that feeling and take it out whenever I needed to remember it, for the rest of my life.

She smelled like espresso with hints of vanilla, an air of sweetness about her skin.

Twenty-Three

For a funeral for a dog, I wasn't quite sure what to expect.

For attending a funeral for a dog with my son, his new girlfriend, my wife who may soon be my ex-wife, along with my brain that couldn't seem to stop thinking about another woman, while hungover again, and so tired I was starting to feel like no amount of sleep would ever be enough...

Well, it was a first.

The vet's office had been closed for the holiday, but Sophia had retrieved the box of ashes the next day, and had texted me to come over.

So, I pretended like this was all normal, and I took a hot shower and drank about six cups of coffee courtesy of my Keurig, and I did.

Thankfully, I had had Independence Day—the whole day—to myself. I used most of it to sleep, dozing in my bed in Room 204, thinking about Lila but managing to summon the willpower to ignore the handful of texts I got from her.

Most of the texts said something about wishing I had stayed that night. One was a picture of her, just her face looking into the camera, a small smile on it, her hair falling softly around her. I looked at it more a few times before finally doing the right thing, which was to delete it. It definitely made me feel something, even though there wasn't anything particularly sexual about it.

Still, there was something disarming about seeing her face in the warm glow of the lamps in her apartment, maybe given all the intimacy we had shared that night, and how close I knew we had come to crossing over an invisible line.

Right, I told myself.

Right, idiot, I repeated to myself—many times.

A boundary that I shouldn't cross.

A boundary that I should stop putting my toes on, just to see how it might feel to take that last step.

And I was fighting the part of my brain that could justify it, too.

After all, Sophia had crossed a line with Ian. It seemed like she'd thought about it for weeks, maybe months. Maybe years. She finally did it, and if we were going to reconcile, there wasn't one part of her that could get mad at me for doing exactly what she had done. She'd be a hypocrite to judge me for doing something she'd done.

But regardless.

I couldn't do it.

I couldn't do it to Lila, anyway. She was an innocent player in my crisis, and I knew it, even if she was still unaware.

Even if the only evidence she had of my circus of drama was that piece of paper she'd found on the floor at JavaHut that suggested I had some serious issues I was working through with a woman.

As I walked around the house to the backyard, I tucked my phone into my back pocket. I had already ignored a text from Carmen. And then a call from Carmen. And finally, I had ignored a voicemail from Carmen.

I knew despite the three-strike policy, it was highly probable choosing to stay with my family for a dog funeral had probably sealed my fate at JavaHut. But I didn't care. I was out of place there the moment I started, and there was no way I could work alongside Lila now, regardless of whether or not Sophia and I reconciled.

If I spent any more time with Lila, I was going to keep falling in love with her, and I wasn't going to let myself lead her down that path.

"Should someone say something?" Sophia asked.

I'd finished digging a hole in the backyard, in the corner, near the large willow tree. When he was a boy, one of Matthew's chores used to be picking up the branches that the willow would shed, and he loved it—he thought it was so much fun. Sophia and I used to exchange laughs at the window, watching him get so excited to do yard work, unaware it was a chore, not a game.

When I was done digging the hole for Benny's ashes, I rested the shovel against the sturdy trunk of the aging willow.

Someday, we'd have to cut that tree down; it had been dying for years.

But not today.

"I can say something," I said after a few moments of silence. Looking over at Matthew, he was holding Portia's hand and looking like he was holding back tears. It was sweet he had wanted her to be there.

They must be getting at least somewhat serious.

Maybe it was growing into more than a summer fling.

I looked to Sophia, and she nodded, offering me the faintest of smiles.

"Dearly beloved," I said.

"Dad!" Matthew said. "No, they say that at weddings."

"Oh," I said. "Yeah. You're right. Sorry. From the top."

Portia giggled, which made Matthew giggle too, and I felt my heart warm up inside me, even though the day itself was approaching eighty degrees and needed no encouragement.

"Friends," I said. "We're here today to honor Benny, who we lost last week, and who we will greatly miss. He was a wonderful dog and a perfect addition to the Averett family. We enjoyed many years with Benny, and we couldn't have asked for a better companion."

No one said anything for a few moments as we stared down at the mound of dirt. We hadn't thought ahead for a grave marker.

When you get a dog, you don't think about it dying, just like when you get married to a person, you never think about it going awry. Not really, anyway. Not in a real way. Not in a way that makes you realize how close you can come at any time to seeing it all get torn apart.

"Does anyone want to say what they're going to miss most about Benny?" I asked. It seemed like a nice thing to hear at a funeral.

"I will," Sophia said. "Benny, I'll miss how you used to jump up and scratch the door when you knew it was time for a walk. Even though now our door is all scratched up, I don't think I'll have the heart to replace it anytime soon."

"Or ever," Matthew said. He smiled a little. "Benny, I'll miss your farts."

Portia burst out laughing, so I chuckled too. "I'm serious," Matthew said. "Remember how he used to wake himself up from his naps? They smelled so insanely bad."

Sophia nodded. "Especially after he got Chinese food. Remember that time you dropped an egg roll and Benny grabbed it?"

We all chuckled, Matthew especially.

"We lit a lot of candles in the house that night," I said. "To help with that smell."

Sophia grinned at me.

Then, to my surprise, Portia looked at me, and then at Matthew. "Benny," she offered. "I didn't know you that well. I was just starting to get to know you. But you seemed like a really sweet dog, and I'm dying to have a dog, but my dad is allergic, so we can't. Anyway, rest in peace, Benny. You were very loved."

"Benny," I said, sighing. "What can I say about you, buddy? You were there for all the good times, and, well, you were a part of our family. We won't ever forget you."

"Amen," Sophia and Matthew said, in perfect unison.

* * *

After we covered the hole with dirt and Matthew packed it down with a shovel, we ambled slowly back into the house. Sophia poured herself a glass of wine and offered one to me, which I sipped half-heartedly. She set out a plate of cheese and crackers, which turned into Matthew throwing a frozen pizza in the oven, once we had settled that I would drive Portia home later in the evening, when her parents were expecting her back.

I was thankful Soph had canceled our therapy with

Dr. Garrett that afternoon. Family emergency.

Although, it felt more like a family reunion.

Matthew and Portia disappeared into the living room for a little bit to watch a movie, until Sophia invited herself to join them with two old photo albums in her arms—the maroon ones I recognized from when Matthew was still a boy.

"I think there are some good ones of Benny in here," she said, which was all Portia needed to hear to be all about looking through old pictures of Matthew, too, when his hair was longer and kind of wild, when his front teeth were missing.

For a while, I stayed in the background, holding my wine and just absorbing the scene. It felt like Christmas morning, or something—everyone gathered around the coffee table, laughing, talking. It was perfect and inviting, and I dreaded having to leave around 7:30 p.m.

"Thanks so much for coming," Sophia said to me. "This was nice. You did a nice job... and yeah. There's no way I could have done this alone."

"It *was* nice," I agreed. "We gave Benny a good send-off, didn't we?"

"More than that...We gave him a good home," she added. There were tears in her eyes.

"He was a good dog," I said.

There was a long moment of silence between us, and I started thinking back to that morning with her in bed, how good she looked and how good she felt. I thought about all the things I wanted to say to her, and I wondered if I stood there long enough, if I could get them to leave my brain and come out of my mouth to the air between us, to her ears.

"Hey, Soph?" I said.

"Yeah?" she said.

"Are you working tomorrow?"

She nodded and sighed. "Yeah. It's going to be a long day, I'm afraid. I'm already dreading it."

"Okay," I said. "Well, maybe I can improve your day."

She looked at me a little quizzically.

"I was just wondering if you'd like to get dinner with me tomorrow night," I said.

"Oh," she said, a little surprised. "Well. I work until seven, so it would have to be late—or at least later."

"That's fine," I said. "I don't mind waiting."

She took a breath in. "Yeah. Okay. Let's get dinner."

"Okay," I said, and I smiled back. I almost let it go at that.

But I didn't.

"Tomorrow at dinner," I said, "I want to tell you I understand what happened, and I want to tell you how sorry I am, and that I don't want anything other than to come back home and work on us, work on moving forward with you. I want to keep going back to Dr. Garrett. I want us to keep talking. Because you and Matthew are everything to me, and tomorrow at dinner, I'm going to tell you I'm not letting go of you as easy as this."

Sophia looked stunned for a moment, and I tried desperately to read her.

Where had that monologue come from?

"Umm," she said finally. Then a smile slowly spread across her face. "Okay. Well, that'll be good then," she said. "I've been wondering how I was going to find a way to tell you it was time to have you come back home so we could do all of that, but I was worried you were still mad at me, and you still might want some time away from me."

I shook my head. "Nope. No thanks. I think I've been away for long enough."

She smiled and I saw that there were tears in her eyes.

I stepped forward and wrapped her in a big hug. "Soph," I whispered. "I love you."

"I love you, too," she said, sniffling.

After a few minutes, I pulled myself away, clearing my throat and yelling to Matthew that it was time for Portia to leave.

Sophia held my hand for a long second before finally letting me go, and I smiled at her as I escorted Portia to the door. There was no doubt in my mind that Portia had clocked our exchange. She had barely waited until she was seated in the front seat of my car before she started in on her cell. I presumed she was texting Matthew by the way she tilted the screen just out of my line of sight.

I couldn't help but smile.

Twenty-Four

There was one more thing to do after dropping Portia off.

Actually, there were two more things to do.

After I backed out of Portia's driveway, giving her one last wave as she went inside, I reached over my head on top of the sun visor and pulled down the object that had been sitting there for several days.

Lila's CD.

I pulled it out of the jewel case and inserted it into the CD player, and then started a slow crawl at twenty-five miles per hour away from Portia's subdivision.

And I found myself smiling.

It was gorgeous. It was soulful, sweet, slow. She had an incredible voice. I didn't recognize the first track, but I did the second and the third—covers, first Adele, then a band I recognized but couldn't name.

I drove around like that for a while, realizing her CD had cycled back to the beginning. There were eight songs on it. It didn't sound like there had been a ton of tinkering, either. It was just her voice—raw and honest

It made me feel like shit for ignoring her texts. I pictured her sitting over in her apartment, checking her phone, wondering why she wasn't hearing from me. Thinking that I was probably never going to even show up for a shift at JavaHut again, which—if I wasn't fired—was supposed to be the next day, bright and early at 5:00 a.m. I had still not listened to the voicemail Carmen had left me, so in all likelihood, I had already been canned.

How could I even talk to Lila anymore, though? The feelings I had were too strong, and I knew it. I'd managed not to tell her a thing about Sophia—our estrangement, Sophia's affair. Either that was a product of how good I was at keeping my personal life always at bay, or it was a testament to how open Lila was to let me just be myself, which I hadn't realized was exactly the balm I had needed this summer.

How could I tell Lila that spending time with her made everything feel clear to me in a way I never expected, even though simultaneously it scared and confused the hell of me? How could I tell her that our connection was a life raft to a man drowning in the ocean?

How could I explain any of that, I thought, as she delivered in my car stereo the beautiful opening lines of Adele's "Someone Like You."

I listened to the CD at least three more times before I pulled into JavaHut's parking lot, looking at the clock after I put the car in park to let my brain tell me why it was dark inside.

Closed.

Of course they were. It was after nine, I realized. I was about to put the car back in drive again, though, when I spotted Lila's green Jeep. It was still parked in the lot. Slowly, I eased the Camry over to her Jeep, but I could see from a few car lengths away that there was no one inside.

I pulled up next to her car and put mine in park, thinking about what my next move should be.

But I didn't have to think very long before my trusty old stupid brain told me exactly where she was, and exactly where I could go to see her.

* * *

She was sitting by herself at the bar, her cell phone in front of her, lighting up her face. It was pretty busy for a Thursday, I thought. What kind of a crowd was this at a fake Mexican restaurant in a strip mall, the day after Independence Day?

People hungover from the 4th maybe. Not the happy hour crowd. Not the dinner crowd.

No, this was a different type of crowd, I realized as the hostess greeted me, and smiled as I signaled to her that what I wanted more than a table for one was a seat at the bar.

This was definitely the pick-up crowd.

Back to the scene of the crime, my brain supplied. *Back to where it all started.*

All the trouble you've managed to get yourself into, all the brain cells you have successfully killed deciding you can't think about anything difficult unless there's a beer in front of you to help you do it.

I told my brain to shut up, at least for the time being.

There were a few other young people sitting at the bar around Lila, drinks in front of them. A few girls sat together in one corner, and a young man in a black t-shirt was chatting them up. One giggled and put her hand on his chest, which made him grin and wag his eyebrows up and down.

I had to smile, and Lila was too focused on her phone to notice me saddle up next to her at the bar.

"Oh. My. God," she said. Her hand left her phone and went to rest over her heart. "You scared the. Shit. Out. Of

259

me."

I smiled at her. "I'm sorry," I said.

"How did—wait, how did you know I was here?" she asked.

She was genuinely confused, and I tamped down the words in my throat that she looked extraordinarily beautiful, too.

She was wearing her hair down, pulled to one side, extra eye makeup, and beautiful feather earrings. A gold necklace hung around her neck, its key pendant drawing attention to her neckline and the boat neck shirt she wore with black pants. She was hands-down the prettiest girl at the bar, and I didn't know what pec boy was doing over there with the girls drinking sugary cocktails.

"I didn't know you were here, exactly," I said. "I was actually just driving around, and I had an errand to run on this side of town, but JavaHut is closed. Then, I saw your Jeep."

She smiled at me.

"Is it okay if I sit down next to you?" I asked.

"It's fine," she said. "Please."

The bartender came over. I looked at her tall draft, asked her what she was drinking. "Not Heineken, I hope," I said, worried.

She smiled. "Nope. Not Heineken. Never again, Heineken. I'm swearing Heineken out of my life, forever. I promise. I've got a Killian's."

"Nice," I said. "I'll take one of those, too. Tall," I supplied to the bartender before he could ask.

The first pull felt incredible, and I told Lila I hadn't one of these in a long time.

"Rough day at the office?" I teased.

"Oh, it was fine," she said. "Stacy asked me if I could close for her."

"That was nice of you," I said.

"You didn't work today," she said, stating the obvious, not mentioning how I'd ignored her texts. "Carmen was bitching about you when I came in. That was your second no call, no show—your second strike."

"No," I said. "I did not work today. I went to a dog funeral."

"Oh," she said, her eyes growing big. "Right."

I took another drink of the beer. "I take that back—err, I amend that a little bit. I *hosted* a dog funeral today. I was the officiant."

"I think officiants are only at weddings," Lila said, frowning.

"Huh," I said. "What is it with me and weddings today?"

"What?" she asked.

I chuckled, took another drink. "Nothing," I said. "It's just a joke."

Whether or not I liked it, I knew this had to be the last time I sat next to this gorgeous woman and drank beer with her.

Not something I should tell her straight away, though, but something I knew I eventually needed to work my way to. One way or another, this had to come to an end. I couldn't keep tempting myself, tempting fate. Sooner or later, I knew that I was just going to fail.

"You're talking about your dog's funeral, aren't you?" she asked. "Is your son doing okay?"

I nodded, took another sip of the beer, which had worked itself into my system, and was doing a very good job of making me feel like the rest of the conversation was going to be okay.

I told her about Matthew feeling responsible for Benny's death, and she empathized.

"I'm sorry," she said. "That must have sucked."

I nodded. "It was sad, but it was nice, in a way. We buried him in the backyard—his ashes. By his favorite tree. *My* favorite tree, actually. And my son's. You know, we got to remember the good times we had with him. We looked at some old pictures."

"Ugh, I'd be lost if Zen died," she said. "She's been with me for so long."

"Yeah," I said. "It really—it really does bring it home. You know, that they don't live forever. I was digging his grave and thinking about that."

"Man," Lila said, taking a drink of her beer. "I'm not sure if I would have agreed to let you sit down next to me if I had known you were going to be such a downer," she said. She winked at me, though.

I chuckled. "I'm not ruining your game here, by the way, am I?" I asked, gesturing to two guys who had joined us at the bar since the time we started talking. One of them had looked at Lila more than once.

She rolled her eyes. "Are you serious?" she asked. "You actually think I would pick up a guy at a bar?"

I shrugged. "Well? Why not? You're young. You're supposed to, aren't you?"

She shook her head, laughing hard, and it didn't escape me that now both guys gave her a once-over, and then me, probably wondering who the hell I was and how I wound up next to Lila at the bar of Excelencia Fronteriza on a Thursday night in July. They looked away casually, and I could tell they were trying to suss out if there were any other girls as pretty.

"I would never pick up a guy in a bar," she said. "Trust me. Once you've worked at a bar, and you've seen how that particular sausage is made, you stay away. In fact, you become a full-on vegetarian."

I just nodded. It would not have surprised me at all to hear that guys hit on her all the time when she was a bartender, but I kept the comment to myself. A fair number of JavaHut customers flirted with her when she worked the register, I had observed.

"Well, technically, this isn't a bar," I said. "It's a restaurant. So, you'd be good."

She took a drink of her beer. "So, wait. You ignore me for days, and then you come and find me, and now you're recommending to me that I hit on a guy, or go home with another guy? No offense Mr. Averett, but you're actually pretty crazy."

I nodded. She hadn't called me *Mr. Averett* since Carmen put us on shift together on my first day. That felt like a year ago, not weeks.

"I am," I said. "You're right about that."

She studied me for a second, and I saw a smile play on her lips.

"So," she said. "You're saying you want to be my wingman now?"

I nodded and smiled back. "I guess so. See anyone interesting?"

"Just one," she said. "But. You know. He's not interested. I checked. Actually," she continued, "I've been checking for a few weeks now. He has been giving me some mixed signals, I think, but I finally feel like it's time to call it—he's not interested in being with me."

I shook my head, took another long swig of Killian's.

"Lila. I would say this to you, if I may. Of course he is interested. He would be the biggest idiot on the planet not to be interested. And he is an idiot, in a lot of ways—you know I am talking about myself here, right?"

She nodded, smiling a little.

"But Lila—this guy—me, I mean—he's just unable, and he's sorry about that. *Really* sorry, actually. And he thinks you'll never know just how sorry he is about that, and he wishes...You know he thinks to himself that if things were different, somehow, by magic, if he were younger, or if he were in a place in his life where he *could* go for it, well..."

She hadn't taken her eyes off me, and the smile on her face was widening.

I went on.

This was it.

"He would want you to know—this guy at the bar, I mean—he'd want you to know—like *really* internalize the fact that he would be with you in a heartbeat, if he could. It would be his honor. This guy you think is interesting can't believe you find him interesting to begin with, and the shock is still wearing on his brain. He was pretty gob-smacked, in fact. That's the whole truth."

She laughed again, and I noticed she'd done that thing where she'd salted her napkin to keep her glass from sticking to it, and my heart actually ached. God, I was going to miss this girl.

She took in a deep breath and sighed.

"That's a good word," she said. "Gobsmacked."

"Not exactly Shakespeare," I said. "But yeah. It fits."

We sat there for a few long seconds, not saying anything, and I knew it was the end of something, that it needed to be time for the end of something, and even though it made sense, it felt sad and bittersweet, and all the air left my lungs slowly as I studied her for what I told myself was going to be the very last time.

"Well. So... now what?" Lila asked.

"Well," I said. "That brings me to my errand."

"Your errand?"

"Yeah," I said. "I came over to tell Carmen I need to put in my notice."

"Are you serious?" she asked.

I nodded. "Yeah. It's time. But they were already closed by the time I got here, of course. Plus, I was taking a gamble Carmen would even be there that late. So... I guess I will just come back tomorrow and quit in person. They *do* say bad news is best delivered on a Friday."

"Oh," she said. "Friday or not, Carmen's gonna be so pissed at you. You no call, no showed twice... and you've only been here, like, not even a full month!" She was laughing, holding her Killian's up to her mouth.

"I know," I said. "And she can be pissed if she wants, but I told her I teach, and so she knew she was just going to have me for the summer. Right? I was going to quit in a few weeks anyway, so it's no big loss for her."

Lila considered this and took another drink. "I guess so. Knowing Carmen, though, she'll still find a way to be pissed."

I chuckled. "I suppose you're right."

"I actually wanted to call in sick today," Lila said. "Sincerely. The fireworks kept me up last night, and I kept drinking, and then... well... Heineken suddenly came in town and wanted to stay with me."

"Oh, wow," I said. "That's something."

I hadn't realized she'd had company the night after I'd almost stayed at her place. Well, the night after I slept in my car on her street. I wasn't sure if I was wrestling jealousy or relief. Both, maybe.

She shook her head. "No," she said. "Trust me. It's *not* something. I meant what I said earlier. He and I are done—like *completely* done. Especially after last night. I absolutely cannot go down that road anymore. No matter what he says."

I picked up my beer and tilted it toward her. "Amen," I said. "I mean, cheers."

She smiled, and we both took a long drink. She was almost on E, so the bartender brought her another tall, and asked me if I wanted another one.

"No, thanks," I said. "I'm okay for now."

"Hmm," she said. "You don't—I mean, are you quitting JavaHut early because of me, though? Sorry if that's awkward of me to ask you, but... I can't help but feel like it's somewhat my fault—"

"It's not your fault," I said. "It's definitely not your fault. You didn't do anything wrong."

She nodded, but she didn't seem convinced.

"I think we're cool," she added. "You and me, I mean. We can work together. I promise. No drama."

"I know," I said. "I'm just done. I want a little time off to enjoy the summer before the school year gets under-way again."

I managed to leave out the part where I had to stop slinging espresso next to her because I was worried I'd eventually just ask her to run away with me.

She nodded, but she seemed sad.

"You should quit, too," I said.

"What?" she said, frowning. "Why?"

"I listened to your CD," I answered.

"Oh, *finally*," she said, smiling.

"Yes, finally, sorry," I said. "What can I say—I've been so busy between running a dog funeral and my burgeoning career as a barista."

Lila chuckled. "I can tell you this now because you're quitting, but you were a pretty shitty barista."

I laughed a laugh that came from somewhere very deep inside. It felt as though I'd been holding it inside for a year, and it came rolling out of me so loudly Lila looked around, embarrassed on my behalf to see who was staring. Several people were raising eyebrows at me.

The bartender gave me a look.

Lila didn't have to tell me that I had just tacitly signaled to the bartender that I didn't need to be served another beer when I'd finished this one.

Which I probably didn't.

"I was, wasn't I?" I said.

She took in a deep breath. "You were too slow at the espresso machine," she said. "And you didn't wait for the pour to be done before pulling them, so they would still be dripping. And half the time, you'd put them in the cup first, like you kept forgetting that you needed to pump the syrup first, like all the freaking time," she said, pounding the bar next to her drink for emphasis. I laughed again.

"It's hard to remember," I said. "In my defense."

She shook her head. "You had some potential, but I think maybe you should stick with what you know best, which is making kids write papers about story arcs and narratives, or whatever, and making them read *To Kill a Mockingbird* and write about what made Atticus a true hero."

"He was a hero," I said distantly, to make Lila laugh. "So was Scout. And Tom Robinson. And Boo Radley, in his own right."

"*That's* what I remember about you," Lila said, smiling. God, she was beautiful. "You liked that book. You admired everyone in that book."

"Well, almost everyone," I said. "Lots of characters to root for in that one."

Man, I thought. *If I were twenty-six.*

If I were single.

If I didn't know better.

If I didn't want a snowball's chance in hell of repairing a marriage I had let fray for so long.

"Speaking of characters to root for," I said. "That brings us back to you—your singing! You're really good."

She took a drink and rolled her eyes. "Thanks," she said.

"I mean it," I said. "I am not just saying that. And you said I would just say that, but I'm telling you, I'm not just saying that. Which is why you should quit JavaHut and go after singing, for real."

She shrugged. "Maybe."

"Do it," I said. "If you hang around that coffee shop too long, you'll just keep hanging around there, and you won't go after what you want. You gotta push yourself."

"Maybe," she repeated. I grinned.

I said, "Let me take advantage of the one thing that's nice about being an old man, here, and tell you, yes, I'm right. Skip ahead two, three years down the road. Do you want to still be at JavaHut? Or do you want to be singing, and doing your vocal coaching thing on the side, for money, or whatever?"

"Singing and coaching," she said.

"So *do* it," I said. I felt like I was on a roll now. It was so much easier to try to fix Lila's problems than to spend even another brain cell trying to sort out my own.

"We'll see," she said.

"Promise me," I said, holding up my beer again, which was almost empty.

She sighed. "It's not that easy," she said. "If I make a promise to you, then..."

"Then what?" I asked. "Then you're really going to have to do it?"

She nodded. "Yeah. I can break a promise to myself—that's easy," she said, rolling her eyes. "But to you? My old English teacher? I can't."

I grinned. "So that's perfect, then," I said. "You'll do it."

She threw her head back and feigned upset. "Okay, fine, fine, fine. I'll do it," she said.

I grinned, satisfied that I had won, and I caught the bartender's eye. "I'll take the check," I said to him, gesturing to my drink and the one in front of Lila, to which he nodded.

"Hey," she said. "Who said I was ready to leave?"

"We're in no hurry," I said. "I don't mind sitting here for a bit longer. If you're not in good shape to drive, I can take you home," I added. "Plus, you have to walk out with me anyway—you told me that CD was on loan. I need to give it back to you. It's still in my car."

Lila smiled. "Oh. That's right. I forgot. Honestly, you can keep it. If you want to, I mean."

"I can?" I asked.

"If you want to," she said, shyly. "I have—like I have other copies of that one."

"I'd love to keep it," I said, and I meant that with everything in me.

"Okay," she said, smiling broadly. "That's actually really sweet. That's a compliment you want to keep that thing."

"You have a beautiful voice," I said. "I kind of like the idea that I can listen to it whenever I want to."

She took a drink of her beer and I had the impression it was her turn to be speechless, that I'd leveled her a little bit.

"So," she said, after a long moment. "You're really going to quit tomorrow?"

I nodded. "Yeah. I have to. It's time, Lila."

"Are you going to put in your two weeks?" she asked. She was studying my face.

"Nah," I said. "I'll tell Carmen that tomorrow is my last day."

"Whoa," Lila said, even more shocked. "She really is going to murder you, you know that, right? You're a dead man walking. And quitting before the weekend? Forget about your dog, you're going to need me to throw you a funeral. You'll get buried in your backyard next to your dog."

I shrugged. "It's okay. I don't really need to use Java-Hut as a job reference, although I'll certainly be apologizing to Carmen tomorrow. And I'll miss the free coffee. It was a good job, you know, gave me something else to do this summer, not teach, not read, not think about all that stuff, and just—you know, just *be*. Work through... work through some stuff," I said, alluding to my homework she had found on the floor.

Lila nodded. I could tell she understood what I meant, and I knew I didn't need to say anything else about it.

We paused for a second as the bartender came back. I pulled a twenty-dollar bill out of my wallet to put in his black pad, which he promptly took. The men at the other end of the bar were looking at Lila and me again, probably wondering if I was lucky enough to be leaving with a girl like that tonight. I smiled to myself.

Let them think whatever they want.

"Yeah. Now it's time to hang up my apron and enjoy the summer before I get back in the classroom. I think I've got some new ideas I want to try this fall."

"Huh," Lila said.

"What?" I asked.

"It's just so weird that tomorrow will be our last day working together. I kind of can't really believe it," she said.

"I know," I said. "It really is."

"Well," Lila said. "You know, we'll miss you at Java-Hut. Charlie especially—he told me the other day how much he likes you."

I chuckled. "That's nice. But hey—pretty soon, Java-Hut will be missing *you*, too," I added. "Right? You're going to leave—you're going to go sing. Someday I won't even need that CD you gave me—you'll be on the radio and I'll smile every time I hear you."

It was an order, not a question, and she smiled at me for saying it.

"Well, that would be the dream," Lila said, smiling. "So, I'll drink to that." She clinked her glass against mine, even though mine was empty. "Here's to you quitting JavaHut tomorrow. And here's to me quitting soon, too."

"Here's to us," I said, setting my empty glass back down on the bar. "You and me. And this summer."

It felt like a gulf of words went unspoken between us then. How could I sum up to her what she'd come to mean to me? How she'd offered me a lifeline this summer, when I hadn't known I had needed one and wasn't sure I had really deserved one?

She knows, my brain said.

She knows.

"Plus," I added, almost making her spill her beer laughing with what I said next. "You won't miss me too much at JavaHut. You know, recently, I heard somewhere that I'm a really shitty barista."

About Atmosphere Press

Atmosphere Press is an independent, full-service publisher for excellent books in all genres and for all audiences. Learn more about what we do at atmosphere-press.com.

We encourage you to check out some of Atmosphere's latest releases, which are available at Amazon.com and via order from your local bookstore:

Tree One, a novel by Fred Caron
Connie Undone, a novel by Kristine Brown
A Cage Called Freedom, a novel by Paul P.S. Berg
Giving Up the Ghost, essays by Tina Cabrera
Family Legends, Family Lies, nonfiction by Wendy Hoke
Shining in Infinity, a novel by Charles McIntyre
Buildings Without Murders, a novel by Dan Gutstein
What?! You Don't Want Children?: Understanding Rejection in the Childfree Lifestyle, nonfiction by Marcia Drut-Davis
Katastrophe: The Dramatic Actions of Kat Morgan, a young adult novel by Sylvia M. DeSantis
Peaceful Meridian: Sailing into War, Protesting at Home, nonfiction by David Rogers Jr.
SEED: A Jack and Lake Creek Book, a novel by Chris S. McGee
The Testament, a novel by S. Lee Glick
Southern. Gay. Teacher., nonfiction by Randy Fair
Mondegreen Monk, a novel by Jonathan Kumar

About the Author

Colleen Alles is a native Michigander living in Grand Rapids. She works at a public library and writes fiction and poetry when she can. Her work can be found in a number of literary journals; two chapbooks of poetry are available through Finishing Line Press. When she isn't  writing, Colleen is herding her young children, cuddling her hound dog, running around her neighborhood, and enjoying good coffee. Or craft beer. This is her first novel.

CPSIA information can be obtained
at www.ICGtesting.com
Printed in the USA
FSHW021554110620
70953FS